DARKENED

DARKENED

BLAKE CHANNELS

Blossom Cove Publishing

For my family –

thank you for believing my dream could be a reality,

even when I didn't believe it myself.

CHAPTER ONE

MY HEAD IS POUNDING, and although the air holds a familiar scent, I feel disoriented. The room comes into focus and I realize the bed I am lying in is my own. This should comfort me, but I also realize that I am not alone. My body goes on high alert as an intruder in a ski mask places a leather-gloved hand over my mouth, overpowering my attempts to scream. I feel hot and cold all at once. The smell of sweat and wet leather stings my nostrils and I feel as if I'm suffocating.

Breathe through your nose. Breathe through your nose.

I struggle to free myself from his grasp. My hands and feet are bound, but I manage to knee him in the groin. He slaps me hard. The sting of the slap is blinding, but the pain doesn't compare to the crushing feeling in my chest. My assailant is on top of me, his right knee pushing into my sternum. I can feel the hard, plastic buttons of my nightshirt forming an impression on my chest as he pins me beneath his weight. I continue to struggle, but with every move I make, I feel the ropes biting into my wrists and ankles.

"Please," I beg, barely recognizing my own strangled voice.

"Do you know who I am?" the man asks.

A thousand thoughts run through my head – each of them equally horrifying. My mind kicks into overdrive, searching for anything familiar; any clue that might reveal his identity. I can feel his hot breath on my skin. The acrid smell of cigarettes and cheap cologne assaults my lungs. The aroma is so thick I can almost taste it, and my stomach churns in protest. The ski mask cloaks the man's features, making him impossible to recognize. I stare directly into his eyes, hoping they'll hold an explanation, and am horrified by what I see. The man has blood-red eyes. Deep, yellow circles surround his crimson irises.

Paralyzed by fear and the increasing weight on my chest, I struggle to speak. "No. Please, you're hurting me."

"Shut up," he yells. His tone is fierce, his voice gravelly. I start to cry. "Tears won't help you," he says viciously. "I don't fall for the games you whores play."

When a woman experiences a home invasion about every other night, you'd think she'd get used to it; become callused somehow. Yet here I am huddled under a down comforter, stomach in knots, and sobbing into my pillow. At least this time wasn't as bad as some of the others. This time I managed to wake up before the intruder threatened to violate me and called me a cock-teaser. I despise that word.

Using my worn nightshirt, I wipe my eyes and dab the sweat from my forehead. *It was a dream. It was just a dream.* I repeat this to myself several times as I wait for my heart rate to return to normal and for the tightening in my shoulders to lessen.

It's been a month since I was attacked, but my bad dreams of that night continue. The police were unable to establish a motive for the break-in and have failed to turn up any leads. The braided rope used to tie me up could be found in any corner drugstore. Nothing was stolen, at least not that I could tell, and despite my assailant's threats, I was not sexually assaulted.

Although the dream is over, I can't shake the irrational feeling that I'm not alone. Heart still racing, I spring out of bed, switch on the lamp on the nightstand, and survey the room. My bedroom door remains locked, the wooden dresser pushed in front of it. The curtains are drawn, and apart from my twisted bed sheets, the rest of the room is tidy. I crouch down and peer under the king-sized bed. *No monsters. No bad guys.* I stand to my feet and stare down at the bed. It once represented so many warm memories with Nate. Now its massive size fills me with an overwhelming loneliness that threatens to swallow me up.

Tearing my eyes away from the bed, I divert my attention to the master bath. The door is slightly ajar, but that doesn't strike me as unusual. Approaching slowly, I cautiously kick the door the rest of the way open before peering inside. I am momentarily startled by my reflection in the mirror above the sink, but quickly recover. My eyes dart to the walk-in shower. To my relief, it's empty.

3

Leaving the bathroom, I make my way to the bedroom door. I slide the heavy dresser aside, press my ear to the door, and listen with bated breath. Hearing nothing, I open the door, fumble for the light switch, and step into the hallway. I check the burglar alarm. It's still armed, but I glare at the keypad. The alarm was installed within days of my attack. It was supposed to make me feel safe. It doesn't.

After checking the remaining rooms in the house, I exhale slowly. I am alone. *Thank God.* I wander back to my bedroom where my relief turns to dread, and I start to panic. *I'm alone, all alone.*

My mind drifts to Nathan Mitchell. I sigh as I sink back on my bed, finding small solace by drawing my knees to my chest and wrapping myself tightly in the plush comforter. *Oh Nate.* We broke up three months ago, just two short months before my attack, but the memory of that day is fresh, painful – like a wound that refuses to heal.

My heart wasn't in it. At least that's what I'd told Nate was the reason I was ending things. But that wasn't the reason at all. The problem was my heart *was* in it; absolutely and unequivocally – so much so that the idea of Nate walking away with it terrified me. Whether he realized it or not, I had given him everything: mind, body, and soul. I convinced myself that if I didn't get out, when he decided to leave, I'd be empty. Lost. Just a shell. What I didn't realize was that by ending things with Nate, I was already lost. I was already empty.

The emptiness consumes me. It surges through my body like a tidal wave. The memory of that day jabs at my heart like a thousand tiny pin pricks – my pride winning out when I told him I was moving on; the hurt expression on his face before he walked away. I had waited for him to call my bluff, to turn back around. He didn't.

As I relive that day in my head, I feel a tear trickle down my cheek and I wipe it away in anger. They say it's better to have loved and lost, but it's during long nights like these that I'm not so convinced. I glance at the clock on the nightstand. 3:00 a.m. *Ugh*... Too early to get up. Squeezing my eyes shut, I concentrate on drifting back to sleep. *Please don't have a bad dream again*, I plead with my subconscious.

When my body does give into sleep, I don't dream of the intruder. I dream of Nate. Only of Nate.

CHAPTER TWO

THE TAUNTING BUZZER OF MY ALARM CLOCK puts an abrupt end to my pleasant dreams of Nate. I switch to the radio, where the weatherman reveals that it will be another overcast day in Edmonds, Washington. Edmonds is a beautiful town to live in with its view of both the Olympic Mountains and the large inlet from the Pacific Ocean known as the Puget Sound; but it's also known for its frequent rainfall. I groan as I swing my feet over the side of the bed and feel the cold bamboo flooring beneath my feet. *At least it's Friday.*

Stumbling to the bathroom, I peel off my clothes and step into the shower. The water is nearly scalding, prompting my stomach to do flip flops, but I welcome it. It helps numb the pain from the night before. I turn to face it head on, closing my eyes as the hot droplets pelt my face and cascade down my body. I want to curl into a ball on the smooth tile of the shower floor and have a good cry, but I force myself to reach for the shampoo instead. I pop open the top, inhaling the sweet fragrance of rose and sandalwood. I reminisce how Nate smelled whenever he showered at my house after sleeping over. The memory is like so many others I have of him – bittersweet.

After a quick shower, I study myself in the mirror. My skin appears paler than normal, a stark contrast to the deep brown of my hair. *My little Snow White*, my mother called me when I was a child. I apply concealer to cover the dark circles under my pale, blue eyes. *Pale.* I sigh, thinking that if I had only one word to describe myself that would be it – *pale*.

I pinch my cheeks for some color, then reach for the blow dryer perched on the countertop. I decide to wear my hair down, hoping the length will mask my tired features. I wander to my closet to get dressed, choosing a simple gray suit jacket with a matching pencil skirt and black heels. I reach for a black camisole, but then reconsider and grab a pink one instead. I can use some color.

Although I didn't have much sleep, I find myself getting pumped for work. I love my job at Danner and Banks Consulting, a small firm on the west side of town. I was hired on as an intern my senior year in college. Now, at 24, I am the youngest Senior Consulting Executive in the firm (by at least a decade if you exclude Lance Danner, the younger of the company's two owners). I have a beautiful corner office with a view of the Puget Sound, and Lance even arranged for the company to pay my tuition while I complete my MBA online. With my private life being such a wreck, I'm proud to have one area of my life going right.

I whip into my parking space at work in my black Mercedes-Benz C300 Coupe (a recent splurge), experiencing the familiar satisfaction at seeing my name and title printed on the sign above my privately reserved spot. *Geez.* I think to myself. *You really are a snob sometimes.* Inching forward, I hear the distinct sound of concrete against metal and I realize that, once again, I've parked too close. After backing up a few inches, I put the car in park, turn off the engine, and climb out. I check the front of the car for damage (thankfully, there is none) and make my way towards the entrance, past the row of neatly trimmed shrubs.

Halfway up the walkway, I stumble. I manage to steady myself, but not before breaking the left heel of my shoes. After hobbling back to my car, I rummage around in the trunk and dig out a pair of kitten heeled Gucci knock-offs. I slip them on, discard my broken shoes in the trunk, and make my way back to the entrance of the building. I hope the start of my morning isn't any indication of how the rest of my day will go.

I pause to greet the receptionist on my way in. "Good morning, Layla," I tell her. She smiles warmly from behind the desk, seemingly pleased that I remembered her name, and I feel partially redeemed for my earlier snobbery.

I arrive at my office ten minutes earlier than usual. Terry Peters, my assistant, is already at her desk and has brewed a pot of coffee. Her chestnut hair is pulled into a neat bun and she maintains perfect posture as she re-straightens the already neatly stacked reports on her desk. The woman is professional to a fault and devoid of any humor – but a damn good assistant. She's perfect, actually. I'm not looking for a friend.

I am hanging up my purse and coat when she enters my office with a cup of steaming coffee and the morning paper. "Terry, you are wonderful," I praise, breathing in the aroma of the strong brew and the hint of newsprint. She smiles faintly and places the coffee on the cup warmer by my keyboard, switches on the warmer, and turns the cup handle towards me. Her movements are crisp and efficient, more robotic than warm-bodied.

I reach up to take the paper from Terry and she pauses midway to handing it to me.

"What's the matter?" I ask.

"What happened to your wrist?" I glance down to see angry marks circling my right wrist. There is also slight bruising. *Oh! Are those rope burns?* I think to myself, noticing them for the first time. *Did I somehow hurt myself when I was having a nightmare?*

"Oh," I find myself saying, "I went out last night and when I got home I was too tired and lazy to remove the chunky bracelet I wore." This is a blatant lie. I didn't go out. There is no such bracelet. I feel both guilt and astonishment at the ease in which the lies pour from my lips. Terry seems to buy my explanation and goes back to her desk. She isn't much for conversation, which is something else I appreciate about her.

Shifting my focus to my computer screen, I prepare myself for a typical hectic day as I try to push the mystery of my injuries out of my mind. I groan when I open my email and find my inbox has nearly reached capacity. I have a strict personal rule not to answer work emails after office hours – but sometimes I wonder if that rule does me more harm than good. After a quick sip of coffee, I start to read through them. The newspaper will have to wait.

I've made minimal progress of whittling down my email when Lance Danner pokes his head in my office. "Got a moment?" he asks. I stare up at him. His towering height and commanding presence often catch me off guard. Lance always has high praise for me, and after years of working together we've become good friends, but his unexpected interruptions make me nervous. He's still the boss.

"Of course," I say, attempting to mask the reluctance in my voice.

"School going alright?" he asks, taking a seat in the chair directly across from my desk. He leans back in the chair, places his hands behind his head, and waits for an answer.

"Yes, great."

"I'll bet you're getting straight A's, despite your work and course load."

I smile at him, but don't respond. He's not wrong. I've been accused of being an over-achiever a time or two.

"I have a question for you, and I hope you don't take it the wrong way." His gray eyes bore into mine, and I realize he is waiting for a response.

"Okay," I say, hoping I don't sound as guarded as I feel.

"You know our PR department wants to revamp the billboards and brochures for the company, right?" I nod, puzzled why he is asking me about it. I don't typically get involved with internal marketing strategies. "Well," he continues, "they would really like to use someone in-house as the face of the company."

"Oh, that's a great idea. Who do they have in mind?" I say, suspecting I already know the answer. With his dark, wavy hair, chiseled good looks, and charming smile, Lance is the obvious choice, but I want to give him a chance to tell me. He always enjoys a dramatic buildup when presenting his ideas.

But Lance's sheepish grin is the only response I need to understand what he is actually proposing.

"Me?" My question comes out as a high-pitched squeak. "Why?"

"You'd be perfect," Lance says. "You have the fresh, youthful image we would like our company to project."

"We? So, you've already run this by Mr. Banks?" Until this moment I have been holding out hope that, as co-owner, Eldon Banks will disapprove of the idea and put an end to Lance's preposterous plan.

"Yes, Eldon is on board. And why wouldn't he be? You're the whole package – brains and beauty." Lance gives me a good-natured wink.

"Beauty?" I scoff as I fidget with the pens on my desk and do my best to avoid eye contact. "I think you're confusing me with Diana down the hall."

"As usual, Emma, you underestimate yourself. Honestly, this would be a terrific opportunity for both you and the company. It's a win-win."

"Lance," I argue, scrunching up my face in disapproval. I press my fingertips to my temples and search desperately for a reasonable alternative. Not finding one, I return my hands to my lap and stare back at him in silence.

"Just, think about it," he appeals, standing to his feet. "I don't want you to feel awkward or pressured. I just think you'd be a perfect fit."

"Okay Lance, I will think about it. Do I have the weekend?" I'm betting over the weekend I can come up with at least ten other employees whose faces would be more fitting on a billboard.

"Take as long as you need. But say *yes*."

"Okay," I say.

"*Okay*, you will?" Lance teases, wearing a cheeky grin as he makes his way to the door.

"*Okay*, I'll *think* about it," I say, shaking my head in mock disapproval of his insistence. I am stalling, but I already suspect this is one battle I'm going to lose.

Terry enters a few minutes later and refills my coffee cup. I make eye contact when I feel her hovering. "So, are you going to do it?" she asks.

It takes me a moment to realize that she overheard my conversation with Lance and I make a mental note to start closing my office door. Doing my best to hide my irritation at Terry's eavesdropping, whether accidental or intentional, I smile up at her, but say nothing. Most likely realizing that I have no intention of revealing anything further, she turns to leave my office.

"Terry," I call after her.

"Yes?"

"Can you please close the door?" This time it's Terry's turn to be annoyed. I see the emotion flicker across her face, and then disappear.

"Of course," she says sweetly. I dismiss her from my mind and refocus my efforts on work before I have the chance to feel guilty.

Hardly an hour goes by before I'm interrupted by yet another knock on the door. "Come in," I say, sounding cross and not bothering to look up from my desk to see who it is.

"Can I get your garbage, ma'am?" a low, timid voice asks.

This time I do look up from my computer screen. A man I don't recognize enters my office, wearing an industrial-gray janitor's uniform that looks two sizes too big for him and has the name "Fred" embroidered in blue thread above the left chest pocket. My first inclination is to be annoyed, but after reminding myself that it is not his fault how my morning has gone, I smile and motion him in.

"Yes, please," I say, scooting my chair back from my desk to allow him full access to the trash bin beneath. "Are you new here, Fred?" I ask, making conversation to entertain my own curiosity.

"Yes, I just started this morning," he says, smiling at me with a mouthful of crooked teeth beneath his thinning moustache. "My name is Robert, actually. The uniform is borrowed until the company can order one for me."

I apologize for my assumption as Robert disposes of the waste from the trash bin and puts in a fresh bag. He nods in my direction before leaving my office, closing the door behind him. I exhale, relieved the awkward exchange is over. Small talk has never been my specialty. Taking another swig of coffee, I dive back into my work.

At quitting time, I am mentally exhausted and feel a dull headache forming. Three hours of meetings, and several more hours of pouring over emails, articles, and spreadsheets has gotten the better of me. Not to mention that my head has been spinning over my morning conversation with Lance. I can't even begin to imagine driving by a large billboard of myself every morning on the way to work. I cringe at the thought.

Doing my best to shrug it off, I grab my coat and purse and dart out of my office, saying goodbye to Terry when I pass her desk, but not bothering to wait for a response. As I barge into the hallway, a portly man with a scuffed briefcase and cheap suit dramatically scoots out of my way, avoiding a human collision.

"*Excuse* me," he says. He makes no attempt to mask his irritation.

Please, as if I would have knocked him over. He has at least 100 pounds on me. "I'm so sorry," I apologize. "I guess I forgot to check both ways before crossing," I explain in my sweetest voice, taking it upon myself to somehow brighten the man's mood.

"Both ways? More like you didn't check at all," he barks.

Inwardly, I stick my tongue out at him as I suppress the urge to let him know that I am a senior executive and can have him fired for his poor and insubordinate attitude. *Bite me.* Outwardly, I smile and apologize again before continuing down the hall. Sometimes taking the high road is tough, but I'm determined not to let the man spoil the start of my weekend.

CHAPTER THREE

TIME IS NOT ON MY SIDE this morning. I check the clock on my cellphone and hurry out of the house. I am going to meet my closest friend, Summer Kensington for our weekly Saturday lunch date. She has been instrumental in helping me get over my attack. *If that is something one ever can get over.*

I first met Summer when we were attending college at the University of Washington in Seattle. She was everything I wanted to be – beautiful, athletic, and outgoing. Most girls in the dorm were intimidated by her seemed perfection, but I found her fascinating. We became best friends in no time.

As different from each other as day is from night, Summer spent her college years coasting through classes and dating whomever she chose while I remained focused on my studies. I graduated with honors. Summer changed majors twice before settling on journalism. Her parents were opposed to the idea, but she stood up to them, convincing them to let her follow her dreams. As much as I agreed with her parents' practicality, I admired Summer for the strength and courage to follow her heart.

Before climbing behind the wheel, I check the backseat, something that has become part of my daily routine. I fire up the engine, adjust my seat, and glance in the rear-view mirror to check the backseat once again. *All clear.* I do have to remind myself to buckle up. Fighting against the restrictive strap is something I've battled since childhood; but given my recent brush with danger, I'd prefer not to tempt fate. After begrudgingly snapping the seatbelt into place, I cross myself and mutter a quick prayer. I'm not Catholic. I'm not sure what I am. But it makes me feel better; temporarily anyways.

As I back out of my driveway, I crank up the radio. The music fills the car, drowning out my worries. My favorite song is playing, and I sing along at the top of my lungs while I drive through traffic. "You're gonna regret this…ooooh," I bellow. The drivers around me probably think I'm crazy, but I don't care. My car is my own fortress of solitude. My sanctuary.

When I pull up to the restaurant, Summer has already secured us a table on the outside patio and is waiting for me. When I approach, she leaps up and hugs me. "I've missed you," she says.

"Summer," I say laughing, "we just saw each other like two days ago."

"I know, but that doesn't mean I can't still miss you."

"You look stunning as usual," I tell her, pulling back from our embrace to study her. She appears elegant in a simple, white dress. Summer does a quick twirl, showing off her long, tan legs. Her blonde hair hangs

16

loosely around her shoulders, framing her pretty face. A floppy sunhat and dark, oversized sunglasses add a dramatic flair to her look.

"If you weren't my best friend, I'd honestly hate you," I say, only half-teasing.

"Touché," Summer retorts, looking me up and down and complimenting my new shoes. She ought to like them. She picked them out after all. We exchange one last hug before taking our seats. To the restaurant patrons around us, we probably appear to be long-lost friends that haven't seen each other in ages.

The waiter walks over and takes our orders. I can see him gawking at Summer as he approaches our table, but as usual, she doesn't seem to notice. Summer orders a salad with light dressing. She is always worried about her figure and I can't fathom why. I order the BBQ pork sandwich and a side of fries. I can care less about my figure at this point. In fact, I can probably tolerate a little more meat on my bones. Surviving the consuming effects of both the *breakup* and the *break-in* caused me to shed a few pounds. But I did survive. These two events may have eroded my foundation and revealed my fragility, but thanks to my work, my family, and good friends like Summer, I'm not completely broken. *I hope.*

"How is work going?" I ask Summer after the waiter walks away.

"Oh, work's work, who cares about that," she says. I admire her nonchalant attitude about her career. After graduation, Summer landed an entry-level position at a local news station and has been there ever since. She loves her job and never mentions the need to move up. It's not that she's not driven. Summer is very driven when she sees something she wants. She just doesn't need to make a ton of money or be a big shot at work to feel fulfilled. I wonder if being career-driven makes me shallow somehow.

"Let's talk about something far more important than work," Summer continues, and I have a sinking suspicion that she's going to start probing into my love life.

"So, have you gone on any dates lately?" she asks sweetly, unfolding her napkin and placing it in her lap.

Suspicion confirmed. "No," I tell her defensively, knowing she already knows the answer to that question.

"What about that one guy we met at that business mixer at the Hilton? What was his name? Clive, was it? He looked like someone who you could just bask in his warmth," she says airily.

"More like whither and wilt in his heat," I grumble. "Summer, the man was intense, and not in a good way."

She sits in silence for a moment. "When are you going to start trying to let yourself get over Nate?" she finally asks. I know she means well but hearing her say his name aloud is like a punch in the gut. I suck in my breath to recover. When I first agreed to go out with Nate, I knew that it was risky. I gambled that I could keep him. I lost.

"I *am* trying."

"No, you're not," she retorts. "You won't give anyone else a fighting chance."

"Oh, yeah, because the guys are just lined up outside my door."

"Would you even notice them if they were?" I stare off in the distance, choosing to ignore her comment. "What about Lance?" she asks.

"What about him? He's my boss. Besides, I thought *you* were interested in him."

"I was. Lance is successful *and* hot. But let's face it, that man only has eyes for you."

"Then you clearly don't know him at all. We are just friends."

"Trust me, guys are never 'just friends' with anyone that looks like you," Summer says. "Besides, are you telling me all of those late nights you pulled – all of the times you two were alone in your office – you've never thought about… you know… anything?"

Silently I reflect on my relationship with Lance. He is attractive. I'd be blind not to notice that. But there has only been friendship and professionalism between us – nothing more. That is if you don't count the one evening, not long after Nate and I broke up.

"Earth to Emma." Summer is strumming her fingers on the tabletop, impatiently waiting for me to reveal my thoughts. For all her admirable qualities, patience is not one of them.

"Well, we did kiss once," I admit aloud for the first time, to anyone.

"What!" Summer grabs her chest as if the news is more strain than her heart can tolerate. I flush at my unexpected revelation and fill her in on the events that led up to the kiss.

୨୦୨୦୨

I was working late yet again, pouring myself into my job to keep from drowning in my sorrows. I was up to my eyebrows in paperwork and hadn't even noticed when Lance walked into my office. I must have looked upset and Lance spoke up from the doorway.

"If he's not willing to fight for you Emma, he's not worth it."

Startled, I looked up. I wanted to argue that Nate was more than worth it; that he was my everything. I searched for the words to explain

19

that being with Nate was like having a soft place to land, and that without him, I was free-falling. But instead the tears began to flow, and I found myself sobbing inconsolably in Lance's arms. He reached up to dry my tears with his long, slender fingers – and out of the blue, he kissed me. He tasted good, and I returned the kiss. When he wove his fingers through my hair and pulled me closer, I closed my eyes and tried to imagine myself with him. For a moment, I had a flicker of hope that I might find happiness with someone else. But when Lance released me from the kiss, I apologized and told him that I was just not ready for anything.

"I understand," he'd said kindly.

৽৽৽৽

"We never spoke of it again," I finish, sighing deeply and drawing my fingers to my lips in memory of the kiss.

For the first time in as long as I can remember, Summer is speechless. "What about you?" I ask, diverting the conversation away from me. "What has been going on with you these days?"

I fully expect Summer to call me out on my diversion tactic, but instead she attempts to regale me with new stories since we last saw each other. She has a talent for making even the smallest of circumstances seem dramatic and interesting.

Typically, I find myself sucked into her stories, but today my thoughts are scattered. I feign interest, but my mind strays again to my recurring dreams. They have become increasingly intense. Instinctively I trace the faint markings on my wrist, wondering how I managed to hurt myself in my sleep. If it didn't sound crazy, I'd swear they were rope burns. Suddenly I realize Summer has stopped talking and is staring at me.

"What's wrong?" she asks, her face drawn in concern. "And don't tell me *nothing* because I know that look Emma Marie Taylor."

I smile at her use of my full name. "Are you thinking about Nate?" she asks. Being truthful, I shake my head *no*.

"You're still having bad dreams, aren't you?" Summer accuses, leaning in intently from across the table. *How does she always know?*

"They're getting worse," I confess, thinking about the man and his horrible red eyes. I sigh, uncrossing and re-crossing my arms before proceeding. "If I tell you something, do you promise not to have me committed?"

"Well, it depends," she teases, trying to lighten the mood.

"I think the guy that broke into my house last month is still after me. I think he's somehow… haunting me." I glance at Summer to gage her expression. If she thinks I'm losing it, she doesn't let on.

"What do you mean?" she prods.

I tell her about my dreams, and about the marks on my wrists when I wake up. Summer reaches across the table, pulling both of my arms toward her. Her brow furrows in concentration. "These look like rope burns," she observes.

I breathe a sigh of relief that I am not the only one who thinks so. "I know," I whisper. "It's like these dreams are, well, somehow real. I think my subconscious is trying to tell me that whatever the intruder was after, he didn't get it, and it's only a matter of time before he returns to get what he came for." I shudder at the thought.

Summer's eyes are wide as she purses her lips together in thought. I glance around, suddenly self-conscious that we appear to be holding hands

21

across the table. "Summer, if you keep holding my wrists, the waiter is going to think we're an item."

She plants a kiss on my right wrist, then shoots a wink at the waiter, who, once he realizes he's been caught lurking, shuffles off to the kitchen. Finally releasing me, Summer says, "I have someone I want you to see." *Oh great, she is going to have me committed.* "I have a friend that I think could help. Her name is Madame Destiny."

"A psychic!" I scoff loudly. Summer hushes me when she spots the waiter making his way back to our table, pitcher of water in hand. She smiles sweetly up at him as he refills our glasses. "Get serious," I say more softly once he is again out of earshot.

"I *am* serious," Summer says. "And she's not a psychic. She's just very... umm... perceptive. My station interviewed her for a human-interest piece about the power of the human mind. She has a real gift." I shake my head in disbelief. For being raised by such grounded parents, Summer really is eccentric.

"Summer, the last thing I need is someone reading my palm and poking around in my already fractured mind. I'm sure I just did something in my sleep when I was having a nightmare."

Summer looks unconvinced, so I try a different approach. "How about if I promise to go to the police station next week, make sure the case is still open? I can tell the detective I suspect my assailant was purposely targeting me for something that he is still after."

"Okay," Summer sighs, giving in. The food comes, putting an end to our topic of conversation. The waiter leaves a bottle of red wine and Summer pours herself and me a generous glass.

"I'd like to get back to our conversation about you dating again," Summer says.

"Oh, c'mon."

"You just haven't been yourself since the breakup."

"I know. And I probably never will be. It changed me." I pause to collect myself. "You know, there's three things I learned about myself since the breakup," I continue, attempting to sound light-hearted. "One, I'm not afraid to cry."

Summer laughs and I take the opportunity to gulp down some wine.

"Two, I am strong enough to be alone."

"Here, here," Summer says, raising her glass and clinking it to mine.

"And three," I pause again, "I vastly underestimated how much I enjoyed having Nate around."

Summer frowns and lets me wallow for a moment in my self-pity. Then she begins to dig into her salad. "Well, on an entirely different matter," she says, breaking the silence, "did I tell you that *I* have a hot date tomorrow night?"

I manage a laugh, grateful for the change in topic, and not at all surprised by her news.

CHAPTER FOUR

HE SITS IN HIS VEHICLE outside of her house and watches her through the partially open curtain sheers. The woman brushes her long, raven hair. Her face is scrubbed free of makeup, giving it a fresh glow that he finds irresistible. She smiles and presses a finger to her lips as if lost in fond reminiscence. The woman is beautiful, but also trouble for him.

His groin tightens as he thinks about the things he'd like to do with her; do to her. He wonders how long he can be content with watching her. The nights are getting lonelier and self-gratification will only take him so far. There have been other women, sure, but none of them compare. None of them taste the way he is sure she will taste or smell the way he knows she will smell. None of them fill the void. He longs for her lips on his and to feel her hair brush against his skin.

His hands travel between his thighs. He closes his eyes, tilts his head back, and imagines she is the one touching him – stroking him. He feels his pulse quicken but resists the urge to unzip his jeans and pleasure himself.

"Patience," he reminds himself. The time will come when he'll need to act – and he knows that time is quickly approaching. Soon she will be his, or she'll cease to be anything. That choice will be left to her.

CHAPTER FIVE

THE REMAINDER OF MY WEEKEND is uneventful, at least while I'm conscious. After my lunch date with Summer, I go home and change into sweats and an old t-shirt, smiling to myself as I try to imagine what Summer's reaction would be to my wardrobe choice. I devote a couple of hours to my studies before I tackle cleaning the house.

With only two small bedrooms and two bathrooms, my house is cozy and relatively easy to maintain. I always thought I'd buy a larger place once I started making real money. But now, it is home. I find it comforting. My home is my rock – my foundation when everything around me starts to crumble. Funny, I used to believe that Nate filled that role.

After I finish cleaning, I walk from room to room, admiring my handiwork and opening the blinds; something I've done less of since my attack, but I love the way the sunlight brightens up the rooms. I pause in the living room and imagine cuddling on the couch with Nate, next to the newly fluffed pillows, but I thrust the thought away. Being without him still hurts so much, and no matter how hard I try to push him from my mind, his memory forces itself back in like an unwanted guest.

On Sunday I drive to Seattle to meet my mom, Susan, for brunch at *Marge's Diner*, a small, family-owned restaurant that we've frequented for years. I bring along a magazine to occupy my time, knowing full well that my mother will be at least ten minutes late and I'll have to wait around for her. Punctuality has never been her strong suit. Despite knowing this fact, I can't bring myself to be anything but prompt.

I take a seat at a corner booth towards the back of the diner. A pretty, young waitress saunters over to take my order. I don't recognize her and decide she must be new. I order a cup of coffee (no cream, two sugars) and a slice of apple pie, hoping my selection will hold me over until my mother arrives.

By the time she finally does arrive, I've polished off the slice of pie, gulped down two cups of coffee, and have read both my magazine and the menu several times. She offers a quick hug and an apology, but no explanation for her tardiness, not that I expected one. She sits across from me and I notice that something has changed. Her typically long hair has been cropped and styled into a pixie cut. "You got a haircut," I say. I'm surprised. My mother has worn her hair the same way for as long as I can remember.

She smiles and uses both hands to smooth down her hair. "Do you like it?" she gushes.

I usually prefer long hair, but the new hairdo makes my mother look even prettier – more vibrant. "It suits you," I tell her. "You look really pretty."

She smiles back at me, appreciatively.

Once we've ordered our food, we settle into relaxed conversation. We chat about my work, the weather, but nothing deeper than that. I know my mom wants to ask if I'm dating again, but she steers clear of the subject.

I do learn that she's seeing someone new. *Shocker.* Perhaps that explains the new hairstyle. My mother is beautiful, and men are easily drawn to her. With her dark eyes and olive complexion, I wonder how it's possible that I'm her biological child. Despite her frequent dating over the years, she never remarried – something I've always found sad. I asked her about it once, but she told me that she gave her heart to my dad and there wasn't enough of it left for anyone else. I never fully understood what she meant until I met Nate.

After spending a few hours with my mother, I head home, fully intending to mow my overgrown lawn. When I reach my driveway, I spot the neighbor kid outside and offer him twenty bucks to mow it for me. Yard responsibilities delegated, I wind up lazily watching TV. Summer calls to remind me of my promise to go to the police station. The girl is persistent when she gets an idea in her head. I assure her that I will be taking Monday morning off work to do just that. I groan at the thought, worrying that I may die of boredom as a result of extending my weekend.

My nights are not as dull. I dream of Nate. I dream of the intruder. Some nights I dream of both. In one dream, I am in a heavily wooded area that I don't recognize. It is dusk, and I am being chased by a man in a ski mask. His angry, red eyes glow through the darkness. Branches whip at my face as I try to outrun my pursuer. I feel as if I've been running for a long time, and my lungs are ready to burst. The man gets closer and I think I can feel his hot breath on my neck, but before he reaches me, another dark but familiar figure appears out of nowhere and tackles him to the ground.

I wake up in a panic but fall back to sleep before I have time to analyze my dream.

My next dream is of Nate. We are walking hand in hand along the waterfront at Olympic Beach, watching the waves gently lap against the shoreline. Nate is telling me a funny story about his work day. His deep, throaty laugh makes me smile as I listen to his account. There isn't any anger between us, only tenderness and laughter.

The sky is a brilliant display of orange and yellow and we stop to watch the sun set over the water's smooth surface. Other than a couple of fishermen on the dock, the beachfront is empty, and Nate leans in to place a tender kiss on my lips. He tastes like peppermint and like only Nate can taste.

"I love you," he tells me. "Maybe I never told you that enough when we were together." My heartbeat quickens in response and I breathe in deeply as we embrace. Nate smells just as divine as I remember, and I bury my face in his chest.

When I awake from my dream, I am momentarily content. I can still feel Nate's hand in mine and taste him on my lips. Then reality sets in, along with an overwhelming emptiness that is all too familiar.

CHAPTER SIX

ON MONDAY MORNING I am exhausted from my restless night. I fire off an email to Terry from my cell, requesting that she clear my calendar for the day. I feel a little bit like I'm playing hooky, but I also know I won't be able to focus at work given the fitful night I endured.

My original plan is to crawl back into bed and get a couple more hours of sleep, but after tossing and turning for what feels like an eternity, I opt for a hot shower instead. I step onto my front porch to enjoy a morning cup of coffee, still sporting my bathrobe. My yard is a sea of grass and flowering trees – a vibrant green with pops of color. A warm breeze flows through the lilac trees and I inhale the sweet fragrance. It's not often that I treat myself to a leisure morning, and I scold myself for depriving myself of the view – something that first sold me on the place. I wave at my neighbor as she jogs by. She offers a wave and a half-smile.

Summer sends me a text to remind me yet *again* about my promise to go to the police station and I respond with a curt text back, letting her know that I have not suffered from amnesia since we last spoke. I follow up with a smiley-face emoji, hoping she will interpret the first text as a joke.

At around eleven o'clock I arrive at the parking lot of the police station feeling nervous and silly. Why should anyone believe me that my attacker is still a threat to me? I have absolutely no evidence. *Why did I come here?* Inwardly I curse at Summer for insisting that I come, even though I know she meant well.

After circling the parking lot twice, I manage to find a decent parking space. When I climb out of the car, I start to second-guess my wardrobe choice. Knowing that I would not be going into work, I decided to try out my new cream dress with the plunging neckline that is a little too risqué for the office. The dress was an impulse buy during a recent shopping trip with Summer. I chose it because it made me feel sexy and confident. But as I ascend the steps to the police station, I tug self-consciously at the fabric, wondering if I look over-dressed (or, perhaps, not dressed enough).

The main lobby is surprisingly quiet. I am glad that I opted for the strappy sandals rather than heels. I can only imagine the loud racket my heels would have made. I take the elevator to the basement, doing my best to ignore the uniformed officers beside me. I wonder why I feel so self-conscious. It's not as if they have any idea why I'm here. I step out of the elevator, taking a deep breath to calm my jittery nerves. I make my way directly to the desk clerk. I recognize him from my previous trips to the police station.

"Rudy, right?" I ask, sounding more confident than I feel.

The freckle-faced desk clerk looks up from his paperwork. He squints at me through his glasses as if trying to place me, and then smiles –

his mouth drawn into a wide, goofy grin. "Emma!" He stands, extending his beefy hand to shake mine. I flash a genuine smile, relieved to see a familiar face. "What can I do for you?" he asks.

"Well, I'd like to speak to the detective about my case. I have some, uh, new information. I think." I can feel my face flush. *Do I really have new information, or just wild theories?*

"Let me look up your case," Rudy says. "I apologize. I forget your last name."

"It's Taylor," I say, "but last time I worked with Detective Adams." I want to speak to the detective before I lose my nerve. *Really, what am I going to tell him?*

Rudy pauses, tightening his lips. "Detective Adams is on leave. His cases have been, um, reassigned." Now it's Rudy's turn to look flustered.

"What happened?" I can't help but ask, my curiosity getting the better of me.

"Err... I'm not really at liberty to say," Rudy mutters, looking around to see if anyone is watching us. He then makes a motion of pressing a bottle to his lips, followed by a "glug-glug," sound, and then winks at me. *Oh, I get it.* Now that Rudy mentions it, I recall that Detective Adams often asked for a drink when he stopped by my house to give me an update on the case. It always struck me as odd since he was still on duty. After typing madly on the keyboard and squinting at his computer screen, Rudy announces, "The new detective on your case is Detective Mitchell."

My heart stops mid-beat. "Mitchell?" My voice is nearly a whisper. *No, no. Please, not Nathan Mitchell.* I feel myself starting to panic as the heat creeps up my neck and warms my ears. I don't think my heart can bear to see him again. When we were still together, Nate was a patrolman, studying to make detective. Could it really be him? "Nathan Mitchell?" I ask more firmly.

"That's correct," Rudy responds. "You know him, ma'am?"

"Um, I know *of* him," I say, doing my best to sound casual. "Does he have a moment to see me?" I silently pray that the answer is *no*.

Rudy holds up an index finger and plucks the phone from its cradle. He dials the extension. His speech is rapid. "There is an Emma Taylor here to see you. Yes sir. Okay, thank you. I'll send her in." Rudy puts down the phone. "I'll show you to Detective Mitchell's office," he offers.

My head is swimming with emotion and anxiety. I want an excuse to flee, but instead find myself being led down a dimly lit hallway towards Detective Nathan Mitchell's office. *Nate. Oh Nate. Please don't hate me.* I have only seen Nate once since we broke up, and that was two months ago. My memory of that night settles over me like a dark cloud.

ೞೞೞ

Summer had convinced me to go on a double date. She set me up with an acquaintance of hers from her work and we went to *Vistas*, a nightclub in downtown Seattle. At first, I was enjoying myself, thanks in part to a couple tequila shots and a generously sized margarita, both of which were incredibly out of character for me.

Taking a break from dancing, I walked over to the bar to order a drink of water. I was trying to catch my breath and my head was spinning, my system rebelling against the considerable amount of alcohol I'd consumed in such a brief span of time.

It was then that I noticed Nate. He was sitting at the bar with another man in a policeman's uniform. Typically, a uniformed police officer would look out of place at a nightclub, but Nate had a way of looking like he belonged wherever he went. I wanted to turn and run the other direction, but I knew that Nate had seen me. Instead, I wielded all the natural and liquid courage I could manage and walked over to him.

The other policeman politely excused himself, and I found myself alone at the bar with Nate. We talked for a few brief moments, but it was strained. "You look really good," he had said. "Single life looks good on you."

I wasn't sure if he meant it as a compliment, but the words cut me deep. "Thank you," I said. My response sounded clipped.

Nate must have heard the hurt in my voice because he leaned in closer and spoke more softly. "No, really Emma, you look good. Different. It's something about your eyes, or maybe your coloring."

He craned his neck to glance over at my date, who by now was looking a little lost waiting for me back at our table. "Or maybe it's your new boyfriend." This time it was Nate's turn to sound hurt.

I knew any extra coloring I had was solely due to the exhilaration from seeing Nate. For some reason I felt dishonest not divulging this information. But once again my pride won out and I remained silent on the issue. We said our awkward good-byes and Nate walked away, leaving a hole in my heart that could never be filled.

∾∾∾

"Here we are," Rudy announces when we arrive outside of Nate's office. I can hear my heart pounding in my ears as I try to imagine the kind of reaction I will get from Nate. I am fairly certain the reception will not be a warm one.

Put on your big-girl panties, I scold myself silently. I then crack a faint smile as I remember that I'm not wearing any panties. My cream-colored dress wouldn't allow for them. The thought gives me renewed strength, and I square my shoulders before walking through the door Rudy is motioning to.

Nate's office is surprisingly organized. Unable to look directly at him, my eyes dart across his modest-sized desk. I notice a picture of him with his parents, one with his brother, but no photo of a girlfriend. I feel a sense of relief, but then scold myself for allowing the sensation. *You broke up with him, remember?*

"Thank you for showing her in, Rudy," Nate says. "That'll be all. Please close the door when you leave." *Oh.* I hadn't noticed Rudy had entered the room behind me. I also hadn't noticed that I had been holding my breath. I exhale slowly and lift my eyes to meet Nate's, but he appears too preoccupied with the paperwork on his desk to meet my gaze.

"Nate, I…," I begin, not sure what to say.

Nate remains seated. For a moment I just stare. He is stunning. His dark hair needs a trim, somehow making him look sexier. I have the sudden urge to run my fingers through it the way I've done a thousand times before, but I clasp my hands in front of me instead. Nate's face sports a little stubble as if he forgot to shave this morning. I'd always admired how he filled out a policeman's uniform, but dressed in a sports jacket and tie, he is just as appealing.

"Please sit down, Emma. It's nice to see you." His voice is hollow. I suspect that it isn't nice to see me at all. Nate finally glances up at me as he motions to a chair. His beautiful green eyes bore into mine. They are like two shiny emeralds and I lose all train of thought.

My heart is slamming in my chest. Gathering my wits, I try once again to speak. "Nate, I'm sorry," I say. "I didn't know when I came in today that you had taken over my case."

"I asked for it," he interrupts. His words nearly knock me over, so I quickly take a seat, reminding myself to sit like a lady. Despite his composed demeanor, I notice Nate's white knuckles as he firmly grips a file on his desk.

"It was only a week or so ago that I came across your case." He puts down the file and runs his fingers over it before proceeding. I glance down, reading the neatly printed label. *It's my case file.* "I wanted to call you, but I wasn't sure…" He pauses and stares over at me. "Emma, if anything had happened to you…"

Nate's voice trails off and I am momentarily stunned. Before I have time to analyze the meaning of his words, his tone changes, but he continues to speak. "What I mean is, once Detective Adams was no longer able to proceed with your case…"

Without thinking, I make a motion with my hand as if pressing a bottle to my lips, imitating Rudy's performance from earlier. Nate tries unsuccessfully to hide a smile before continuing. "When Detective Adams' case load was redistributed, I thought it made sense for me to handle this case given my familiarity with the… umm… victim and her surroundings."

Oh, I think bitterly. *That's all I am to you now. Another victim in your stack of case files.* I now regard the files on his desk with disdain, realizing my case is no different to Nate than any of the other manila-colored folders. Regretting my decision to come to the police station, I feel the tears well up in my eyes. The silence in the room is growing uncomfortable.

"Congratulations on making detective," I say lamely, clearing my throat. "At 28, I'd say that's pretty impressive." I try to sound casual, but I know my voice is all wrong. My throat feels tight, constricted.

Nate makes a grunting sound, looking a little embarrassed by my praise. "What did you want to see me about?" he asks.

"Huh? Oh, yes, I wanted to discuss my case, but I can see you're very busy." I hurriedly stand to go, knocking over a container of pens perched on Nate's desk. I can feel the flush on my cheeks, but I ignore it and head for the door. I do not offer to clean up the pens.

"Emma," Nate calls after me.

Almost to the door, I turn around to face him. And just when I think my heart can't drop any further, he speaks. "I always have time for a friend," he says softly. His words sting. *A friend.* We used to be so much more, and like a fool I ended it.

"It's okay," I say. "Perhaps another time."

I am practically running as I bolt out of his office and head to the stairwell, avoiding the generically blue-clothed patrons of the elevator. I scurry across the lobby and push through the double doors, squinting into the bright sunlight. Once I am safely out of the police station and alone in my car, I start to cry, reeling from the aftermath of my encounter with Nate. Deep sobs rack my body as I fight for self-control. The bitterness and pain that I've felt over the past three months fills my car like a thick fog. How pitiful. I left this man before he had the chance to hurt me, and I only ended up hurting myself.

I cry for several minutes before composing myself. Once I am certain that I'm okay to drive, I head for home, thankful that I took the rest of the

37

day off. I promise myself a date with a bowl of strawberry ice cream and a low budget sci-fi movie and I feel a little better.

CHAPTER SEVEN

I AM AT HOME STUDYING when my doorbell rings. Groaning to myself, I put down my textbook and walk to the door. My irritation evaporates when I open the door to find Nate on my front porch. His hair is wet from the rain and I stand on my tiptoes to wipe a damp strand from his forehead. He flashes an unexpected smile, revealing a perfect row of white teeth and a faint dimple on his right cheek. Feeling my legs start to wobble, I press my palm to the wall to steady myself.

Nate steps through my front door and I hold my breath, expecting him to be angry. Instead he pulls me close to him, gently pushing the hair out of my face. Tears spring to my eyes without warning. I fight to hold them back, but I'm unsuccessful. They stream down my cheeks as I begin to speak.

"Nate, I'm so sorry. I didn't really want to leave you. I thought you didn't love me. I was trying to leave you before you left me. I…"

"Hush. Baby, it's okay. Don't cry. It's okay." He pats my hair and kisses me softly. I am filled with relief. *Will we ever really be okay?*

Before I have a chance to say anything, Nate scoops me up and throws me playfully over his shoulder. Squealing in delight, I nimbly pound my fists into his back as he carries me into the bedroom. The moonlight shines through the windows between the partially open curtains, dancing across the floor and illuminating the bed. Nate pulls back the covers, setting me down gently as he leans in to kiss me. My pulse is racing, and I close my eyes and meet his kiss with equal fervor, breathing in his scent. *Nate, I've missed you so much.* I want so badly to tell him, to show him.

Suddenly something feels wrong. The kisses start to hurt, and Nate's intoxicating scent is replaced by the smell of stale cigarettes and an overpowering cologne. I open my eyes and am inches away from my masked attacker. Two burning red eyes stare cruelly back into mine. I blink rapidly, hoping by some miracle that the image of Nate will reappear.

When that doesn't work, I desperately try to push the man away, but he presses me down onto the bed and leans in to kiss me again, scraping his teeth against my lips. I attempt to scream, but his lips overpower mine. His ski mask feels rough against my face. I claw at him, but my efforts are futile.

Pinning me down, he binds my hands with rope. I feel the familiar sting on my wrists. Next, he binds my feet at the ankles, but not before I land a solid kick. The man bellows loudly but doesn't back off. I struggle against the ropes, but they dig deeper into my skin. I buck and fight, but the man's strength is far superior to my own.

The room begins to spin, and I know at any moment I am going to be sick. My stomach lurches and I close my eyes to stop the spinning, but it grows increasingly intense. "Please, please," I beg.

CHAPTER EIGHT

WHEN I SNAP OUT OF MY NIGHTMARE, it takes me a few moments to realize that the screaming is coming from me. I clamp my hand over my mouth to stifle the sound. My stomach lurches without warning and I run to the bathroom, making it as far as the sink before I vomit.

Reaching up with a trembling hand to wipe my mouth, I notice the angry red marks that circle my wrist. The marks are darker than before, and this time I feel the sting of rope burns. Through tear-filled eyes, I study my face in the mirror and can't help but think that my lips appear swollen.

I slowly trace my lips with my index finger, remembering the gentle kisses from Nate – followed by the brutal assault on them by my unknown assailant. *How is this possible?* I start to shake violently before throwing up again.

My nightshirt is damp with sweat and clings to my body, so I discard it on the bathroom floor. I pull on a clean t-shirt and sweatpants. I tug my hair back into a loose ponytail, brushing back the hair that is sticking to my forehead. After splashing water on my face and brushing my teeth, I call Summer. She always knows what to do.

She answers on the second ring, sounding more chipper than I would expect at such an early hour. "Can you please come over?" I blurt out.

"Right now? What time is it?" Summer sounds more confused than annoyed. I hear rustling on the other end of the line, as if she's fumbling around for the alarm clock.

"I'm sorry to wake you. I just really need to talk to someone. Do you mind?"

"No, I'm just really touched that you thought of me," Summer replies.

"Really?"

"No, it's called sarcasm. Don't ever call me at this hour again," she scolds, but she's laughing. "I'll be right over."

Summer sits just inches from me on my living room sofa as she examines my wrists and listens intently to my latest nightmare.

"I'm told that nightmares are common after a home invasion," I tell her.

"Yeah, but typically nightmares don't result in bodily harm," Summer argues. She purses her lips together. "That settles it. I'm making you an appointment to go see Madame Destiny tomorrow."

I don't argue. What can it hurt at this point?

I've tried everything to get whole after what happened to me. Therapy first (still trying, actually), but the sessions generally turn to Nate instead of the break-in, suggesting that perhaps I'm more traumatized by

43

our breakup than I'm willing to admit. I tried church. I wasn't brought up in a religious household, but my mother recently found a church she loved and insisted I give it a try. It made me feel a little better, but my need to sleep in on Sundays and spend the day in my PJs eventually won out.

Correction, I've tried *most* everything. Now, bring on the psychic.

CHAPTER NINE

MADAME DESTINY IS NOT AT ALL as I imagined her. I had pictured someone in long, flowing robes and decked out in gaudy jewelry. Instead, she's sensibly dressed in a pair of fitted jeans and a pretty, teal blouse. Her light brown hair is pulled up neatly and I can't help but notice that she's surprisingly attractive. She is also younger than I imagined, probably no more than forty.

She invites Summer and me in, where we take our seats on a plush, white couch in her brightly lit living room. I survey the room, intrigued that there are no crystal balls, star-patterned draperies, or dangling beads. With its neutral color pallet and cozy furnishings, the house is quite inviting. Aside from a wilted plant in the corner, the surroundings are pristine.

"Tell me why you're here," Madame Destiny prompts, taking a seat across from us on a sofa chair and tucking her legs beneath her.

You're the psychic. You tell me. I push the mean thought away and walk her through my attack and the days leading up to this moment. While trying to remain calm, I relay the details of my most vivid nightmares. It's not until Madame Destiny hands me a tissue that I realize I've been crying. Summer sits beside me, squeezing my hand reassuringly.

When I am done talking, I feel a little relieved at being able to share the intricacies of my nightmares with someone. I glance over at Summer, whose face is drained of color. I realize that this is the first time she has heard the full depths of my dreams. I feel guilty for not having confided in her more.

Madame Destiny remains quiet and I'm not sure how to interpret her silence. *Great, even the psychic thinks I'm crazy.* After some time, she speaks.

"I have seen this before, but it's very rare," she begins. "When two people have a very deep, unresolved conflict between them, the conflict spills over into their subconscious worlds. They create a sort of new realm which is very real, to both of them."

"Wait a minute," I interrupt, "are you telling me that the reason I'm seeing this guy in my dreams is because we both want to be there?" I am reeling at the news. It leaves a sour taste in my mouth.

"It's not that you both *want* to be there," Madame Destiny corrects. "It's almost that you *need* to be there." She looks pointedly at me. "You, Emma, have a need to find out why this man attacked you. You can't rest until you have a reason. Is this correct?"

I nod numbly. "Yes."

She continues. "For whatever reason, your assailant also has something to settle with you."

My fears are being confirmed. "How do you know?" I ask.

Madame Destiny rises from the sofa chair and crosses the room to a large bookcase, selecting an enormous leather-bound book from the middle shelf. She blows the dust from the cover and I make a face. With its raised symbols and crinkled, weathered pages, it looks like a book of spells and I begin to wonder what I've gotten myself into.

She flips through the book until she finds what she is searching for. "You see," she says, squeezing between Summer and me on the couch and pointing at a page in her book, "it's called dream darkening. This man appears in your dreams because of your *combined* unfulfilled needs. That's the only way this works. Like I said, there must be a very deep, unresolved conflict between *both* parties."

Madame Destiny proceeds to talk more in depth about the strange phenomenon of someone's dreams being *darkened*. I am skeptical at first, but the more she explains, the more I find myself starting to believe her. The testimonials in her book are eerily similar to my own experiences.

"You must be very careful," Madame Destiny says. "There are no rules in this realm you have created, and there is no way to know how deep your unresolved conflict goes."

"What do you mean?" I ask, fearing that I already know the answer to my question.

"This man that darkens your dreams, there is no way for me to know how badly he can hurt you. You are venturing into uncharted territory here. From what you have told me, your dreams are becoming progressively violent. If your dreams continue to intensify, or if this man discovers that his nightly encounters with you are more than just a twisted dream, I fear the worst for you."

"What do I do?" By now I am pleading for an answer.

47

"You have to resolve the source of the conflict," she replies firmly. "And only you can reveal that source from within yourself."

What? How?

Summer and I leave Madame Destiny's house in numbed silence. I clutch the heavy book she forced into my arms when she insisted that I do my own research into the phenomenon of my darkened dreams. Climbing into Summer's car, I am filled with mixed emotions. I am relieved that someone believes me, and am even more relieved to have some answers. *Crazy answers*, I think to myself, but answers. On the other hand, the thought that this masked intruder can somehow take over my dreams and even physically hurt me terrifies me to the center of my being.

"Thank you," I say to Summer, finally breaking the silence.

"For what?"

"For suggesting that we do this."

Summer gives me a huge grin and I sense that she is pleased with herself. "Well, I always know best," she declares.

"That's what my mom used to say." *Used to* – past tense. And I get that gut-wrenching feeling as I realize that, like my father, one day my mother will also be gone. I push the morbid thought away. "Anyway, I wouldn't get too cocky. Even a broken clock is right twice a day," I tease.

When we reach my place, Summer walks me inside. I set the bulky book on the coffee table, eyeing it skeptically and wondering what answers it holds. Summer checks each room with me, dramatically pulling open closet doors and looking under beds. I smile to myself. Summer always did have a flair for the dramatic.

"Want me to stay over tonight?" she asks. "I can pop popcorn and we can stay up late watching chick flicks."

The idea sounds appealing, and I'm touched by the sweet gesture, but I also don't want to take up anymore of Summer's time. "Nah, I'll be fine," I say, trying to sound fearless. "Besides, you probably have another one of your hot dates tomorrow and you'll need your beauty sleep," I tease.

Summer smiles and I realize from her expression that she actually does. I shake my head in mock disapproval. "Okay, where did you meet this one?"

"At the gym. I love a man that looks good all sweaty."

"Dang, maybe I should get a gym membership," I say.

Summer laughs and hugs me close before leaving. "Stay safe," she orders affectionately.

After watching Summer drive away, I begin my nightly routine. I check that all the doors and windows are locked and verify the burglar alarm is set. I wander to the kitchen where I empty the dishwasher and pour myself a glass of water.

I bring both the water and Madame Destiny's book into my bedroom and push my dresser in front of the door. I am annoyed at the drag marks that scar the bamboo flooring, but my typical obsession with perfection is overshadowed by my growing need for extra security. I shove the book under the bed. I know I should do some research, but I'm too tired. Or maybe I'm too chicken.

Exhausted, I stumble to the bathroom to brush my teeth and wash my face. I grab an old nightshirt from my dresser drawer and slip into it. Nightly ritual finally complete, I go to bed alone and scared, regretting that I didn't take Summer up on her offer to stay over.

My imagination chooses tonight to work overtime, and I huddle under the covers like a child during a thunderstorm. Each time I think I hear a noise or see a shadow, I think to myself that I should buy a massive guard dog. Or maybe I'll do better with a small companion dog. I can probably get past the pet hair on my furniture – then again, maybe not. While mulling over this dilemma, I eventually fall asleep.

CHAPTER TEN

I ROLL OVER IN BED to find Nate lying naked beside me.

"Hello there, sleepy head," he says. He casually drapes an arm across my body and I wonder what became of my pajamas. I snuggle closer to him, and he strokes my hair.

"I wish it could always be like this, Emma. I miss you, baby. I miss us."

My heart melts in reaction to hearing the words I've waited months for him to say. I lean in to kiss him and before I realize what he's doing, I'm pinned beneath him. Nate stretches his body over mine and inhales deeply. "You smell amazing," he murmurs in my ear.

My body responds, and I kiss him feverishly as I trail my fingers down the curve of his spine. "I need you," I confess. My boding is aching from his absence and my own carnal desire.

Nate smiles and his lips rove across my cheek, down my neck, and towards my breasts. I squeal in delight as he teases my taut nipples with his tongue. My nails dig into his back and I arch toward him, my entire body begging to be possessed by this man. "I want you so bad." I am practically pleading.

Nate raises his mouth from its gentle assault on my nipple to offer me a mischievous smile, his dimple fluttering on his cheek. Then his mouth moves further down my body – lower, and lower still.

"No…yes!" I beg as my hips involuntary arch towards him.

My need intensifies as Nate continues to pleasure me with his tongue. I reach down, tugging at his hair. I need him inside me. My desire for him consumes me.

As if sensing my thoughts, Nate lifts his head, kisses me chastely on the forehead, and then pushes himself inside me. *Yes!* I am overcome with emotion, but I will myself not to cry. *Nate, don't ever leave me*, I scream in my head.

Nate moves slowly at first, teasing, tormenting. But then his pace begins to quicken, and I match him with my own urgent rhythm. He whispers something in my ear that I can't make out, but I love the feel of his breath on my skin.

My breathing becomes raspy as the intensity builds. I find my release as his mouth closes over mine, muffling my deep moans. I revel in my victory when Nate finds his own release.

He pulls me closer to him, looking deep into my eyes. "Do you have any idea how beautiful you are?" he asks.

I don't agree with him, but I love to hear him say it just the same. I smile, edging in closer to him. I close my eyes, exhausted by our lovemaking, yet knowing I will never get enough of him.

My eyes open and I'm alone in my room. The side of the bed where Nate used to lie is now empty. My heart sinks when I realize it was once again only a dream. Ordinarily I would feel relieved after dreaming about Nate instead of my attacker. But lately the heartbreak I feel after dreaming of him is taking more of an emotional toll than the terror from my nightmares.

While lying in bed and playing back my dream in my head, I have an overwhelming need to see Nate. I want to talk to him about my nightmares and what Madame Destiny said. But most of all, I have a molten desire just to be close to him. I run my fingers over the bed sheets, tracing the spot where Nate rested his head only moments ago – only he hadn't been here, I remind myself. It was just a dream.

My first thought is to skip work and drive straightway to Nate's office to see him, but I know I am being irrational – irresponsible even. *You can go see him after work*, I reason with myself. This temporarily subdues my need and I spring out of bed to grab a shower.

CHAPTER ELEVEN

THE WORKDAY GOES BY IN A BLUR. I meet with the other executives to go over the marketing campaign. If anyone thinks it's a bad idea, they politely keep it to themselves. I still hate the idea of being the face of the company, but in light of everything going on in my personal life, I no longer spend much energy dwelling on it.

Lance pops by my office to invite me to lunch, but I decline the offer. He looks a little put out, but I don't care. I get the impression he's not used to being turned down by the ladies. In fact, I may very well be the first.

After closing the door to my office so I'm not disturbed during lunch, I fight the urge to take a little catnap. I want to see Nate. My need to dream about him is becoming like a drug to me. And like a drug, the physical and emotional letdown after coming down from such a dream almost negates the benefits of my temporary high. *Almost.* I lean over to take a bite of my sandwich and a strand of hair falls across my left eye. I tuck it behind my ear, reminiscing about the way Nate used to do that for me. *Good grief, I need to get a grip.*

Terry knocks softly at the door. I am annoyed, but I know if she is interrupting, it must be important. "Come in," I say, trying to hide my irritation and returning my half-eaten sandwich to its plate.

"I'm sorry," Terry apologizes, "but I have Mr. James on hold for you."

Tyrell James is an important client, so I nod my approval and answer the phone. "Mr. James, how may I help you?" I ask, doing my best to refocus my thoughts.

Tyrell's words are clipped as he explains the urgency of his call. His video game company, *Angry Gamer*, was set to unveil its latest game, *Mobster Island*, within the month. The marketing campaign, packaging, and pricing were developed under the direction of Danner and Banks Consulting.

My heart sinks when Tyrell tells me about a competitor that announced the launch of a virtually identical game just this morning. The disappointment I feel isn't just for my client. I myself logged several consulting hours on the project, so any setback feels very personal.

"Someone must have been leaking information to them," Tyrell rants.

"Mr. James, you're not implying that someone here at Danner and Banks Consulting would violate the nondisclosure agreement?" My tone denotes an equal amount of defensiveness and concern.

"Of course not!" Tyrell replies gruffly. "I think the leak is on my end. I intend to launch a full investigation amongst my staff. In the meantime, I need your guidance on our next move."

I discuss the rival company's product with Tyrell some more, taking notes and promising to look into the situation promptly. "We'll fix this," I reassure him before hanging up. My voice conveys more confidence than I truly feel.

I spend the rest of the afternoon doing research and putting together a revised recommendation for Tyrell. Typically, I would use the firm's administrative staff to do the grunt work, but this is the distraction I need. Not to mention, if the leak is on our end, I don't want to risk additional information being relayed back to the competitor.

My research reveals that several aspects of the rival company's game, *Mobster's Cove* (they didn't even try to get original with the name), are not as polished. According to blogs leaked from test groups, the game has several bugs, but the company released it prematurely in hopes of beating *Angry Gamer* to the punch. Furthermore, their product is over-priced, and they are marketing to a younger demographic than what my firm's thorough research found was suitable given the maturity of the game.

Picking up the phone, I call Tyrell to discuss my findings. I propose a change to his company's overall marketing approach, a change that will focus on all the positive things *Mobster Island* has that *Mobster's Cove* does not. "If we play this right," I explain to him, "we can actually use their premature product launch to our advantage. We can market your product's strengths, ergo highlighting the weaknesses of your competitor's product." Tyrell is pleased with my recommendations, and I promise to follow up with a summary he can take to his internal marketing department. Crisis avoided.

I'm reasonably certain no one on my staff would violate a nondisclosure agreement; NDAs are a foundational element of any consulting business. But to give the matter due diligence, I call Terry into my office. "Can you give me a list of everyone that billed time to the *Angry Gamer* project over the last fiscal quarter?" I ask.

Terry looks like she wants to question why, but instead she agrees to pull the information together by the next morning.

I leave my office at four o'clock on the dot. I feel like a kid on Christmas as I hurry to my car. *Nate!*

CHAPTER TWELVE

I MAKE IT FROM MY OFFICE to the police station faster than anticipated, fueled by my burning desire to see the man I still find irresistible. Nate looks up as I walk into his office. His dark hair looks a little disheveled and I can't help but notice how tired he looks. *Hot and haggard.* I smile to myself as I think about my dream from the night before. His appearance would be just about right had he really spent his night the way my over-active imagination played out just a few hours earlier.

"Why do you look like you swallowed a canary?" Nate asks, and my wayward thoughts come to a screeching halt.

"Err… no reason. So, any news?" I ask, ignoring the growing warmth on my cheeks.

"No." Nate sounds frustrated. *At me?*

"Nate?" I pause timidly but start again before he can answer. "I have a strange theory and I want you to hear me out."

"I'm listening," he answers, sounding amused. I wonder if he thinks that I've been playing detective.

"You're going to think this sounds crazy," I begin, taking a seat across from him.

"Try me."

"In my defense, it really isn't my theory. I heard it from someone else."

"Emma," Nate says impatiently, "just tell me." His green eyes soften as he waits for me to continue.

I sigh before proceeding. Unable to look him in the eye, I stare down at my hands and begin to tell him about my nightmares and about the marks on my wrists when I wake up. I even tell him all about going to see Madame Destiny and her theory about my dreams being *darkened* by my assailant. *So embarrassing!*

Nate listens intently while I talk. He doesn't smirk or laugh. He even jots down a few notes as I speak. When I am finally done talking, I look up at him. I study his expression, but his face doesn't give anything away. For what seems like an eternity, we sit in silence.

Nate leans back in his chair, running his hand over his chin. I stare back down at my hands, struggling with the compulsion to snuggle up on his lap. Finally, he speaks. "So, you think this guy keeps showing up in your dreams because he has some unfinished business with you?" I still can't tell if Nate is taking me seriously.

"Yes," I say, trying not to sound defensive. "I think there was a reason he was in my house. I think he tied me up to make it look like he wanted…. umm… something else."

59

Unmistakable anger flashes across Nate's handsome face, but I continue. "I think he was looking for something in my house."

"But what would it be?" Nate asks. He sounds genuinely interested. *Is he really considering my theory?*

"I'm not sure. That's where you come in Detective." I smile coyly, playfully fluttering my lashes.

Nate stands up from behind his desk and circles around to where I'm seated. He walks slowly to me and crouches down beside me. Without warning, he clasps my right hand in his, pulling it closer to him to examine my wrist. The faint markings are still visible. "Do these hurt?" he asks, tenderly tracing the marks with his fingertips.

"No," I say, feeling the need to reassure him. My pulse quickens at his gentle touch.

Nate frowns, his brow furrowing. "And you have no other explanation for how you got these marks?"

"No!" I pull my hand away. This time I am defensive.

"Relax, Emma," Nate says. "I believe you."

"You do?" I am stunned. "Why?"

Nate pauses. "I noticed those marks on your wrists when you first came in here, Emma. At first I thought you'd found someone else who knew how to make good use of police-issued handcuffs."

Nate looks up at me and gives me a questioning look. I flush scarlet as I recall the sensual games he and I used to play with his handcuffs.

"Frankly," he continues, "I think I prefer this Madame Destiny's theory to the alternative." He smiles mischievously, his eyes dancing with humor.

"Get serious," I challenge. "Why do you really believe me? I'm the one telling you and *I* don't know if I believe me."

"Seriously? Let's just say that recent events have led me to believe your theory is plausible."

Recent events? I wonder what he is referring to. I want to ask him that very question, but his phone rings, reminding me that Nate has a demanding job that I am keeping him from.

"I will let you go," I say, standing to go. I can tell Nate wants to say something, but instead he nods and picks up the phone.

As I turn to leave, Nate puts his hand over the receiver and looks up at me. "Emma."

"Yes?"

"You look pretty sexy in that dress."

Shocked by his casual flirting, I manage a little curtsy and a wink before leaving his office. I am all smiles when I step into the elevator.

CHAPTER THIRTEEN

I AM CURLED UP NEXT TO NATE on a blanket at Olympic Beach, feeling the slow rise and fall of his chest and listening to the steady rhythm of his heartbeat. The morning breeze feels cool and refreshing against my skin. Nate strokes my hair and kisses my shoulder, making me feel warm all over.

"You know, someday you're going to have to let me go here too," he tells me, slowly caressing my cheek with his fingertips as he stares off into the distance.

He sounds as forlorn as I've been feeling, and the tears well up in my eyes because, as much as it pains me to admit it, I know that he's right. "Why did you leave?" I finally ask.

Nate pauses as if my question confuses him. "You told me to," he answers softly. I lift my head off his chest and turn to face him. When I look in his eyes, I don't see any anger. All I see is pain – deep pain swimming in brilliant pools of green. *Even the beautiful ones are damaged*, I think to myself. And the guilt rips through me because I know I damaged him.

"I lied, Nate," I confess. "Please come back to me."

He is silent, and a heavy morning fog surrounds us. I know I am just inches from his face, but I can scarcely see him. "Nate!" I scream out as the dense fog envelopes us. I reach out for him, but he is no longer there. The blanket is empty, and I am alone in the suffocating mist. "Nate! Nate! Please, please come back to me!"

I wake up screaming Nate's name and feeling the moisture of my tears on my cheeks. I reach for my pillow, give it a tight squeeze, and wish with everything within me for it to be Nate. Frustrated, I toss my pillow aside and roll out of bed to face the day.

CHAPTER FOURTEEN

WHEN NATE STROLLS INTO MY OFFICE, I smooth my skirt from behind my desk. Opening my purse, I take out my vanilla-flavored lip gloss and apply it slowly to my lips. Nate used to tell me how much he liked the taste when he kissed me. I am being flirtatious, and I hope that I am being subtle enough. Then again, part of me hopes that I'm not.

I smile sweetly up at Nate as he approaches my desk. "Vanilla?" he asks, his eyes dancing with humor.

"Yes," I say innocently, feeling a slight blush creep across my cheeks.

Nate grins, shaking his head. "You're really moving up in the world," he says, gawking at the view from my office and pointing his finger at my fancy title printed on the door.

I shrug, unsure how to respond. "So, um, what are you doing here?" I ask, attempting to break the awkward pause.

"It's nice to see you too," Nate says sarcastically, but he is smiling.

"I'm sorry," I say. "I'm just surprised to see you, that's all." I start to feel flushed and I wonder if it's obvious to Nate, the powerful affect he has on me.

Nate clears his throat and seems uncharacteristically hesitant. "I just wanted to say that it's been great seeing you lately and I also wanted to let you know that I'm going to do everything I can to close out your case. I am personally handling every facet of the investigation."

"Do you feel an obligation because you're familiar with the *victim?*" I know I am being unpleasant but am unable to help myself.

"That's not how I meant it."

"Isn't it?" I raise one eyebrow – at least I attempt to.

"I see that you are just as frustrating as ever," he tells me.

"And I see you still have a way with words." By this point Nate and I are both smiling – fully aware we are being ridiculous. Our heated exchange has turned to playful banter.

"In all seriousness," I say, "thank you for everything you're doing." Nate takes a step towards me, then seems to change his mind. Instead, he nods; then, without another word, he walks briskly out of my office.

Nate and I start to see a lot of each other after his quick retreat from my office. He often stops by to take me to lunch to talk about the case. For some reason, I am never disappointed when he tells me there hasn't been any major developments. Just being able to talk to Nate outweighs my vested interest in his investigation. I know I should be more apprehensive about the lack of progress; it is my neck on the line after all.

The ladies at the office gush whenever Nate stops by. I can't blame them. The man is an Adonis with a rare gift for oozing confidence without appearing brash. "You're so lucky," they croon. I know I should tell them that Nate is just a friend, but I don't want to advertise his single status.

I can't help but wonder if his visits are an excuse to see me, but I tell myself not to get my hopes up. Nate is a detective and is just doing his job. Sometimes I catch him staring at me during lunch and I want to ask what he is thinking about, but I don't have the nerve. We restrict our discussions to my case and casual conversation about our families. Our brief exchanges, although pleasant, always leave me wanting more.

When I don't hear from Nate for a few days, I instigate a meeting by stopping by the police station under the guise of checking in on the investigation. I walk into his office unannounced and catch a glimpse of a clear, plastic bag with an article of clothing in it. Nate shoves it in his desk drawer and flashes me a nervous grin. The familiar print of the fabric and the apologetic expression on Nate's face tell me all I need to know. It is an evidence bag from my case – my nightshirt the police confiscated to check for DNA and fibers. A dull roar begins in my ears and I absentmindedly run my fingertips over my sternum, half expecting to feel the indent of the buttons the intruder left when he buried his knee into my chest. Nate coughs uncomfortably.

"I'm sorry, I was just reviewing some of the evidence from your case, trying to see if we missed anything."

I offer him a tight smile. Relief floods me that my nightshirt was one of the only pieces of evidence the cops seized from my home. In the nightstand by my bed was a letter I'd started to Nate all those months ago – a feeble attempt to explain why I ended things with him and, in a late-night moment of weakness and sleep-deprivation, about a half-page of

66

scrawled words, begging him to take me back. When the police combed my room that night, I was mortified they might find the letter and, for some reason, bag it as evidence. My face flames as I recall that moment. It was irrational, of course, to think the letter would be confiscated as evidence, but I had feared it all the same.

"Anything new to report?" I ask, straightening my shoulders and hoping the redness in my cheeks has subsided.

"Not yet," he tells me, sounding defeated.

I find myself offering him encouragement while he summarizes the angles of the case he's pursued over the past several days. He says he has additional leads to follow, I suggest names of my neighbors he might re-interview, but it's clear the department is no closer to solving the case than the day of the home invasion. After a fruitless, yet somehow gratifying exchange, I offer my good-byes.

"Hey Nate, do me a favor," I say, casually looking back over my shoulder as I make my retreat.

"What's that?"

"When you're done with this case, and that shirt is no longer evidence … burn it."

Once a place of solace, my home has become a domicile of discontentment. The quiet atmosphere provides the ideal setting for Nate to invade my every thought. I do my best to fill my evenings to keep my mind off him. Summer takes full advantage by convincing me to be her workout partner, although she knows that I loathe exercise.

"Summer, I don't want to go to the gym," I whine for the third time in a week. I know I sound like a schoolgirl trying to get out of an early bedtime.

"Oh, come on," Summer urges. "They're doing hot yoga tonight and I really want to go." Now it is Summer who is whining. "We'll go for sundaes afterwards."

Summer knows my weak spot. "Isn't that counterproductive?" I tease.

"I won't tell if you won't tell," she promises, and I find myself giving in.

When the hot yoga class is finally over, I am covered in sweat and have extended my body in ways I never knew possible. I wonder if any of the yoga poses could be used in bed with Nate. I bite my lip, trying to hide a smile as I attempt to reign in my errant thoughts.

"Sundaes?" Summer asks, a little too chipper for my taste. I glance over at her. Her tight ponytail remains intact, not a hair out of place, and she looks as if she barely exerted herself. I am amazed at her seemingly effortless perfection.

"At this point, all I want is a shower," I say. She laughs as we head for the locker room.

Feeling better after a quick shower and a change of clothes, we agree to go out for coffee at *Hal's Stomping Grounds*, our favorite local coffee shop.

"Hello ladies," a chipper voice calls out from behind the counter.

"Hi Tom," I call back. Tom is a long-time employee of the coffee shop and always treats Summer and I like family.

"The usual?" he asks, flashing a toothy grin behind is ever-growing beard. With his whiskered face and bold tattoo that snakes up his forearm, Tom's outward appearance is a fierce contradiction to his warm persona.

"Of course," Summer and I respond simultaneously.

After making our drinks, Tom rings us up using his employee discount. "You know you don't have to do that," I tell him, dropping a generous tip in the jar to make up the difference.

Tom winks and hands us our drinks with our names neatly written on each cup. A smiley face is drawn next to my name.

"I told you he likes you," Summer tells me as we take our seats at a corner table. I ignore her comment and instead begin to fill her in on my reoccurring visits with Nate.

"I just wish Nate thought of me as more than a friend," I sigh.

"Oh, come on Emma," Summer says. "It's obvious the man still cares about you. I mean, really, how many other cases do you think he has where he visits the person at work? You know, they did invent something called a phone – not to mention email."

I want to believe what she's saying is true, but I can't really be sure. Despite Nate's cheerful disposition when we talk, I can tell how guarded he is now and I hate that I am responsible for that. As much as I would give to be back together with Nate, for now I will have to settle for a casual friendship.

Noticing Tom approaching our table, mop cloth in hand, I attempt to switch the subject. "Can I get you ladies anything else?" he asks, wiping the already clean tabletop and offering us a couple of napkins from the pocket of his apron.

"What is your opinion, Tom?" Summer asks mischievously, thwarting my attempts to change topics.

"On what?"

"If a guy constantly stops by your office on *business* rather than simply picking up the telephone and giving you call, would you say his intentions go beyond friendship?"

I see a hint of annoyance flicker across Tom's face and it makes me feel guilty. I kick Summer from below the table. Tom recovers quickly, and his good-natured mannerisms return. "It depends," he tells us. "But I would bet if a guy constantly goes out of his way to do extra things like stopping by the girl's office or, say, leaving little drawings on her coffee cup, then yes, he probably would like to be more than friends." And with that, Tom winks in my direction and walks away, leaving both Summer and I speechless.

CHAPTER FIFTEEN

"WHERE IS SHE?" HE ASKS ALOUD. Only today he's not angry, only curious. He circles the block to pass by the woman's house once again. When she finally pulls into the driveway, he is pleased to see that she is by herself and not with her blonde friend. He likes to see the woman all alone – vulnerable.

He watches the woman exit her car and ascend the steps to her front door. She pauses on the top step and cocks her head to the side, looking around. She looks momentarily uncomfortable, as if she knows she's being watched, and he leans forward in his seat to get a better look at her. To him she represents beauty, grace, and innocence – innocence that reminds him of his childhood. He clinches his fists at his sides in response to the burst of mixed emotions the memories of his childhood evoke in him. By all accounts, he had a good upbringing, with respectable parents and a stable home environment. But no one ever knew the demons he battled within.

His family wouldn't have understood – his dark thoughts, his secret desires. "She would understand," he mumbles to himself as he strains his eyes to catch a glimpse of the woman through the curtains. His efforts are futile. The curtains are shut tight.

He wonders if he should try to break into her house once it gets dark. He is aware of the sign for the alarm company boldly posted in her front yard, and although it is an enormous deterrent, he is certain he can find a way to circumvent it. Resisting the urge to pull into her driveway, he makes one final pass before heading home.

CHAPTER SIXTEEN

I AM ABOUT TO WRITE OFF THE WORKDAY morning as uneventful when I receive an unexpected visit from Eldon Banks. He enters my office without knocking. I suppose he doesn't have to knock, he is half owner of the company after all. "What can I do for you?" I ask politely.

No matter how hard I try, I can't help but find him intimidating. His silver hair is slicked back in a ponytail. He's dressed in black slacks and a gray shirt. A gray and black bow-tie completes the ensemble. Typically, I find a bow-tie clownish, but Eldon even manages to make that look intimidating. Realizing that I have been staring and that Eldon still hasn't answered my question about why he is in my office, I try again.

"Did we have a meeting?" I ask, knowing full well we did not.

Eldon removes his round glasses and rubs the bridge of his nose. He places the glasses back on his face and starts to speak at an exasperatingly slow and deliberate pace, as if he's patiently explaining a simple fact to a child. "Lance has it in his head that he'd like to expand our consulting services to areas I feel are, well, beyond our mission scope. You often have his ear. I'd like you to talk him out of it."

"This is the first I've heard of this," I say, hoping to avoid being caught in the middle of a dispute between my two bosses.

"I'll have my secretary provide you the information within the hour. I'm counting on you to resolve this with Lance before the end of the week."

"But...," I try to object.

"If you're as good as Lance always says you are," Eldon interrupts, "I trust this won't be an issue." He stares coldly down at me. The gauntlet has been thrown.

"Yes, sir," I say. It's the best response I can come up with.

Eldon smiles. At least I assume it's a smile. The left side of his mouth curls upwards. If his eyes didn't look so triumphant, I might mistake the expression as a grimace of pain.

"I won't let you down," I say lamely before he walks out of my office. "I won't let you down?" I repeat sarcastically under my breath once I'm alone. "What a suck-up," I scold myself.

The report I receive from Eldon's secretary has me chuckling to myself. Lance actually suggested that we broaden our consulting services to the adult entertainment industry. I can just imagine Eldon Banks providing input to our clients as he casts withering looks from behind his glasses and self-importantly adjusts his bow-tie. This is one argument that I think Eldon might have a good point on though. I don't like to think of myself as a prude but studying up on the adult entertainment industry so that I can provide my expert feedback is something I might find a tad uncomfortable.

Unsure how to approach Lance directly, I dial the number for his secretary instead and request that she schedule Lance and me in a lunch meeting later that day.

At lunchtime, Lance meets me in the lobby. "Really? We're going to a hotdog vendor? Is that how you want to spend our first date?" He winks at me, clearly teasing.

"I have business to discuss with you, Mister," I say.

"Uh oh," Lance says, but he doesn't look at all concerned. We walk about a block before we reach the food trucks. We order sausage dogs and sodas and I continue making small talk as I search for a way to broach the subject.

"Eldon came to see you, didn't he?" Lance speaks up, his mouth full of food.

"What are you talking about?" I stall, not sure what to say.

"I knew it," Lance says. "You're a horrible liar. He wants you to talk me out of my new idea."

I feel my face redden. "Well, Lance, you have to admit, it is a little… out there."

"You wouldn't be interested in studying up on the business?" I can't tell if he's being serious.

"You know I'll work hard for any of our clients, but to be honest…" I trail off when I catch him snickering.

"It was a joke," he tells me.

"What?"

"It was a joke. Eldon is so straight-laced and unwilling to pursue new interests, so I wrote up a preposterous plan that I knew he'd never go for."

"Why?" I ask, starting to laugh.

"To let him think he won an argument. We'll balk and argue, and then I'll finally concede. Once he thinks he's won one, he might be more amenable to my next idea, which is far less scandalous."

"Well, can we at least pretend that I helped talk you out of it?"

"Eldon give you the ol' 'I'm counting on you' speech?" Lance asks. His goofy grin is spread from ear to ear.

"As a matter of fact, he did."

"And bringing me to a hotdog stand to talk me out of it was your best plan?"

"Hey," I say, "it was the best I could do on such short notice."

"You've got to admit; my idea would have allowed all of us to look at porn at work and claim we were just doing research." I nearly choke on my sausage dog, then hit Lance in the arm.

"Grow up," I tease.

Arriving back at the office after lunch, I notice an impressive vase of fresh cut flowers sitting on Terry's desk. "Secret admirer?" I ask her. I've never heard Terry mention a boyfriend.

"No, actually they are addressed to you," she says.

"Oh," I respond in disbelief. I am instantly excited. *They must be from Nate*, I think to myself. I eye the card, wondering if Terry already read it, unable to contain her curiosity. Then again, she doesn't strike me as the overly-curious type.

Lifting the flowers from Terry's desk, I bring them to my office and close the door behind me. I set them down in the middle of the round table next to my desk. I breathe in the sweet aroma before reaching for the envelope where my name is written in flawless calligraphy.

I pull out the card, anxious to read the message Nate has left for me. My excitement turns to dread when I begin to read. The words, *I am watching you,* glare back at me from the unsigned paper, extinguishing my excitement. My knees buckle, and I sink to the floor.

After collecting myself, I call Terry into my office to ask what delivery company dropped off the flowers. I try to appear composed, but Terry is taken back by my adamant request.

"What's wrong?" she asks. She looks as if she pities me, and I am immediately frustrated by her belaying my urgency.

"Who dropped these off?" I repeat more forcefully.

"Um, I believe it was *Edmonds in Bloom*," Terry says, looking confused.

I offer her a quick apology and explain to her about the card. I typically like to keep my private life just that around the office, but I know that Terry deserves an explanation for my outburst.

Less than thirty minutes later Nate is in my office, pacing back and forth. "I'm fine, Nate," I repeat for what feels like the hundredth time. "I just thought you should know since you are working on my case, but I am sure you have more pressing matters to get back to."

"Well, crime is down, so..." Nate jokes, but he is still frowning.

"I was sort of hoping the flowers were from you," I blurt out, hoping to distract him with my unexpected confession.

It works. Nate stops pacing and walks over to me, closing the gap between us in a few quick strides. "I wish I would have thought of it," he says earnestly.

Locking his eyes with mine, Nate strokes my cheek. He is standing inches from my face and I think he's about to kiss me. My heartbeat quickens, and I close my eyes and tilt my head in anticipation.

Nate abruptly takes a step back and clears his throat. "Well, I'll call the delivery company and see if I can track down the person that ordered these flowers. If he called it in on a credit card, it should be easy to trace. Then again, if he paid cash he would have had to place the order in person. Maybe we'll get lucky and the flower shop will have video surveillance."

I nod in approval, disappointed that he didn't kiss me. I wonder if he saw me close my eyes and am mortified at the thought.

"What's wrong?" Nate asks.

"Nothing," I lie. I feel the tears creep into my eyes and am angry with myself. Frowning, Nate steps towards me again, leaning in so close that his lips brush my hair. I'm not sure if it's my imagination, but his breathing sounds labored.

"I should have been the one that sent the flowers," he whispers in my ear. His confession sends shockwaves through my body. Before I have a chance to respond, he plants a quick kiss on my cheek, then abruptly leaves my office, leaving me flushed and unsteady.

CHAPTER SEVENTEEN

NATE CALLS ME AT HOME to tell me the flowers were a dead end. The order was placed from a burner cellphone and paid for by a prepaid Visa card that can be picked up at any local grocery store. I can tell Nate is just as disappointed as I am. I was hoping this would soon be over – the case anyways, not our interactions with each other.

"I did give them a piece of my mind about delivering flowers with such a threatening message," Nate grumbles.

"What was their excuse?"

"The girl at the store who writes out the cards actually thought it was a romantic message. I'd hate to know what her love life is like."

I let out an unladylike snort before thanking Nate for the call. Uncomfortable silence follows as I try to find an excuse to keep him on the line. I love hearing the smoothness of his voice.

"Are you free for dinner tonight?" he asks after a long pause. My heartbeat quickens.

"Why?" I ask before I can stop myself. I wonder what Nate would possibly want to discuss over dinner. He just said the flowers were a dead end.

Nate sounds strangely unsure of himself. "Well, if you already have plans."

"I'd love to," I interrupt, fearing he will change his mind.

"Great, I'll pick you up in an hour." Before I can respond, he hangs up.

I call Summer to tell her about the dinner invite and to ask for advice on what to wear. I am practically hyperventilating as I rush around my bedroom getting ready, all the while with my cellphone plastered to my ear.

"Calm down," Summer tells me. "You don't want to scare the poor man away." She is teasing me, but I know that she's right. I take a few cleansing breaths to steady myself.

By the time Nate arrives, I'm dressed to kill in an outfit Summer picked out over the phone. She has helped me pick out practically everything in my closet, so she's committed my wardrobe to memory – at least the pieces she considers worthy of being seen in public.

Nate is prompt, something I always appreciated about him. He strolls into my house wearing tan slacks and a white, button-up shirt. I stare down at my feet to keep from gawking. "Ready?" he asks.

When we reach his car, he opens the door for me, and I slip inside. When he gets in the car, my heartbeat quickens when he leans toward me. *Is he about to kiss me?* Instead, he reaches for my seatbelt and slides it across my shoulder and lap. He must read the startled expression on my face, because he stops mid-way.

"I'm sorry. Old habit," he explains, clicking the seatbelt into place. We both laugh uncomfortably. With all he's witnessed as a police officer, it's always bothered Nate that I never remember my seatbelt. When we dated he often slipped it on for me, then rattled off a lecture on seatbelt safety statistics. It gives me a pleasurable thrill at how quickly we've slipped back into old habits.

Nate takes me to dinner at a quiet Italian restaurant. The linen tablecloths and candlelight seem a bit out of place for our current relationship status.

After a glass of wine, we start to loosen up. We talk about our maturing careers and our families but are careful to steer away from any discussions about dating. That is, until I can't stand it any longer.

"So, are you seeing anyone?" I blurt out. I can feel myself blushing at the question, but I keep my eyes level with Nate's.

Nate looks almost relieved that I opened the door to this line of questioning. "Nah," he says. "I mean, I've been on a few dates lately, but nothing serious."

Although comforted with his response, I feel a twinge of jealousy at the thought of him dating anyone else, no matter how inconsequential. I wonder how far the dates went. An image of Nate in bed with another woman pops into my head and it churns my stomach.

"What about you?" he asks, staring at me intently. The image vanishes. I am flattered that he seems genuinely interested in my response.

"No one special," I say, shrugging my shoulders and trying to sound casual. I don't want to tell him that my one and only date I've had since we broke up is the one he saw me on just a few months ago.

Nate leans back in his chair and smiles. "Don't look so pleased at the news of my pathetic love life," I tease. Nate laughs and reaches for the check.

"Oh, no way," I argue, reaching across the table to grab the check from him. My hand brushes his and I feel a jolt of electricity run through my body. "I can pay my half," I finish, pretending that I am not affected by our brief touch.

"I know you can. I've seen your fancy office."

I roll my eyes. "Seriously, I'll get mine."

"Emma, let me," he says. His voice is soft, but firm. I don't argue, but instead quickly thank him. Nate's always been so old school, something I find alluring despite my voiced objections.

Nate drives me home, and as the silence settles over us, my nervousness returns. I fiddle with the door handle, then the radio. When we reach my house, I clamber out of the car at a fleeing pace. Nate steps out of the car and walks me to my front door, careful to keep some distance between us while matching my brisk pace.

"I had a really good time," I tell him as my shaking hands struggle to put the key in the lock.

"I did too. We'll have to do it again some time." *Some time.* His offer is noncommittal. He offers me a brief hug, but there is no warmth in his embrace, and before I can say another word, he places a swift kiss on my cheek and walks away.

I let myself in and close the front door, resting against it. With a heavy heart, I sink to the floor and let my body absorb the pain. It courses through my veins and sends shockwaves to my heart. I close my eyes and will the pain to subside. I am strong. I can live without him. I know this.

There's just one problem – I don't want to. I want so much for Nate to come in and hold me like he used to. My mouth still yearns for the taste of him; my body pleads to feel his warmth. I know our dinner was progress, but it also made it abundantly clear how different things are now from how they used to be.

Reduced to tears, my wallowing is interrupted by a brisk knock at the door. I scramble to my feet, straightening my clothes and wiping my eyes. I look through the peephole. It's Nate!

I throw open the door. Before I can ask Nate what he forgot, he pulls me towards him. He places a hand on the side of my neck, lacing his fingers through my hair while stroking my cheek with his thumb. My heart is racing, and he leans in and plants a long, fierce kiss on my lips. "To hell with pride," he growls as his lips possess mine. "It's overrated anyway."

I stand on my tiptoes, close my eyes, and revel in the warmth of his mouth against mine and the rapture of his hands on my skin. I edge my body closer to his and tip my head back as his lips brush my throat. He growls with desire into my ear before his mouth once again claims mine. Then, without warning, he releases me and takes a step backwards, leaving me breathless.

"I would like to see you again tomorrow," he says. My skin burns from the fire of his touch. "Stop by my office after work?" Nate phrases it as a question, but I sense it's more of a command.

I nod in response and Nate walks back to his car without another word. This time when I close the door, I am all smiles. I have a new glimmer of hope that the two of us can once again become more than friends. For the first time since my attack, I forget my nightly ritual and head straight to bed. I am certain that I'll dream of Nate.

CHAPTER EIGHTEEN

TRUE TO MY WORD, I STOP BY THE PRECINCT after work. When Nate said, "after work," he didn't specify a time. I wanted to stop by at two... perhaps three. It took a great deal of willpower to wait until 4:30. A woman must at least *try* and play hard-to-get.

When I pass Rudy's desk on the way to Nate's office, I offer a friendly wave but head straight past him. "Detective Mitchell is expecting me," I call over my shoulder.

Nate's door is shut, so I knock firmly and wait for an answer. I hear shuffling from inside, then his door opens. I'm taken back when I see that he's not alone. A tall, shapely woman with shoulder-length red hair opens the door to me. I stare at her. She's pretty, perhaps a little too dolled-up, but I suppose a lot of men are drawn to that look. The woman is wearing a short, black dress that hugs her curves in all the right places. The neckline is low, exposing a hint of a lacy bra.

I straighten my spine and look her directly in the eye to show her that I'm not threatened by her. I know women are always throwing themselves at Nate, but I'm not going down without a fight.

"Excuse me," the woman says cheerily, stepping past me into the hallway. "I'll be in touch," she calls over her shoulder to Nate. I can't help but watch her strut away in her four-inch heels.

"I didn't realize I had to take a number," I say sarcastically once the woman is out of earshot. Not wanting to sound like a jealous lunatic, I smile sweetly and take a seat across from him. My imagination is working overtime and I wonder if Nate had me come here just so I could witness how he's moved on.

"She's a client on one of the cases I'm working," he explains.

"So am I," I say pointedly.

"You know you're more than that," he says, shooting me a warning look.

This time the smile I offer is genuine. "So, what did you want me to stop by for?" I ask.

Nate stares blankly at me but says nothing.

"Last night. You asked me to stop by after work," I remind him as my confidence wavers.

He continues to stare at me as if confused, and amid the agonizing silence, I feel my cheeks burn. All the excitement I'd built up towards this moment comes crashing down around me. "You forgot," I say, the hard realization setting in. I fiddle with the hem of my skirt and rise from my chair.

"Well, I…," Nate begins.

"No, it's fine," I interrupt, trying to mask my humiliation and irritation. "I just remembered that I have somewhere to be," I say, heart in my stomach.

Nate looks like he wants to say something, but he just stares as I turn towards the door. I can feel the anger bubbling inside as I try to make sense of why he would have me come here, only to give me the brush off.

"You know," I say, swallowing the lump in my throat as I turn to face him. "You asked me to come here. I came. Now you can't even remember why you summoned me here? I've got news for you; I'm a very busy person. I don't have time for your little games." I square my shoulders and place both hands on my hips.

"Can I talk now?" Nate asks. I can hear the irritation in his tone and I wonder what right he has.

"Oh, I think enough of our time has been wasted here today." I storm out of his office before he can witness the tears well up in my eyes. I refuse to give him the satisfaction.

Alone at home with my thoughts, I can't wait to go to bed. Once I fall asleep, I know in my dream world everything will be okay between Nate and me. The anger we share won't exist there – there's no place for it. I also know when I fall asleep I run the risk of dreaming about my attacker, but it's a risk I'm willing to take.

After dinner, I turn in early. I brush my teeth and select an emerald green negligée from my bottom dresser drawer. I know it's ridiculous, but it makes me feel closer to Nate. I lie down in bed, fluff up the pillows around me, and squeeze my eyes shut.

Before I drift off to sleep, I'm reminded of the lyrics from an old Everly Brothers song my parents loved. "Only trouble is, gee whiz, I'm dreamin' my life away..."

It's true, but I don't mind.

Nate seductively enters my dreams – just as I anticipated. "I've been waiting for you," I tell him when he enters my bedroom.

"Have you?" He sounds more playful than surprised.

"What took you so long?" I tease, kicking away the covers to reveal my sleek nighty.

He grins and raises an eyebrow. I motion him over to me, using only my index finger. Nate obediently walks to the edge of the bed. He leans down to kiss my cheek, but I turn my head so his lips land on mine.

"You did that on purpose." This time he does sound surprised.

He leans down to kiss me again, then pauses. "I didn't forget," he says.

"What?"

"Earlier today, when you came to my office. I didn't forget. I was just searching for a good excuse for having you stop by. I had all night to come up with one. I guess I fell asleep and never did." He captures me with his intense gaze and I can tell he's being sincere – and that he needs me to believe him.

"Oh," I shrug, taking his hand and pulling him down onto the bed. "Well, I guess you should have said so. We could have just avoided our little argument."

Nate grins and shakes his head. He stretches his body over mine. For a timeless span, we make love as Nate caresses my body and covers me in kisses. I squeal when he suckles on my neck, chuckling at the mark he leaves behind.

"What are you, fifteen?" I tease.

CHAPTER NINETEEN

MY ALARM CLOCK IS BUZZING IN MY EAR and I groan as it pulls me away from my dream. I would like to go back in time to meet whoever invented such an annoying noise and have a stern talk with them. I stretch before forcing myself out of bed. Rubbing the sleep from my eyes, I walk to the bathroom and stare at my reflection in the full-length mirror. Smiling to myself, I relive every moment of my dream in my head – the warmth of Nate's lips against mine; the strength of his hands when they caressed my body.

Suddenly I do a double-take and lean in closer to study my reflection, carefully examining my neck. A hickey? I have a hickey! The realization hits me like a truck. I remember Madame Destiny's words, *"When two people have a deep, unresolved conflict..."*

The obvious truth was right in front of me the whole time and I didn't even see it. My beautiful Nate, who clouds my thoughts by day, also darkens my dreams by night. All at once I am elated. Hurriedly walking to my closet and pulling on clothes, I now know what I have to do.

I stroll through the door of Nate's office, unannounced and unapologetic.

"Emma, this is a nice surprise," he says, and I know he means it.

"Why did you believe my theory about the intruder?" I challenge.

"What?" It's evident he is both startled and confused by my question.

"You heard me. Why did you believe it?"

Nate continues to look confused. "I told you."

"But I want the real truth," I demand, my hands on my hips to emphasize that I'm all business.

"Emma, like I said..."

Growing impatient, I pull back the collar of my jacket to reveal the mark on my neck. The mark that Nate left in my dream the night before. In *our* dream.

"Oh," is all Nate can manage as I see the realization setting in. He leans back in his chair and his green eyes burn with shock and desire.

"Yeah, *Oh*," I say, doing my best to hide my amusement. Before I can think of anything clever to say, we are interrupted by a knock on the door. I turn to see a young cop standing in the doorway.

"I'm sorry to disturb you Detective Mitchell, but the mayor is here to see you." Nate nods in the cop's direction, both acknowledging and dismissing the young officer.

I raise my eyebrows to show that I am impressed. "I'll let you get back to work, but I trust this conversation isn't yet over," I say. And with that, I leave Nate's office without uttering another word. I can feel his awestruck stare as I walk elatedly out of the room.

In meetings all day at work, I don't even have time for a lunch break. When I return to my office, I have several messages, but none are from Nate. I am disappointed after this morning's big reveal, but I remind myself that he has a demanding job too.

After a long day at the office that I thought would never end, I slip behind the wheel of my car and wonder to myself yet again why Nate hasn't at least called. I felt victorious this morning. Now all I feel is uncertainty. Determined not to dwell on it any longer, I crank up the radio to drown out my thoughts as I head home to hit the books.

CHAPTER TWENTY

I AM DEEPLY ENGROSSED IN MY ECONOMICS curriculum when my phone rings. "Yeah," I answer casually, welcoming the interruption and fully expecting it to be Summer.

"Is that any way to talk to the detective working late on your case?" The voice on the line is masculine, but smooth as honey. My heart skips a beat. *Nate!*

"What are you doing?" I try to sound nonchalant.

"Oh, nothing much. You know, just hanging out on your front doorstep." *Oh crap!* I spring to my feet and look out the peephole. Nate is standing on my front porch, looking dreamy as usual. I pull open the door, all smiles as I invite him in. I know I'm not containing my excitement, but I don't care.

Nate strolls casually into my living room and takes a seat on the couch without being prompted. He unclips his badge from his belt and tosses it on the coffee table. "Make yourself at home," I say sarcastically.

He grins mischievously, kicking off his shoes and putting his feet up on the coffee table, next to his badge. I recollect all the times I got after him for putting his feet up on the table. Now I just want him to stay like this forever. Pushing aside the memories, I finally ask, "So, are you here about the case?"

Nate's expression turns serious. "Emma, I think we both know I didn't come about the case." I feel the familiar heat rush to my face.

"I see." I take a deep breath and sit next to Nate on the couch. I think it will be easier sitting next to him. That way I can look straight ahead instead of getting lost in his inviting green eyes. "I don't know where to begin," I confess, staring down at my hands.

"Then let me," Nate interjects. He turns towards me, looking directly into my eyes. Our knees are touching, igniting the passions of our shared, erotic dreams.

"Emma, I can't forgive myself for what happened to you. I should have stayed here to protect you. Even though you stopped loving me, I should have stuck around to make sure you'd be alright."

I cut him off immediately, clasping both of his hands in mine. "Oh my God, Nate, is that what you thought?" I am stunned. "I didn't tell you that I was leaving because I didn't love you anymore. I told you that I was leaving because I wasn't sure that you loved me." As soon as the words are out of my mouth, I know how foolish they sound. Nate looks confused, so I continue.

"I know how silly that must sound to you. But I knew you could have any woman you wanted, so why would you choose to stay with me? I felt it was only a matter of time before you moved on and I knew I'd be wrecked if you left me unexpectedly, so I wanted to leave you on my own terms." Tears stream down my face as I stumble through my explanation. Nate tries to brush them away, but I stop him.

"Please, I need to get this out," I tell him. "After I told you that it was over, I saw the look on your face and for just a moment, I thought there was a chance that you might actually want to stay. When you walked away that night I knew I should stop you, but my pride wouldn't let me undo what I'd said. I've spent the past several months being miserable without you."

My rambling explanation is silenced when Nate pulls me closer to him and presses his lips to mine. He's gentle at first, but his kisses become more urgent. For a few wonderful moments, I return his passions, drinking in his irresistible scent of soap, aftershave, and hint of leather. But then self-doubt creeps in and I go rigid, chilled at the thought of losing him again.

"Emma, what's wrong?" he asks, feeling me stiffen in his arms. I pull away. "Talk to me," he urges. He cups my chin in his hand, forcing me to look up at him.

Tears sting my eyes as I search for the words to express what I am feeling. Nate is so gorgeous, and caring, and wonderful. Being without him is a pain I've learned to shoulder; one I no longer wish to carry. But as euphoric as I feel being in his arms again, I know it can't last. He'll eventually move on and I'll be shattered.

Finally, I respond. "I don't know how to act when I'm with you. Part of me wants to give into you completely. It would be easy to do. But the rest of me wants to run the other direction. If we got back together and you ever walked away again, I don't think I could handle it. I just…," I trail off, lost once again for words.

94

Nate smiles, but his expression is pained. He pulls me gently towards him, kissing me square on the mouth. "Me too," he whispers breathily in my ear.

"What?" I tilt my head to the side to get a better look at him, trying to gauge his expression.

"Seriously, Emma, do you have any idea what you do to me, how you make me feel? You're beautiful and incredibly smart. I think I'm in control of my emotions, then you walk into the room and I'm shattered. All I want is to be with you. Don't you get it? *I'm* the lucky one. As long as you want me to stay, I will stay. You're exactly who I want to be with. I'd have to be crazy to leave."

I sit in stunned silence, absorbing Nate's words. How can he possibly want to be with only me? I feel the tears threaten to spill over again. "Oh, baby no," Nate sooths, pulling me onto his lap. "Please don't cry."

I sniff and smile up at him. "I'm crying because I'm happy," I tell him. "I can't believe you feel that way about me. I know you tried to tell me before, but I guess I didn't really believe it until now. I've been such an idiot. I love you like crazy Nathan Mitchell." The words are out of my mouth before I can take them back. *Uh oh! Too soon?*

"And I love you, Emma Taylor." Nate doesn't miss a beat. *Nicely done*, I praise silently.

"So, where do we go from here?" I ask.

"I'd be interested in exploring some of the things we did last night," Nate responds. I blush, knowing I've been bolder in our dream realm than I normally would.

"Or, we can take it slow," he says, sensing my hesitation. Gently stroking my hair, he leans in to kiss me and this time I don't resist. I press in closer to him, my arms wrapping around him. His warmth ignites a fire in me that has remained dormant for months – at least while I'm awake.

"Nate," I say shyly, coming up for air.

"Yes?" he asks.

"You can darken my doorway or my dreams anytime."

He laughs as he takes my hand and leads me towards my bedroom. I want to challenge him on his definition of *taking it slow*, but I don't want him to change his mind. I'm perfectly happy with his interpretation.

When we reach my bedroom, he shuts the door behind us and locks it. The click of the lock is like a definitive, unspoken agreement between us – that there's no turning back. I meet Nate's gaze with hesitation and am relieved to find the passion I'm feeling mirrored in eyes. His look of molten desire matches my own.

"If you're having second thoughts, you should tell me now," he warns.

I shake my head as the lump rises in my throat. "Make love to me," I say.

It's the only prodding he needs. He crosses the room towards me and sweeps me into his arms – his lips clamping down on mine. My arms are pinned in his embrace, but I manage to bring my hands to his chest. I place them softly, careful not to push. I don't want him to misinterpret my movements as a struggle.

His hands travel under my shirt and I raise my own hands above my head, allowing him to easily slip my shirt off. He discards it on the floor, then looks at me. Challenging me. "Your move," he says.

I unbuckle his belt, slide it from the beltloops, and toss it in the corner. I then unzip his jeans, but don't go any further. "Check," I say, eyebrow raised.

Nate's patience appears to be wavering. He slides his index fingers into my beltloops and jerks me towards him. My pulse is racing and my body temperature climbs. His lips crush mine, but it's not enough to distract me from the feel of his hands skimming my waist before he unbuttons and yanks my jeans down to my knees.

Quivering with anticipation, I sit on the edge of the bed and finish removing my pants. I kick them off and they land next to my shirt. I steal a glance at my lacey black bra and panties, thankful that I put on a matching set earlier this morning. Scooting back towards the headboard, I motion Nate to join me on the bed.

"Checkmate," he growls, but I'm not sure who he's declaring the winner of this match. Hopefully both of us. In an instant he is naked, on the bed, and pulling me up towards him until we're both kneeling, face-to-face.

His hands cup my breasts and I skim my fingertips down his bare torso. I can hear Nate's labored breathing in response to my touch. He unclasps my bra and my bare nipples harden in the chill of the room. I tremble when his fingers travel to the edge of my panties. He gives them a tug, and I lie back on the bed while he jerks them from my body.

Nate shakes his head in appreciation of my nakedness and I smile shyly. "Are you cold?" he asks. The air holds a chill, but my body is on fire, so I shake my head *no*.

He smiles and stretches his naked form over mine. He buries his face in my hair and I lift my head to kiss his neck. He tilts his head towards mine and my lips rove over his jawline. I plant my mouth on his and his tongue sweeps mine. Unexpectedly, Nate roles over, taking me with him so that I'm now on top.

"You're going to make me work for it?" I say, squirming as I struggle to sit up straight.

Nate's hands once again reach my breasts, then travel to my waist. He positions my hips and eases me down until our bodies finally meet and he fills me. I arch my back and a throaty moan escapes my lips. He rises to press his lips to my throat, all the while moving beneath me as we search for our desired rhythm. My arms circle his neck and we move together. Closer. Higher.

My fingers twist in his hair and his hands cup my buttocks. With each thrust he has me soaring. We climb higher and higher until I feel my resolve slipping away. Nate buries his head in my hair once more and I moan my desires in his ear.

"Oh Nate, please, please," I cry out and he deepens his thrusts until I feel myself tighten around him, then find my release. He covers my mouth with his, muffling my cries. We continue to move together, and when his hands cradle my face and his eyes lock mine, I see every semblance of his control dissolve as he reaches his climax.

We collapse onto the bed and he curves his body against mine. His skin is slick, and his hair is damp. I close my eyes, content and not wanting the moment to be over. *Will he want to go back home?*

"There's nothing you can do to get me out of this bed," he murmurs in my ear, answering my unspoken question as he drapes one leg over mine.

"Stay," I say.

"Gladly." He kisses my bare shoulder and nuzzles my neck. As I drift off to sleep, I wonder if he'll be in my dreams. But he doesn't need to be. He's where I needed him to be all along – in my life, in my room, in my bed.

CHAPTER TWENTY-ONE

OUR RELATIONSHIP ESCALATES in the days to come. In many ways, it's as if our breakup never happened – although I sense Nate is keeping his guard up at times. I can't blame him. I know I wounded him. We do our best to keep our relationship professional in public, especially since he remains the lead detective on my case, but I know Terry, my assistant isn't fooled. She's brighter than most people give her credit for.

As our newfound relationship is kindled, my nightmares are partially subdued. Mostly I have sensual dreams that Nate and I share by night and reenact by day. When I do wake up screaming from a bad dream, Nate is there to hold me until I fall back to sleep.

"We're going to get this guy, Emma," he promises.

My first night back at Nate's, I am amazed at how stylish his home is decorated. His once eclectic and sparse décor has been replaced with contemporary furnishings and a tasteful selection of modern art. When we dated before I was constantly prodding him to let me give his place a woman's touch. Since our breakup, I can see that he's stepped up his decorating game and I secretly hope it wasn't another woman's touch that helped him do so. While considering this, I study the sofa table behind the couch and run my fingers over the smooth finish.

"My mother," Nate says aloud, breaking the silence.

"What?"

"The decorating," he says, motioning around the room. "My mother helped me. She insisted the place was *downright depressing.* Her words."

I'm not sure why, but I feel my cheeks redden as I try to comprehend how he read my mind. "It's lovely," I tell him.

In his master bedroom, Nate is giddy as he takes my hand and leads me into his walk-in closet. He brings me to a section of empty hangers, with an equally empty shelf beneath it.

"For the nights I con you into staying over," he explains. "What do you think?"

"I think I'm going to need another shelf," I tease, but I'm grinning from ear to ear as I stand on my tiptoes to give him a well-deserved kiss.

"Have dinner at my parents with me tomorrow?" Nate asks just a few hours later. I feel like a bomb has been dropped and I'm silent as I contemplate his request. I know this is a giant step for us, but the thought terrifies me. It has been months since I have seen Nate's family and I wonder what he has told them about our breakup.

"Oh, I see what's going on here," I say, trying to buy myself some time before I commit. "Was making space for me in your closet your way of buttering me up before asking me?"

"Maybe a little," he admits, flashing a mischievous grin. "Is that a *yes?*" he asks more seriously, taking me by the hand to plant a kiss on my wrist. I'm not sure that I am ready to face Nate's family, but I also don't want to disappoint him. His green eyes search mine for an answer.

"I'd love to," I say. It's a mild lie but warranted given the situation.

As I get ready for the dinner with Nate and his parents, the anxiousness rises in my stomach like proverbial butterflies. I choose a black pencil skirt and coral blouse from my closet. The doorbell rings and I know it's Nate. I grab a pair of pumps and a light jacket before opening the door.

"You look beautiful," Nate says, waiting on the doorstep to be invited in. He is casually dressed in a pair of jeans and a black button-up shirt with gray pinstripes.

"So do you," I say breathily, motioning him in and suddenly feeling dull in comparison.

He pulls me in for a long kiss, cradling my face in his hands. "You are sexy as hell," he whispers in my ear, and I smile, no longer feeling so plain.

I lean in to deepen the exchange but change my mind. "Hey, if we keep this up, we'll never make it to your parents' house," I say, gently pulling away. When Nate groans in protest, I remind him that dinner was *his* idea.

It's an hour drive to Nate's parents' house. I fiddle nervously with the radio, a habit I find annoying when others do it, but Nate never seems to mind. "Relax," he says, "my parents have always loved you."

Forcing a smile, I do my best to look unflustered, clasping my shaky hands in my lap to steady them. Nate casually reaches over to hold my hand, lifting it to his lips and giving it a quick kiss that sends shockwaves through my body.

When we finally arrive, Nate's mom, Nancy, flings open the door and greets me with a warm hug. She doesn't seem at all concerned about messing up her perfectly set blonde hair as she embraces me exuberantly. Nate's dad, Martin, follows suit. I can't help but notice how similar he smells to Nate. Dismissing the awkward thought, I hug him back and thank them both for the dinner invite. I barely make it through the front door before I'm nearly bowled over by a large German Shepard.

"Bear," I say, leaning down to let the canine plant a sloppy kiss on my cheek. I guess the dog doesn't hold a grudge either.

While Nate takes Bear outside to play fetch, Nancy gives me a quick tour of her home to show me the remodel and the addition being constructed. With her flawlessly pressed outfit and polished nails, she looks out of place amidst the tools, debris, and sheetrock dust. As we move from room to room, she carries on about how much her family has missed me, and I'm relieved at her kindness. It's certainly more than I deserve.

Nate's brother, Brandon, is another matter. He acts cold at dinner, glowering at me across the table with his dark, brooding eyes. I am taken back because he and I have always gotten along. I find an opportunity after dessert to confront him.

"Brandon, can we talk outside?" I ask.

"Sure," Brandon says, shrugging his broad shoulders and sounding noncommittal.

We walk out to the veranda and take a seat beside each other on the patio sofa. Bear wanders out after us and plops down at my feet. I am silent, not sure where to begin. It takes me by surprise when Brandon is the one who starts talking.

"You really hurt him, you know," he says quietly, running his hands through his black hair. I feel like I've been punched in the gut. Any forgiveness I previously afforded myself is rendered invalid.

"Nate will probably never admit it," he continues, "but he was a wreck when you left him. I've never seen him like that." Brandon's voice rises, and he stares pointedly in my direction. "It was hard to see him so — so gutted. I was so angry with you for doing that to him. I don't think I can handle seeing him go through something like that all over again." My heart is breaking. I was so worried about protecting my own heart, I never stopped to consider how my actions might hurt Nate. I find it astonishing how two people so in love can do so much damage to each other.

"Brandon, I promise that I will never, never hurt Nate like that again. I was so stupid. I didn't even realize I meant so much to him." My excuses seem lame.

"Emma," Brandon sighs, "it's obvious how he feels about you. At least, it seems obvious to everyone but you."

It takes all my self-control not to cry. I am not looking for the sympathy vote here. "Brandon, please just let me explain," I say. My face is on fire as I launch headlong into my pathetic explanation of why I ended things with Nate all those months ago. Somewhere during my ramblings, I cross the valley of regret and make a hard right onto Atonement Avenue, spilling my heart and apologizing profusely for the pain I know I caused.

"You see," I finish, "I honestly thought it was just a matter of time before he left me. I guess I thought I was protecting myself." I shove my hands into my jacket pockets, feeling ridiculous at hearing my own misguided logic aloud.

Brandon's expression softens. "Are you sure you're as smart as Nate says you are?" he teases. And suddenly the old Brandon is back. "Just be good to him," he says. He pulls me in for a hug and pats my head affectionately.

"Am I interrupting something?" I pull away from Brandon's embrace to find Nate staring at us. Nate is doing his best to look appalled, but I can tell he's messing with us.

"I'm sorry Nate, it was only a matter of time before she realized I was the better brother," Brandon says, standing to his feet and flashing a mischievous grin. Without warning, Nate pounces and the brothers are wrestling in the grass. Bear runs in circles around them, barking and tail wagging. I sink back onto the patio sofa and breathe a sigh of happiness.

As we drive away, I lay my head on Nate's shoulder and smile to myself, pleased with how the evening went.

"I told you my family loves you," Nate says.

My smile widens. "Will you be staying over?" I ask, feeling a bit uncertain.

"Well, I do have a few other offers…"

I punch him playfully in the arm. "Okay, okay, you win. I'm all yours," Nate answers. "But tomorrow, you're coming to my place."

CHAPTER TWENTY-TWO

IMMERSED IN RESEARCH FILES, a knock on my office door disrupts my thoughts. "Come in," I invite, grateful for the interruption.

The door opens, and a wave of nausea hits me. It takes me a moment to reorient myself and I realize that I smell the familiar scent of cheap cologne – the same cologne worn by the man who attacked me in my house.

Once I force myself to focus, I recognize the visitor as Andrew Higgins from the mail room. I find it odd that I've never noticed the cologne before and am finding it hard to picture this lanky, young kid as my attacker.

"Ma'am?" I shake off my thoughts, realizing that Andrew must have asked me a question. He continues to stand awkwardly in the doorway.

"I'm sorry, what was that?"

"I asked where you would like me to put your mail. Your inbox looks pretty full."

I motion to the small table. Andrew carefully moves aside some paperwork to make room for the mail. "New cologne?" I ask, unable to suppress my curiosity, all the while trying to sound casual.

"What? Oh," he says, looking a little sheepish as he lifts his shirt color and sniffs. "The bathroom has a ton of cologne samples. I thought I'd try some. I'm picking up my date after work. Is it too strong?"

"No, it smells good," I lie, plastering a smile on my face. Andrew thanks me and walks out of my office. I study his lean frame as he leaves.

"I mean, it's obvious he's too scrawny to be the man who attacked me," I tell Nate, recapping my encounter with Andrew while we get ready for bed. "But I can't shake the feeling that the cologne might be a clue."

Nate remains quiet as I continue to ramble.

"Do you think it's just a coincidence, or do you think it's possible the man who attacked me is someone I've worked with?" I shudder at the thought.

"It's possible," Nate says, rubbing his chin in thought. "Maybe we could find out who supplies the samples. If there's a vendor giving out samples to all the local businesses, it could just be a coincidence. But if not…"

"I can ask Terry, my assistant, to find out," I interrupt, excited that we may have a break in the case.

"Some detective I am," Nate grumbles. "It seems like you're always the one bringing in the new evidence." I can't be sure if Nate is truly upset, but I wrap my arms around him and kiss him on the mouth. The distraction works, and Nate changes his focus from my case to… well… other parts of me.

I wake up early. I can't wait to get to work so I can ask Terry to check into the cologne samples. Nate is sleeping peacefully, so I slip out of the house without disturbing him. I arrive earlier than expected and the office building is nearly empty, so I take the opportunity to do some snooping around myself. I approach the men's room, my eyes darting around the hallway to make sure no one from a nearby cubicle is watching. Like most of the building, the hallway is empty.

Stopping in front of the door to the men's room, I look around once more before knocking on the door. When no one answers, I slowly ease open the door, poking my head in to be extra certain the room is vacant. My pulse quickens, and I feel a rush of excitement. *I could get used to this detective stuff*, I think to myself.

Before making my way to the bathroom counter, I glance under each bathroom stall door to check for feet. I chuckle to myself, knowing how ridiculous I am being, but I'm also enjoying the thrill. On the bathroom counter there is a small basket filled with cologne samples. I pick through the basket until I am certain I've selected one of each type. I drop the samples into my purse and hurry out of the men's room.

Just as I am swinging open the bathroom door, a man that I recognize from the payroll department is approaching the door and he gives me a strange look. Startled and embarrassed, I explain that I must have the wrong room. He offers a partial nod, partial grunt, and I scurry back to my office. I stop at the cabinet next to Terry's desk and grab the bag of coffee beans next to the coffee pot. *To cleanse the palate.* I roll my eyes, knowing that I am making more of an adventure out of my little inquiry than needed – but loving every exhilarating moment of it.

Closing the door to my office, I spread the samples across the small table. My phone rings, but I let it go to voicemail. I meticulously open each sample and smell the contents, sniffing the coffee beans between each sample. When I open the fifth sample, I realize the coffee beans were not necessary. The familiar wave of nausea engulfs me. I read the label with trembling hands. *Indulgence for Men.* I drop the sample packet on the table as if it bit me. My legs are quivering, so I sink into my desk chair.

My phone rings again, and this time I answer it. "Emma Taylor speaking."

"Oh, aren't you so professional?" I hear Nate joke from the other end of the line.

"Oh, sorry. I didn't check my caller ID."

"I tried calling you a little bit ago. You were gone when I woke up this morning. Everything okay?"

"Yeah, sorry. I was going to leave a note and then it slipped my mind. I just had some, uh, work to do." I am excited to tell Nate about my little investigation, but I want to wait until I have more information.

"My place tonight?" he asks – or demands, I'm not sure which. But either way I oblige before hanging up the phone.

No longer feeling as rattled, I decide to conduct an internet search to see just how widely distributed *Indulgence for Men* is. I can hear bustling outside my office and I realize Terry must have arrived. Wanting to avoid any questions, I rise from my chair and scoop the samples back into my purse before going back to my internet search.

I feel a bit deflated when I learn that one can pick up *Indulgence for Men* at any Wal-Mart, and about a half-dozen other chain retail stores. I'm interrupted by a knock at the door, which puts a temporary halt to my investigation. "Come in," I say, expecting it to be Terry with my morning cup of coffee.

Instead it's one of the janitorial staff coming to empty the trash. I start to wonder just how many janitors our small company needs. While my garbage is being emptied, I use the opportunity to ask about the samples. "Um, excuse me, but can you tell me about the cologne samples in the men's room?"

"What about 'em?" the man asks politely. He scratches his head and I sense he's contemplating why I would know, or care, what's in the men's room.

"Oh, I was just curious. Who puts them there?"

"We do. Us janitors."

"Oh?" My curiosity is peaked.

"Yeah. You know *Victor's* department store down the street?"

"Yes."

"Well, a few times a year they send out a big box of samples to lots of the local businesses here in Edmonds. I think they reckon it'll drum 'em up some business," he explains. "For me, all they've succeeded in doing is giving me headaches." I thank him for the information and he leaves my office. He probably thinks I'm a nut.

The news squelches both my investigation and my spirits. I was looking forward to having something to report back to Nate. Now I'm too embarrassed by my failed attempts to even mention it. Bummed, I refocus my energies on my real job and decide to leave the detective work in Nate's experienced, capable hands.

CHAPTER TWENTY-THREE

NATE AND I LIE NAKED in his king-sized bed as he covers my body with kisses. "You are beautiful," he says, kissing my right shoulder. "You're smart." He plants a kiss on my stomach and I squirm with anticipation. His chin stubble tickles my skin as his lips rove to my thigh. "You're sexy." My heart is racing wildly.

His phone rings, interrupting our little game. "Don't answer it," I groan.

"I have to babe. It could be about a case."

"I know, I'm just trying to be selfish," I pout as I run my hand playfully up Nate's thigh, an attempt to persuade him not to take the call.

Nate is smiling when he answers the call, but then makes a face and hands the phone over to me. "It's for you," he says, and I detect a hint of irritation in his voice.

"Hello?" I answer, shocked that someone would know to call me at Nate's.

"Hi, Emma, sorry to bother you, but I need a major favor tomorrow."

"Lance?" I ask.

"Yes." He sounds amused, as if he's party to some private joke where only he knows the punchline.

"How did you know to call me here?" I ask. Nate coughs into his hand.

"Well, I tried to call your cellphone first," Lance explains, "but when I couldn't reach you, Terry told me that I should try this number."

My brow furrows in mild annoyance at the intrusion. I know Terry has taken several messages from Nate, but I am amazed she remembered his number by heart. I am taken back, realizing how much I've failed at keeping my relationship with Nate under wraps.

I look uncomfortably over at Nate before continuing. "I see. So, what do you need?" I try to sound casual, but I can feel Nate's eyes boring into my head.

"Am I interrupting anything?" Lance's playful tone echoes in my ear.

"That would be none of your business," I reply, knowing what Lance is insinuating and doing my best to sound stern. "What can I do for you, Lance?"

"I am going to wine and dine some potential clients in the morning and I want you to be with me."

"Why?" I ask, intrigued.

"Well," Lance says, clearing his throat, "I originally thought it was just going to be two execs from the firm I've been wooing, but now they are bringing their girlfriends, so I want to bring you along to make the meeting feel more casual."

112

"How very *Pretty Woman* of you," I tease, momentarily forgetting Nate is next to me. Nate coughs again and I glare in his direction.

"Where is this meeting at?" I ask, making a concerted effort to sound more professional for Nate's sake.

"We're going to meet at the yacht club and then take my boat out for a spin."

"You own a yacht?" I exclaim in disbelief.

"It's a little one." Lance tries to sound modest.

Laughing at Lance's failed attempt at humility, I agree to meet him at six-thirty the next morning. I hand the phone back to Nate. I can tell he's trying to look nonchalant, but underneath that cool demeanor, he is simmering.

"What?" I ask, even though I think I know.

"You, my dear, are a flirt," he tells me, returning the phone to the nightstand before turning to face me. He is smiling, but his voice is strained.

"Me?" I am dumbfounded. A moment ago, I was convinced he was annoyed that someone had called me at his house. I'm shocked that he's jealous of my perceived flirting. "What are you talking about?"

"*How Pretty Woman of you*," he mimics, batting his eyelashes and doing his best to imitate the inflection of my voice.

"If that is supposed to sound like me, I really need to take some extra estrogen," I say.

A faint smile creeps across Nate's face, but quickly vanishes. "I'm serious baby. You need to be more careful. You may be unintentionally sending Lance the wrong message."

I smirk at his irrational trepidation. "That's ridiculous. Lance and I are just friends." I snuggle closer to him to ease the tension between us.

Nate leans in and nibbles on my ear. "*I* know that. But someone may want to clue poor Lance in." There's an air of mischief in his tone and I turn my head to kiss him square on the mouth. He leans in closer, lengthening the kiss.

"Well," I say, coming up for air, "since everyone at my work already seems to know that we're dating, why don't I just put a poster-sized picture of you in my office so there isn't any question?" My words are dripping with good-natured sarcasm.

"That's all I ask," Nate teases as his hand strokes my cheek and he pulls me in again for a kiss. I deepen the kiss and resolve myself to the fact that, regardless of how early I'll need to get up the next morning, neither of us will be calling it an early night.

CHAPTER TWENTY-FOUR

SIX-THIRTY IN THE MORNING comes awfully early. I am thankful that I remembered my jacket as I huddle on a bench outside of the yacht club and wait for Lance. He appears with two gentlemen I've never met and two bleached-blonde women that I assume are the girlfriends. My first instinct is to secretly nickname the women Bimbo Number One and Bimbo Number Two, but then I feel guilty, so I smile sweetly and extend my hand to introduce myself.

Lance is wearing a form-fitting t-shirt and shorts, which compliment his athletic build. I can't help but feel overdressed in the pale-yellow dress I threw on this morning. Lance hands me a coffee from *Hal's Stomping Grounds*. It makes me smile. I've missed that place but have been unable to bring myself to face Tom after his little admission. "I figured you'd need a double shot," Lance tells me as I take my first sip.

"You figured correctly," I say.

I follow Lance down to the boat launch where I get my first glimpse of his yacht. It's enormous and beautiful. *Sir Lancelot* is stenciled boldly in blue across the massive white stern. I resist the urge to tease Lance about the self-important name he chose for the vessel. "Um, *this* is a *little* one?" I ask aloud.

Lance shrugs. "Well, compared to some," he says, trying once again to sound humble but unable to mask his obvious pride.

A smile tugs at the curves of his mouth and I chuckle to myself as he helps me on board. Upon closer inspection, the two men appear to be in their mid-fifties and I wonder to myself why they are not yet married. I soon learn that one of the men, John, is indeed married and the girl with him is his mistress. I go back to thinking of her as Bimbo Number One and feel somewhat justified.

Lance takes us out on the Puget Sound for several hours and I am amazed with his ability to charm the perspective clients. One minute he has them in stitches with his impressions of Popeye and 'Captain' Jack Sparrow, and the next he is closing a hefty contract deal.

"Nicely done," I tell Lance after we see our new clients off and we are walking towards our cars.

"I couldn't have done it without you," he tells me.

"Liar," I say. "I'm happy it worked out, but I can't help but think we made a deal with the devil."

"How so?"

"Well, it's bad enough John brought his girlfriend and not his spouse – but come on, did you see his perfectly manicured nails, heavily starched shirt, and military haircut? Mark my words, that man beats his wife."

Lance chuckles, slapping his knee. "Seriously Emma, you have quite the imagination."

I shrug my shoulders. "Hey, I just call it like I see it," I say, but I am laughing because even I am not convinced of my dramatic declaration.

We both pause next to my car and I get the sense that Lance wants to say something more, but he keeps quiet. "I'll see you back at the office," I say.

"Huh? Oh, yes. Wow, it feels like the day should be over, but it's not even noon yet."

"I know, I'd take the rest of the day off, but I have a ton of work to do."

"Don't work too hard," Lance adds, opening my car door to help me in.

I call Nate on the way to the office. "How did it go?" he asks. His voice is surprisingly cheerful, and I wonder if he's gotten over whatever misgivings he had the night before.

"It went really well. We just snagged a new client," I tell him excitedly.

"And did Lance snag a new girlfriend?" *And there goes the jealousy again.*

Ignoring Nate's comment, I proceed to tell him all about the incredible yacht. I know I'm being somewhat wicked and fueling his jealousy, but I can't help myself. I'm annoyed that he can't just trust me.

Nate does a decent job of feigning interest. "Your place tonight?" he finally asks once there's a break in my chatter. I agree and offer to get off work early and prepare a delicious dinner.

"Don't oversell your culinary skills," Nate warns playfully before hanging up.

I arrive at work just as most of the employees are heading out to lunch. I detour to the ladies' room to brush out my tangled, windswept hair before heading to my office. When I unlock my office door, I am taken back at seeing Robert, the new janitor, behind my desk.

"Excuse me!" I say, alarmed and questioning his presence in my office.

"I'm sorry, ma'am," he tells me. "I was emptying your trash bin." Robert lifts the garbage can and retrieves the trash bag. I look around for his janitorial cart and spot it in the far corner of my office.

"Thank you, Robert," I say curtly, "but typically I request that the janitorial staff only enter my office while I am here." I know I must sound like a condescending snob, but I dislike the thought of a virtual stranger poking around my office while I am away.

"I apologize, ma'am," he tells me, looking uncomfortable. "I have keys to all the offices and nobody told me of your preference."

I suck in my breath and purse my lips while I study him. His story is plausible, and his actions, most likely, are completely innocent. "It's okay," I say more calmly. "You just startled me, that's all."

Robert quickly replaces the bag in my trash bin and leaves my office, avoiding eye contact as he wheels his cart past me in retreat. I sit down at my desk, trying to evaluate if I'm making a bigger deal of something than I should. I could have sworn it looked like Robert was doing more behind my desk than just emptying the trash, but now I'm not so sure. I dial Lance's extension. He answers on the first ring.

"Didn't I just talk to you?" he asks good-naturedly.

"I know, sorry." I want to tease him that I couldn't stay away, but I remember Nate's concerns about me being overly flirtatious, so I resist the urge. "Do you think you can stop by my office for a moment?" I ask.

I am skimming through the contents of my desk, trying to determine if anything is missing or out of place, when Lance raps at my door. "I hope you don't start making a habit of summoning your boss," he says with a sober expression, but I know straight away he's teasing.

Chuckling, I motion for him to close the door. "Do you know Robert, our new janitor?" I ask conspiratorially.

"Yes. Eldon personally hired him."

"What? Why would Eldon... err... Mr. Banks bother with the hiring at that level?"

"I'm not sure. It's some friend of his uncle's or something like that. Why? Is something wrong?"

Suddenly feeling stupid for distrusting someone the co-owner of the company hand-picked, I try to brush it off. "Oh, not at all. He just looked familiar to me, that's all."

"You called me down here to talk about the janitor?" I can tell Lance is amused. Confused, but amused.

"Of course not!" I insist. My eyes dart around the room as I try to come up with another excuse for requesting that Lance come to my office. I spot a file for a potential client that one of my research staff pitched just days earlier. I haven't even had time to review it, but I scoop it up and hand it to Lance.

"This came across my desk the other day and the potential client, *Aidleman, Inc.*, is pretty intriguing." I silently hope that I remembered the name correctly, but I continue as if I am well-versed on the company and the contents of the file. "I was hoping you could give me your thoughts. Perhaps we can put our heads together on the best pitch to get them on board."

Lance looks at me strangely, opening and shutting the file. Then he smiles, shaking his head in confusion as he exits my office. I feel like an idiot and pray to God my research staff did their homework, knowing I am in jeopardy of looking like an even bigger fool if they didn't.

CHAPTER TWENTY-FIVE

MAKING GOOD ON MY PROMISE to Nate, I leave work early to make dinner. I hit the supermarket to pick up a few things for a new shrimp and scallops recipe I am anxious to try. Remembering Nate's healthy appetite, I grab a couple of steaks from the butcher.

Rounding the corner towards the check stands, I spot Tom, from the coffee shop, browsing the magazine aisle. For a moment I wonder if he followed me, but then dismiss the absurd thought. I turn to head the opposite direction, but think better of it, scolding myself for being such a coward.

"Hello, Tom," I manage instead.

Tom turns to face me, and his eyes light up. "Hi, Emma. How've you been?" He gives me an awkward hug – awkward for just me or for both of us, I can't be sure.

"I've been great. How about you?"

"Great. I haven't seen you around lately," Tom points out. "I hope my little comment from the other day didn't scare you off."

Feeling myself blush, I am unable to deny the allegation. "Tom, I'm sorry. I'm not used to flattery like that. That's more Summer's department. I should have handled that more maturely."

Tom laughs. "Oh, Emma, it's totally fine. If you just want to be friends, that's cool. No need to stop drinking good coffee over it."

I can't help but laugh, grateful at how laidback Tom is being about everything. We exchange another hug, less awkward this time, though I can't help but wonder if Nate would disapprove. Maybe I am a flirt. Dismissing the thought, I promise Tom that I will return to the coffee shop soon.

By the time I get home, I am exhausted and feel a slight headache coming on. I pull into the driveway and collect my briefcase, purse, and the bag of groceries before shutting the car door with my hip and heading inside.

I enter the kitchen, setting my keys and the bag of groceries on the kitchen counter. Only then do I notice the bouquet of red roses on the island. Remembering the flowers and the terrible card from before, I begin to shake. *How did he get into my house?*

Pulling my cellphone from my purse, I frantically dial Nate's number as I rush back outside. "Nate! Nate! Come quick. He broke into my house. He left me flowers. He…"

"What? Emma, slow down."

"He left me flowers again, Nate!" I am practically screaming. My body is trembling, and my legs feel like rubber.

"Emma, Emma. Calm down. It's okay."

"No, you don't understand. He could still be here. How did he get in?"

"Baby, *I* left the flowers."

I pause on the front porch. "What?"

I am sitting on the front porch steps, knees pulled up to my chest, when Nate screeches into the drive and jogs over to me. He sits beside me, and I rest my head on his shoulder. "I am sorry again about the roses," he says, stroking my hair. "I snuck them in while you were at work. I didn't think…"

"Don't. Please don't apologize for doing something nice for me," I tell him. "I overreacted. Dangit, this guy is really messing with my head. I even misread roses from my boyfriend as something sinister."

"That's okay," Nate chimes in. "Next time I'll just buy you jewelry."

This inspires a laugh from me, and I stand to my feet and turn to head inside, the knot in my stomach subsiding. Nate holds the door open for me. When we enter the living room, he sinks into the sofa, but I continue towards the kitchen.

"No, don't worry about it," Nate tells me when he realizes I still intend to cook. "We can just order pizza."

I shake my head in protest. "Are you kidding me? And let the shrimp and scallops go to waste? I don't think so."

Leaving Nate in the living room to watch the news, I head to the kitchen to unpack the groceries, relieved to find the seafood is still cold. Turning on the stove, I lop off a half a cube of butter, place it in a large skillet, then set the skillet on the stove. Settled into a rhythm, I turn the oven to broil, season the steaks, and pop them into the oven. I chop fresh

123

parsley and shallots and combine them with lemon juice, a small amount of sugar, and various spices until I have perfected the marinade for the seafood.

Once the scallops and shrimp are sautéing in the butter, I caramelize more butter, then add seasoning and more fresh cut shallots to serve as the sauce to pour over the scallops. I do cheat on the sides, emptying a bag of store-bought green salad into a bowl and buttering the rolls I picked up from the bakery.

After setting the table and plating the food, I invite Nate to join me in the dining room. "Are you sure you didn't have this catered?" he teases, taking in the spread.

"You may want to hold any compliments until you actually taste it. You're my guinea pig tonight. I'm trying out a new recipe."

I study Nate's expression as he takes his first bite. I see a smile spread across his face and I know that he likes the food. I take a bite. I must admit, it's pretty good.

"I'm impressed," he tells me.

"Oh, just wait. This isn't the only thing new I'm going to try on you this evening."

CHAPTER TWENTY-SIX

WE'RE LYING IN BED snuggled up to each other when Nate starts to talk out of the blue. "You know, when we first broke up, I drove by your house almost every night for several weeks," he confesses.

"You what?" I ask, sitting up in bed. Nate never struck me as the stalker type. It's kind of hot.

He grins. "It's true. Unfortunately, I rarely saw your car in the driveway."

"I spent a few nights at my mom's," I admit. "And I also took a trip."

"A trip? Where? By yourself?"

I grin back at him. "I know. It surprised even me. I didn't even take Summer. I just booked a ticket to Kauai and spent a full week there by myself."

Nate looks mystified and somewhat impressed. "Wow, I just hit the bars every night to drown my sorrows. I'm so original." We both laugh.

I tell Nate about all the sites I saw, and the interesting people I met. I leave out the details of the nights I cried myself to sleep or the long, lonely walks on the beach. I remember sitting at the top of Waimea Canyon and staring down at the rugged terrain. While everyone around me marveled at its unique beauty, I sat all alone and was miserable – because that's what I deserved to be.

"Earth to Emma," Nate says, interrupting my thoughts.

I smile at him. "I was just thinking about how much better the trip would have been if you were there," I tell him honestly. "I really missed you."

Nate leans in and kisses me sweetly. "We'll just have to make it a point to go together. Since you've been there before, you can be my own personal tour guide." I giggle when Nate leans in unexpectedly to plant another kiss on my neck.

"Since it's confession time," I say, "do you remember that time you saw me out on a date?"

"How can I forget?" Nate's expression turns sour.

"That was my *only* date while we weren't together." I decide my brief kiss with Lance does not qualify and choose not to mention it.

"Good."

I hit Nate playfully on the leg. "If it makes you feel even better, it was a horrible date."

"I figured as much."

"Oh, how so?"

"You drunk-dialed me that night," he says in matter-of-fact fashion.

"I did not," I argue. I search my memory for that night, but everything after the nightclub is a blur.

"You did. You called me about two a.m., woke me from a sound sleep, and scared me half to death."

"What did I say?" I am both mortified and intrigued.

Nate slides his hands up my thighs and towards my waist, bringing me closer to him so that our faces are inches apart. "You told me that you still loved me." He looks at me with intensity, waiting for my response to his admission.

"And how did you respond?" I ask, eager for his answer.

"I told you that if you felt the same once you sobered up, to give me a call."

"And I never called," I say, stating the obvious.

"Nope. You never did." Nate is smiling, but I can see the pain he tries to cover.

Not wanting the evening to take a dismal turn, I wrap my legs around his waist and drape my arms around his neck. "Well," I say seductively, "I'm here now."

"Hmm... I guess we can start making up for lost time."

CHAPTER TWENTY-SEVEN

WHENEVER NATE STAYS OVER, I find it hard to go to work the next day. I only want to stay in bed with him and feel the warmth of his nakedness against my own bare skin. "You are turning me into a lazy employee," I tell him when I finally roll out of bed.

Sauntering to the bathroom, I turn on the shower. Nate joins me. Now I know I should try to be strong since I'm already running late, but I also know it's futile to resist his naked physique. "I find your lips very kissable," Nate growls, pulling me towards him under the steamy water. I kiss him back, giving into the fact that I'm going to be even later to work.

While wolfing down my breakfast, I take the opportunity to sort through the growing stack of mail on the kitchen counter. I grumble to myself when I open a neatly printed invitation to a family reunion. My mother's side of the family makes it a point to get together at least every other year, overkill as far as reunions go in my opinion. What starts out as a friendly gathering of relatives usually ends with my aunts fighting, my grandmother playing peacemaker, and every relative over fifty asking when I'm going to settle down, get married, and have babies.

Nate comes up behind me, putting his arms around my waist and nuzzling against my neck. "What's up?" he asks casually.

With exaggerated revulsion, I hand over the invitation. "What's so bad about a family reunion?" he asks, turning the invitation over as if expecting to find something printed on the back that might explain my reaction.

"Have you met my family?" I respond, only half joking. "There's only so much drama I can take all in one setting."

"Oh, come on, it could be fun." I don't answer. "I can come with you," he offers. I am touched by how sweet Nate can be and wonder how many boyfriends would so willingly offer to face an entire flock of their girlfriend's relatives.

"You'd do that for me?" I am moved, yet somehow not completely surprised.

"Well, it may cost you," he teases, leaning in to nibble on my ear. *I may never make it to work.*

At the office, I once again mull over the list of names Terry provided of staff that worked on the *Angry Gamer* account. I think back to a situation a few months prior where it appeared that confidential information about one of our clients, *Moxley's*, was leaked to a competitor. I devoted several of my own hours, along with numerous hours of my administrative staff, to going over the files but did not find any evidence that the leak came from inside our company.

I wonder if this latest situation is a coincidence, or if I should compare the names Terry provided with the names of people that worked on the *Moxley's* account. Deeply engrossed in thought, I barely notice when Lance knocks on my door.

"Come in," I invite.

"What do we have here?" he asks, surveying the mess of paperwork on my desk. I am hesitant to accuse employees, or to stir up any unwarranted panic, but I feel obligated to tell Lance about the recent breach. After I relay my conversation with Mr. James, Lance's expression is strange. I wonder what he is feeling. Betrayal, perhaps?

"Mr. James really feels like the leak came within his own company. I am just trying to be thorough," I say, reassuring him.

Lance looks mildly relieved. "Well, I'm sure you're right. Just keep me posted, okay?" I nod in agreement.

"On another note," Lance says, "how does tomorrow sound for the photo shoot?"

"On Saturday?" I say, resisting the urge to groan aloud.

"Sorry, Emma, it's the best I could do. The photographer wants to do the photo shoot in this building, citing authenticity, but he wants as few distractions as possible."

I try to sound positive. "Sure, that should work. I don't have any plans." What I want to say is that I had plans to spend the day in bed with Nate, but I keep that fact to myself.

Lance looks pleased. "Great, then I'll see you tomorrow morning. The photo shoot will be in the main conference room. Nine o'clock?"

After trying out another new recipe at dinner, resulting in a meal that only mildly passed as edible, Nate and I snuggle up together on the couch at my place. "Sorry about the dinner," I say. "Just when I thought my cooking skills had improved."

He laughs, squeezing my hand. "Oh, it wasn't so bad."

"Liar."

"What should we do tomorrow?" he asks, expertly changing the subject as he absentmindedly twirls a strand of my hair between his fingers.

"Oh, I have that dreadful photo shoot in the morning," I say, wishing for the thousandth time that I hadn't agreed to it. The thought twists my stomach into knots.

"Photo shoot?" Nate inquires, clearly confused, and it suddenly occurs to me that I never mentioned it to him.

Without Lance around to hear me, this time I do groan. "Yes, the one that my boss convinced me to do…" I trail off when I notice Nate's expression.

"He what?" His face turns red and he drops the strand of my hair that he's been playing with.

I am confused by his outburst. "Yes," I say more firmly, lifting my chin in defiance. "*We* executives at the firm have decided we need a new marketing campaign." I emphasize *we* for effect. "My bosses would like me to be the face of the company. I'll be representing our company on billboards and brochures."

I'm surprised by my tone. I've been dreading the idea since Lance first pitched it, but now I find myself defending it. I am almost prideful. *What is Nate's problem?*

"Oh," Nate responds, sounding remorseful. He goes back to looking calm – almost angelic.

Now I get it. Suddenly I'm a little horrified. "What kind of photo shoot did you *think* I was talking about?"

Nate looks uncomfortable. "Um, I'm not sure."

I know I should probably make a bigger deal of the situation and prod him to respond to the question that I already know the answer to – forcing him to hear aloud for himself just how ridiculous the thought of me doing an off-color photo shoot with my boss sounds. Instead, I laugh and climb into his lap. "My big, handsome, jealous man," I tease.

Nate chuckles and playfully musses my hair before planting a kiss at the nape of my neck, sending a pleasurable thrill through my body.

CHAPTER TWENTY-EIGHT

I FEEL SOMEONE LEANING OVER ME, but I keep my eyes squeezed shut and remain perfectly still. "Are you sure you're asleep?" I hear a man with a gravelly voice whisper. His breath is hot against my skin and the hairs on the back of my neck stand on end. My heart beats wildly and the pounding in my chest is so loud that I wonder if he hears it.

Hovering over me, he smashes his lips down on mine. My survival instincts kick in and I struggle against him, bucking and scratching. I scream and curse as I twist my body from side to side to escape him. But when he digs his knee into my sternum, I go still. The crushing pain is more than I can bear, and I feel as if I'm suffocating at the pressure of his weight on my chest. I feel helpless as everything begins to go dark and a loud ringing starts in my ears.

I wake up in a panic, gasping for air as adrenaline surges through my body. My nightshirt feels sticky, so I strip it off and discard it on the floor.

I'm not crying this time. Perhaps I'm getting braver. I snuggle closer to Nate, put a pillow over my head, and squeeze my eyes shut. I pray for peaceful sleep. But peaceful sleep continues to elude me.

I face my attacker in defiance. He edges closer until his face is just inches from mine. Without realizing it, my trembling hand moves slowly towards him and I gingerly touch the black ski mask. The man narrows his red eyes from behind the disguise, but he doesn't try to stop me. His cold stare suggests he might be daring me. My movements are gradual at first – deliberate. Then, in a moment of boldness, I tug upward on the mask, determined to expose my attacker's identity.

CHAPTER TWENTY-NINE

I WAKE UP EARLIER THAN USUAL to prepare for the photo shoot. I didn't sleep well. My dreams were restless, and I awoke several times drenched in sweat. Each time I was aroused from sleep, I found Nate lying peacefully beside me, one arm draped across my waist while he snored softly. I take a long shower to clear my head. My dreams come back to me in small waves of color and I can't escape the gnawing feeling that something important happened that I am supposed to remember.

While toweling off, I grimace when the towel glides over my chest. I glance down. A large, purplish bruise covers the lower half of my sternum. I trail my fingers across my discolored skin, wincing in pain and alarm at how tender the area is. I wonder how I will manage to hide this from Nate. I can't possibly show it to him. It would only make him angry that he couldn't protect me. I suspect my dreams may affect him more than they do me.

I tiptoe out of the bathroom and into the bedroom. Nate is still fast asleep, so I slip into my robe, quietly retrieve Madame Destiny's hefty book from beneath the bed, and creep past him and into the hallway. I still have some time before I need to finish getting ready, so I sneak to the living room to do some much overdue research about the paranormal events that plague my evenings.

Madame Destiny was right when she said that the darkening of dreams was rare. The thick book she lent me only contains a few chapters devoted to it. There are personal testimonials and a few meager, probably less-than-reputable, studies about the phenomenon. I focus on the chapter about controlling dreams through self-hypnosis.

After retrieving a pen and paper from the end-table, I jot down a few notes, fold up the paper, and tuck it into the pocket of my robe. I glance at the clock on the wall, realize I am now in danger of being late to my own photo shoot, then slide the thick book under the couch.

When I return to the bedroom, Nate stirs, but he doesn't open his eyes. I return to the bathroom to finish getting ready. I don the outfit Nate helped me select the night before. My original plan had been to have Summer come over and help me, but Nate insisted that he knew better than anyone what looked good on me. Personally, I think his opinion may be a little biased, but I decided to trust his judgment.

Once I am ready, I re-enter the bedroom and find Nate awake and throwing on jeans and a t-shirt. "You're up early for a Saturday," I observe.

He lets out a low whistle, looking me up and down. "Well, I thought I'd go with you to the photo shoot – make sure there isn't any funny business going on."

Nate must read the angry expression on my face because he starts to laugh. "I'm kidding, Emma. I promised Brandon I'd hang out with him today."

I sigh, relieved, and Nate crosses the room to pull me into his arms. Placing my hand on his chest, I suddenly wish that neither of us were dressed. "I can cancel with Brandon and go with you though, if you need me to," Nate offers, his tone more serious – almost hopeful.

"I think I'll be self-conscious enough having to be photographed. Watching my boyfriend glaring in the background may make things just a bit more awkward." I wink at Nate and pretend not to notice the flicker of emotion on his face. I can tell he still doesn't like the idea of me going but is trying his best not to show it.

I arrive at my workplace about five minutes to nine and head straight to the main conference room. The photographer, Jake, is a young man in his early twenties. He has a deep French accent but something about it makes me suspect that it's an act. In addition to his camera and assorted backlighting, Jake comes equipped with an assistant named Tara – a boisterous young woman who is adamant about touching up my hair and makeup. I immediately dislike her, but I don't argue as to not be thought of as a diva.

Tara spends the next twenty minutes invading my personal space. When she finally steps back from her bothersome hovering to admire her handy work, I grab her compact mirror to sneak a peek at my reflection. I'm sporting twice the makeup I usually wear, and my hair has been twisted into a sophisticated up-do. When Jake announces that he's ready to start taking pictures, I'm surprisingly relieved.

Lance comes in to watch the photo shoot, but Jake artistically dismisses him from the room. Lance is not used to being told what to do, especially at his own company, but I give him a pleading look and he obediently waits in the hallway.

The photo shoot goes surprisingly well. Jake does a great job of putting me at ease. I pose crossing and uncrossing my arms at the photographer's prompting. I smile until the muscles in my face hurt. Jake must take a thousand pictures before he wraps things up.

"With that many photos, you've got to have at least one good one, right?" I ask nervously.

Jake smiles. "The camera loves your face. It will be hard to choose." I wonder again if his accent is fake, but his words are reassuring.

"I'll bet you say that to all the girls," I quip.

"Only the pretty ones."

From the far corner of the room Lance clears his throat, and I wonder how long he's been standing there. "Are we done here?" he asks Jake. Lance's words are clipped, and I can't help but think that he seems jealous.

"Yep, just finished," Jake says shortly. I don't hear even a hint of an accent. *Busted.* "I should have the proofs for you in a day or so." The accent has returned, and I smile to myself.

I thank Jake, who kisses my hand before leaving. "Oh brother," Lance says, rolling his eyes. I jab him playfully in the ribs.

Lance and I go out for a late breakfast to celebrate. I would rather go to breakfast with Nate, but I know he already made plans with his brother.

"So, that wasn't so bad, right?" Lance asks me, his mouth full of waffles.

"No, it actually went pretty well," I say.

"He didn't get fresh with you, did he?" Lance is smiling, but I get the impression he is not fully joking. I laugh it off and change the subject. Male insecurity and jealousy seems to be going around these days.

Nate is waiting for me on the porch, cup of coffee in hand, when I get back to my place. "Didn't you tell me that you were going to spend the day with your brother?" I ask.

"I spent the morning with him. It's close to noon," he replies, glancing down at his watch for dramatic affect.

"Impatient much?" I tease, giving him a quick kiss. He sets down his coffee and pulls me closer to deepen our exchange.

"Maybe I missed this," he says, his lips still brushing mine.

"Does this mean you're staying over again?" I ask, my voice hopeful.

"Oh, babe, I wish I could. You have me for the rest of the day, but I actually need to go into work this evening. In fact, I'll probably be working all day tomorrow too. The SPD sent over a ton of paperwork for a case that we're working together and I want to get up to speed on the material before our meeting on Monday."

"SPD?" I ask, trying my best to mask my disappointment.

"Seattle Police Department," Nate explains.

"Ah. Well, I guess I'll just have to make good use of the time I have with you."

"That's my girl."

Nate follows me inside. "I just ate a late breakfast, but would you like me to fix you lunch?" I offer.

A strange look flashes across Nate's face and I can tell he's deducing that I went out to eat with Lance. Sometimes dating a detective is exasperating. Nothing gets past him.

Walking to the kitchen, I pretend not to notice Nate's expression. He reaches for my hand and spins me towards him. "Oh no, you're not getting off that easily." His tone is playful but holds a hint of displeasure.

I coolly pluck an apple from the fruit bowl on the kitchen island. "I have nothing to hide, and you need to learn to trust me." I take a large bite of the apple as I stare into Nate's eyes, holding his gaze – challenging him.

"Oh, I trust you. It's this guy Lance that I don't trust," he says. The image of me kissing Lance surfaces and I wonder fleetingly if not telling Nate constitutes a lie by omission.

I brush the thought away and decide that telling Nate about a kiss that meant nothing will do more damage than good. Instead I flutter my eyelashes in mock exasperation. "Lance is a friend. He's also my boss. So, I need you to be okay with us spending time together and trust that there is nothing between us."

"Oh, Emma," Nate says, smiling as he strokes my cheek, "sometimes you are adorably naïve. Trust me, as a man, I know his intentions are not pure."

"And what about your intentions?" I ask. "I'm counting on *your* intentions not being pure."

"They rarely are," Nate says, taking my hand and leading me to the bedroom, obviously no longer concerned about lunch.

In the privacy of my bedroom, Nate starts to undress me. "What's this?" he asks, pausing halfway through unbuttoning my blouse.

Uh oh. In my excitement, I forgot all about hiding the bruise on my chest. "Oh, I uh…"

"Emma, what happened? Who did this to you?"

I say nothing and watch the expression on Nate's face as he apprehends the truth. "You had a nightmare last night," he says. His eyes darken, and his jaw tightens. "And you didn't tell me," he finishes. He looks more hurt than angry.

I take a step back. "It doesn't feel as bad as it looks. Really."

Nate steps toward me, folding me into his arms and kissing me. His hands fist in my hair as he presses his body closer to mine. "I'm here for you, Emma," he says urgently. "You don't have to hide anything from me." He pulls back from me just enough to lean down and kiss my exposed chest. My heart flutters and my body temperature climbs. I can see in his eyes just how much he cares about me – and I wonder how I didn't see it all those months ago. His nimble fingers trace the outline of the bruise. "I love you Emma," he tells me, pulling me closer and crushing his lips down on mine.

Nate's hands move once again towards my partially unbuttoned blouse, but he stops and gives me a questioning look, as if waiting for permission. When I nod my head, he finishes undressing me, then strips off his own clothes. His eyes flash with desire and appreciation as his hands skim across my naked body. We fall together into bed, drinking each other in. Nate is gentle and loving and more than I could ever ask for.

"I want you," I tell him, unable to resist, and I can hear the deep urgency in my own voice.

Nate growls in response and enters me. I moan, arching my body to meet his and wondering if I'll ever get enough of him. With each

141

maddening thrust I soar higher and higher. Sweat glistens on his brow as we move together towards a common goal.

"Tell me again that you want me, Emma," Nate whispers in my ear.

"I want you. Only you," I tell him. "Please..." I am begging for my release.

As our steady rhythm increases, my hands move to his hair. It's soft and slick and my fingers twist in it as my body responds to his every move. Nate's mouth is against my neck and I can hear his labored breathing as we start to climb. When I reach the pinnacle, Nate's lips cover mine. I moan softly into his mouth and he growls seductively. We fall apart in each other's arms – he is my undoing and I am his.

Nate rolls onto his back and pulls me close. Laying my head on his chest, I emit a deep sigh. It's a content, enraptured, and fully satisfied sigh.

CHAPTER THIRTY

SUNDAYS ARE A DAY OF REST, but someone forgot to tell Summer. I grumble to myself as I get out of bed. Today is spa and shopping day. Summer has been ecstatic about it for days. I am dreading it. I must have had a weak moment when I agreed to go with her.

At first, I was excited about the idea. In theory, a day of relaxing and being pampered sounded fabulous. Work has been crazy, and I haven't spent as much time with Summer as I would like. But then I realized that I would have to sit still for hours as I was waxed and clipped and groomed in all sorts of unimaginable ways. The idea makes me shutter.

My phone rings. When I realize it's Summer, my eyes widen in amusement, certain that she is reading my thoughts from her house and is calling to ensure that I don't back out of our plans. "You excited?" she croons.

I put on my best game face. I know how much this means to Summer and I also know that I need to learn to relax. This really could be fun. "Yep," I say, trying my best to sound chipper.

Summer offers to pick me up in thirty minutes, so I rush to get dressed. I don't have to do my hair or my makeup since it'll soon be done for me, so that helps brighten my mood.

My phone rings again and this time it's Nate. "Hi babe," I hear him say casually from the other end of the line. It always makes my heart skip a beat. *My Nate.*

"Hi babe," I tell him. "What time are you going to work?"

"I'm actually about to head out the door now. I got a lot done last night, so I figure the sooner I get in, the sooner I can get out and see my girl."

"And who would that be?" I feign ignorance, but my heartbeat quickens in anticipation of seeing him again. I missed him last night. He probably spent half his night at the office, and I didn't even get to dream about him. My only solace is that I didn't dream at all. That means no nightmares and a good night of sleep.

"What are you up to today?" Nate asks. I pause. As much as I am dreading the day, I am excited to see Nate's reaction to my makeover and I have been keeping this day a secret.

"Oh, Summer and I will probably just shop a bit. Maybe get some coffee," I trail off. I'm a horrible liar, so I offer partial truths. We will do a little shopping. And I'm certain there will be coffee at the spa.

"How did Summer talk you into shopping?" Nate asks, and I can't help but smile to myself. He knows me well.

"I offered," I say in mock defensiveness. "I miss spending time with her."

"Not as much as I'm going to miss you today," he says.

"Me too." Suddenly my doorbell rings. "Crap," I tell Nate, "Summer is here. You just made me late, so I'll have to find a way to make you pay for that later."

"Promise?" I laugh, we say our quick goodbyes, and I hang up.

Summer and I pull up to the new *Serenity Spa* in Seattle. After feeding the parking meter, we take a tour of the spa. Summer is practically jumping up and down with excitement. I, on the other hand, do my best to hide my look of horror when we pass the waxing room. The flickering candlelight and classical music, which I gather are soothing to most, are putting me a little on edge.

Back at the front desk, Chantelle, the receptionist, hands Summer two sheets of paper. "Your schedules for today," she explains.

I wasn't aware we had anything prescheduled and I glance in Summer's direction. She silently reads over the schedules before smiling sweetly and handing me mine. I glance down at the list of services I'll be expected to participate in.

"A Brazilian bikini wax?" I squeal. "No way!"

"It's not up for debate," Summer says. "Trust me. This is my area of expertise." She gives me a big smile and I know there's no arguing.

The next several hours are a whirlwind. I love the massage. I hate the bikini wax. I am assigned a personal stylist. She waxes my eyebrows and cuts and styles my hair. She applies my makeup and shows me the best color combinations to use around my eyes. Summer and I top off our visit with a mani-pedi. Surprisingly, I am feeling pretty good.

"You are enjoying yourself," Summer says from behind her magazine as our feet are being massaged with warm seaweed mud. It is not a question, and I can hear the triumph in her voice.

"Besides the, uh, waxing," I say, "this has been pretty great."

I stare at myself in the full-length mirror in the lobby of the spa. I almost don't recognize my reflection. Although my length hasn't changed much, the stylist worked miracles on my hair. The subtle layers frame my face. I lean in closer to examine my makeup, impressed that my blue eyes no longer look so pale.

"You truly look beautiful," Summer says. For once, I believe her. I really do feel pretty. Summer also looks beautiful – but that's nothing new.

"Just one more stop," Summer says in a sing-song voice as she climbs behind the wheel.

"Ugh," I groan.

"Oh, come on," Summer whines. "You have to get some new clothes to go with your fabulous new look."

An hour and a half later, I am weighed down with packages and impressed with Summer's ability to speed shop. I am wearing a new dress and heels and love how feminine the new outfit makes me feel.

"I cannot wait until Nate sees you," Summers says excitedly as we walk to her car. I secretly can't wait either.

"Thank you for making me do this, Summer."

"We have to test out your new look," Summer says.

"What are you talking about?"

146

"We are heading to *Hal's Stomping Grounds*," Summer announces. "Let's see how Tom likes the new you."

I want to point out that our little shopping excursion was supposed to be our last stop, but I must admit that I am eager to get a male reaction to my transformation. "Well, I did promise Tom that I would stop by again."

When we enter the coffee shop, Tom is his typical cheerful self, calling out our names from across the café. Only this time, instead of waiting for us, Tom comes out from behind the counter and gives me a bear hug. "Someone is looking particularly scrumptious today," he tells me, playfully ruffling my hair.

The bell above the door of the front entrance rings and Tom and I both turn to see a pretty, young woman entering. "Hello, Carmen," Tom calls out to her. "The usual?"

I smile, glad that I'm not the only girl Tom has taken an interest in. My guilt is absolved. "We actually have to get going," I tell Tom, forgetting all about ordering coffee and pulling Summer towards the front door.

"You look great," Tom tells me again. "Don't be a stranger."

Pacing the floors in my living room, I am all nerves waiting for Nate to get off work. I invited him to come by and take me to dinner. When he knocks on my door, I nearly jump out of my skin. I start to move toward the door when a thought hits me. *What if he doesn't like the way I look?*

The thought stops me in my tracks. Nate is always telling me how perfect I am. What if he doesn't like the change? I start to panic, but still force myself to open the door. One look at Nate removes all feelings of dread and self-doubt.

He sweeps me into his arms and his lips crush down on mine. "You look beautiful Emma," he says. I feel triumphant. I give a little twirl, showing off my new dress and shoes. Nate reaches up and strokes my hair. "Emma, you've always been sexy, but *damn*."

I giggle and kiss him again. "I wanted to surprise you," I say. "Summer made me go to a spa day with her, and actually, I was pretty surprised at how much fun I had."

Nate is practically gawking. "Are you sure we have to go *out* to dinner?" he asks.

We don't go out. We don't even make it past the front room before Nate has me out of my new dress. We head for the couch. I love my newfound confidence as I kiss him. I remove my panties and am confused at Nate's shocked expression. That is until I remember my wax treatment from earlier. I smile seductively at him, raising an eyebrow.

"You're going to be the death of me," he says. He takes my hand and quietly leads me to the couch, pulling me down on the sofa with him.

"You're cooking me dinner after this," I whisper in Nate's ear.

Snuggled up next to Nate on the couch, I gaze at him and he kisses the top of my head. "What's with the strange look?" he probes.

"I was just thinking about how I used to consider you a gentle lover," I tell him.

His expression turns somber. "Oh, babe, did I hurt you?" His voice is soft, concerned.

"If hurting me means that you just gave me more pleasure than I knew possible than, yes, I'd say you did," I answer, grinning at him.

Nate looks relieved and I punch him playfully in the arm. "Get a grip big guy, I'm not *that* fragile."

"Oh really," Nate responds, and I squeal as he lifts me up and gently tosses me back onto the couch. *Round two.*

CHAPTER THIRTY-ONE

BACK AT WORK, I AM EMBARRASSED at the fuss everyone makes over my new look. I thought I'd love to get the kind of attention I often see Summer get, and while I am flattered, it also makes me uncomfortable.

Just before noon, Lance taps on the door to my office and I invite him in. "I just came to see what all of the fuss was about," he divulges as he circles behind my desk.

"And?" I ask, standing to my feet.

"Hmm... I'm not sure that I see a difference," he says, looking me up and down. I give him a playful shove. "You know I'm teasing," he continues, "but you've always been beautiful to me." I know Lance and I are good friends, but his spirited compliments often fluster me.

I am relieved when the work day is over. On the way out, I pass the main conference room and see Eldon Banks and Robert, the janitor, having what appears to be a heated discussion. Their conversation comes to an abrupt halt when I walk by. Eldon casts his typical hard stare in my direction while Robert looks apologetic. I wonder to myself if Eldon is regretting his decision to hire a family friend. I offer a passing smile to both men before continuing down the hall. My smile is incited by amusement as opposed to any real desire to show myself friendly. *Oh, the consequences of nepotism.*

I drive straight from the office to Nate's house. I know that I will beat him home, but I want to surprise him. He is the only one I don't mind drooling over me.

When I hear Nate on the porch, I answer his door wearing only my panties and a silk scarf. He smiles at me, but he looks drained and I can tell he is upset. "What's wrong?" I ask, my face falling.

"Nothing, babe, you look very sexy," he says, as if feeling the need to reassure me.

"Nate, tell me," I urge, temporarily forgetting my lack of clothing.

He tugs at the scarf around my neck and gives me a devilish grin. "Maybe if you put some clothes on, I can concentrate and tell you," he says.

I discard the scarf, throw on one of his white dress shirts, and sit next to him on the living room couch. "You look tired, Nate," I tell him as I finish buttoning up the shirt.

After some prodding, he tells me about a new string of seemingly related carjackings he has been working on in cooperation with the Seattle Police Department. "Someone died today," he says. "These carjackings have been going on for a few weeks now, but this is the first time someone has been killed. It was a young woman. She had three little kids and a husband. It was hell breaking it to the family."

Nate puts his head in his hands. I pull his head into my lap and comfortingly stroke his dark hair. I lean down to kiss his forehead and am temporarily lost for words. "I am so sorry," I offer lamely.

"As a cop I've seen a few things," he continues, "but when I saw how this guy reacted when I told him about his wife, it made me think about you and how I would react if someone told me that kind of news."

Nate sits up and his face is just inches from mine. "I don't know how someone ever gets over something like that," he says in earnest.

I am shocked at how vulnerable Nate seems. He is usually so composed and strong. Squeezing behind him on the couch, I wrap my legs around him. I gently massage his shoulders and plant a kiss on the back of his neck. "I'm not going anywhere," I tell him.

When he nods off on the couch, I carefully cover him with a blanket before slipping away to prepare myself a sandwich, comfortably moving about in his kitchen. I make one for him too, but I wrap it and place it in the fridge for later.

Nate's home phone rings and I answer it without thinking. "Is Nate there?" I hear a woman ask. I feel a chill run down my spine, my jealousy threatening to get the better of me.

"May I ask who is speaking?" I do my best to keep my tone even.

"Yes, this is Detective Williams," the woman responds, and I'm flooded with relief.

"Nate is sleeping," I say more kindly. "Would you like me to wake him?"

"Yes, if you could. It's important," the woman replies.

152

I gently nudge Nate awake. I wonder if he'll be annoyed that I answered his phone. If he is, he doesn't let on. "It's Detective Williams," I say, handing him the phone.

Nate grabs the phone and rises from the couch. He is pacing during their brief exchange. When he hangs up the phone, he looks upset again.

"Emma, I'm so sorry, I have to go."

I want to know more about what's going on, but I know that Nate is in a hurry. "I understand," I lie.

"I'm sorry that our evening didn't turn out the way you planned," Nate says. I silently agree, remembering the scarf and panties.

"Oh, Nate, don't worry about it. I'll give you another chance," I say lightly, trying my best to hide my disappointment.

I expect a quick kiss, but instead Nate pulls me close to him, kissing me long and hard while smoothing my hair with his masculine hands.

"Go do what you have to do," I say, out of breath when he finally releases me.

"You're amazing, you know?" he says, turning to go. "You'll be here when I get back?"

Realizing how much he wants me to stay, I can't help but feel warm all over and I smile up at him. "Of course," I say, pushing him gently out the door.

When Nate returns, it's after midnight. I pretend to be sleeping, not wanting him to feel bad that I waited up for him. He eases into bed beside me and slips an arm around my waist.

"I love you, baby," I hear him whisper in my ear, and it tugs at my heart. He kisses my bare shoulder. I breathe a contented sigh, still not giving away that I am awake. Nate is asleep within minutes and I am left wondering about the carjacking case and why he was out so late. I realize this may be the first of several nights like this and I wonder how well I will handle it.

CHAPTER THIRTY-TWO

IT'S A TUESDAY NIGHT and while Nate is working late (yet again), I hold a secret planning meeting with his family and Summer. Nate's birthday is coming up in a few days and I want to throw a surprise party for him. His family is quick to get in on the plan. Nancy provides the names and contact information for several of Nate's friends from the academy, as well as friends he currently serves with on the force.

The hardest task is figuring out how we are going to throw a surprise party for a detective that doesn't miss a thing. Brandon is adamant that he can get Nate to the party without him becoming suspicious.

"And how do you plan on managing that?" I ask, not bothering to mask my skepticism.

"We've been playing basketball together lately. I'll just tell him that he and I need some one-on-one practice at the gym. I mean, he is getting older. He's rusty."

I laugh. "Hold on," I argue, "I've seen Nate when he gets home from playing basketball. He is covered in sweat. Do we really want him to arrive at his own surprise party that way? Or do you want to arrive that way, for that matter? What will the ladies think?" I tease.

"We'll grab a quick shower at the gym," Brandon suggests. I'm still not convinced that he can pull this off, but I agree to his plan.

"I would love to hold the party in your newly finished addition if that works for you two," I say to Martin and Nancy.

"That would be perfect," Nancy gushes. We agree to keep the menu and decorations simple, but if I know Nate's mother, that will probably change.

On the morning of Nate's birthday, I make him breakfast in the buff. He chuckles when he enters the kitchen. "Birthday suit for the birthday boy," I explain, shooting him a wink as I scurry about the kitchen.

After I slip into a nightshirt and we sit down to eat, I do my best to sound casual when I ask what he'd like to do after work for his birthday. "Oh, I forgot," Nate says, "Brandon wanted to get together and shoot some hoops this evening. I actually forgot that it was my birthday."

Doing my best to look disappointed, I study Nate's expression for a hint that he's onto my little plan. As usual, his face doesn't give anything away.

"Of course, if you want to do something, I can cancel," Nate offers.

"Oh, no, don't be silly. It's your birthday and your brother will want to see you. We can do something later."

"Are you sure?"

"Yes, totally," I half reassure him while still attempting to sound disappointed. I'm a terrible actress, so I hope I'm not overdoing it.

Nate pushes aside his breakfast and stands from the table. "Of course, we don't have to wait until after work to do something for my birthday," he says. Grinning, he crosses over to me and plants a kiss on my lips.

I feel desire stirring within me as I rise from the table and lean into him. "Why, whatever did you have in mind?" I ask innocently, allowing him to lead me towards the bedroom.

Nate calls after work to say he's headed to the gym to meet Brandon. I tell him that I'll be home waiting for him, but, in truth, I am speeding to his parents' house to set up for the party.

When I arrive at Nancy and Martin's, I realize there was no need to speed. Nancy already has the place completely decorated. There are long buffet tables covered with linen tablecloths. Several round tables are positioned around the room, also covered with linens. Beautiful carnation centerpieces adorn each table.

"Wow, you've really outdone yourself," I say when I enter the spacious addition and look around.

"Is it too much?" Nancy asks, nervously ringing her hands.

"Oh no, it's perfect," I tell her, although I can't help but feel like I'm attending a wedding reception instead of a birthday party.

"Where's Bear?" I ask, looking around for the drooling beast that I've grown quite fond of.

"I took him to the dog sitter. I wasn't sure how he'd handle a house full of people," Nancy says. She waves her hands around the room. "Now the band will be here at five-thirty, and the catering will arrive at six o'clock," she tells me. *Oh, good heavens, a band?* She continues to rattle on about the menu and the people she added to the invite list after we last spoke. I can't help but smile to myself. It's obvious how much Nancy loves her boys and would do anything for them.

"Where's Martin?" I ask.

"Oh, he thinks I make too much of a fuss, so he decided to go play basketball with the boys."

I secretly agree with Martin, but I don't let on, although the amused smile I can't quite cover up might give me away.

At fifteen minutes after five, the guests start to arrive in groves, followed shortly by the band. We huddle in the great room of the new addition, waiting in eager anticipation for Nate's arrival.

As promised, Brandon delivers Nate at exactly fifteen minutes to six. Nate appears genuinely shocked when he walks in on his surprise party. He crosses the room towards me and pulls me into his arms for a kiss – unconcerned about who might be watching. "Did you do all of this?" he asks.

"Well," I say, "your mother took my plot a little further than originally planned." He laughs genially, and I stand on my tiptoes to kiss him again.

Nancy makes her way to where we are standing, and I take a step back, suddenly conscious of the room full of people. Nate wraps his mother in a tight hug, lifts her off her feet, and twirls her around. "The party's perfect, Mom," he says after setting her back down. I know it's a mild lie – Nate likes crowds about as much as I do – but his assertion makes his mother gush with excitement and pride.

158

A few minutes later Nate introduces me to Tony Garza, a detective that he is working with out of the Seattle Police Department. Tony is a bit older, but handsome for his age. The respect Tony and Nate afford each other is unmistakable, and I feel a jealous twinge at the amount of time they must get to spend together. I wonder if I ever come up in their conversations.

"Nate has told me so much about you," Tony tells me, as if reading my thoughts.

"All lies, I'm sure," I say, laughing.

"Well, he got your beauty right. I must admit, I thought the guy was prone to mild exaggeration," Tony confesses, slapping Nate affectionately on the back.

Nate laughs and squeezes my hand. "I would never lie about such things," he says good-naturedly whilst pretending to be insulted.

I want to remind him about the mild untruth he told his mother only moments earlier, but I bite my tongue. Instead, I steer the subject away from me. "So, how often do you guys get to work together?"

"I have probably spent more time with Nate over the past month than with my own family," Tony says. "After spending this much time with him, I have to ask Emma, how do you do it?"

I laugh and offer Nate a playful smile before responding. "Well, it's my cross to bear," I say, feigning despair.

Another man I don't recognize saunters over and extends his hand towards me. "I'm Frank Jefferson," he says. His voice is friendly enough, but something about him puts me on edge. I also can't shake the feeling that I've met him somewhere before. I glance up at Nate, but he doesn't seem to notice anything out of the ordinary.

Cautiously, I extend my hand to shake Frank's. "I'm Emma Taylor," I tell him, trying not to appear anxious. I quickly return my hand to my side and fight the urge to wipe it on my new party dress.

"Frank and I went through the academy together," Nate explains. "We go way back."

Not wanting to appear unfriendly, I offer a smile before politely excusing myself to check on the catering.

Nate introduces me to several more friends throughout the evening. I wasn't even aware that Nate knew so many people. The house is bursting at the seams.

"You have a lot of great friends," I tell Nate when we arrive back home.

"Yeah, I guess I really do," he agrees, looking thoughtful. I want to mention my uneasiness around the man who introduced himself as Frank Jefferson, but I don't want to insult one of his friends.

"Thanks for planning that, babe," Nate's voice breaks into my thoughts.

"Well, were you surprised?" I ask, dying to know if his family and I managed to best the great Detective Mitchell.

A faint smile tugs at the corners of Nate's mouth. "I knew it!" I accuse. "You knew the whole time!" I try to appear disappointed, but I always knew it was inevitable.

"Aww… but it was still very sweet of you and my family to try," he says.

"I do have one surprise for you that I'll bet you haven't guessed," I tell him.

"What would that be?" Nate asks, curiosity piqued. I say nothing as I head into the bedroom, knowing Nate will follow.

In the bedroom, I slip out of my dress, revealing black, lacy lingerie complete with garters and silk stockings. Nate steps back in shock, and, unlike at his surprise party, this time I'm certain the surprise is genuine. He lets out a low whistle, then moves towards me. I squeal in delight when his lips come down hard on mine, the warmth of his body pressing up against me.

I can feel Nate's quickening heartbeat pounding against my flesh and it turns me on to feel the affect I have on him. Nate strips off his shirt and tosses it carelessly in the corner. I tug at his belt buckle, impatient to feel his naked form against mine.

He kisses my shoulder, then drops to his knees to kiss me between my thighs. I moan with anticipation as he pulls at one of the garters with his teeth. "Do you mind if I rip this off you?" he asks with animalistic instinct.

Although I don't answer, I'm certain that my expression reveals he's welcome to get me naked the quickest way he knows how. Nate removes each garter with his trained mouth, then gently pulls down my lacy panties. His mouth moves towards the nakedness between my thighs, but I tug at his hair until he stands to look at me again.

"It's your birthday, not mine, remember?"

Nate groans when my hands slowly travel over the zipper of his pants. Despite my trembling fingers, I manage to unbuckle his belt and tug down on his jeans. He kicks out of his pants and I smile with satisfaction at the sight of his taut manhood. Nate leads me to the bed where he finishes removing my lingerie.

We fall together into the bed, Nate easing himself inside me as I lift my hips towards him. My lips are on his neck, begging him to consume me. His pace quickens with every thrust, a perfect match to my growing urgency. At last we collapse together, spent from our love making.

"Happy birthday," is all I manage before drifting off to dream.

CHAPTER THIRTY-THREE

"I THINK IT'S TIME TO CLEAN out your wardrobe again," Summer tells me one Sunday afternoon as she flips through the clothes hanging in my closet, narrowing her eyes and smirking each time she finds something that she doesn't approve of.

"Summer," I groan. "We just did that!"

"We cleaned out your closet like six months ago," she corrects me. "And frankly, I'm not sure how some of these outfits made the cut."

I laugh, keenly aware that fashion is not my strong suit. "Okay," I give in. "But try to leave me with something to wear to work tomorrow."

"I'll certainly *try*," Summer says.

Exhausted by our efforts, I stare at the impressive stack of clothes and shoes piled in the middle of my closet. I survey all the empty hangers and shake my head.

"This means I'm going to have to go shopping again," I grumble aloud as the realization hits me.

"Think of this as a healthy cleansing," Summer says. I make a face, but I can't help but laugh. "Come on," she says, "we'll hit the donation center on the way to the mall. Just think of how charitable I'm helping you become. And don't worry, I let you keep your precious sweatpants."

After several exhausting hours of shopping with Summer, I am back home re-organizing my bedroom closet when the burglar alarm goes off. Gripped with fear, I reach for my cellphone to dial 9-1-1. *No! Please, no!* It's dead. I forgot to charge it. Searching my room for somewhere to hide, I rush over and lock the bedroom door, pushing my dresser in front of it. The alarm goes silent. The intruder must have disabled it.

Panicking, I run into the bathroom, bolting the door behind me. I study the tiny bathroom window, trying to assess if I can squeeze through it. I hear a pounding on my bedroom door and I bite down hard on my lower lip to keep the scream from escaping from my throat. When my teeth sink into my lip, I taste blood. It begins to pool in my mouth, but I ignore it as I desperately rack my brain for a plan. The best I can come up with is the shower. I step into it and turn to face the bathroom door. My blood is pounding as the banging on the bedroom door continues. I inch closer to the shower wall, pressing my palms against the cold, smooth surface. Then I squeeze my eyes shut and wait for the inevitable.

"Emma! Emma!" It takes me a few moments to recognize Nate's voice. I clamber out of the shower and unbolt the bathroom door just as

Nate crashes through the bedroom door, sending the dresser toppling to the floor. *So much for my extra security.*

I run to Nate, shaking and sobbing. "Someone's in my house," I cry hysterically.

"No, Emma. That was me. I accidentally set off the alarm when I let myself in," Nate explains. "It took me a few tries to remember the code..."

Nate looks around the room as if realizing for the first time just how vulnerable I would have been if he had indeed been an intruder. "What was your plan? That flimsy bedroom lock?" He waves a hand in the direction of the broken door and collapsed dresser. "Then what? Did you hide under the bed?"

"I hid in the bathroom," I say lamely.

Nate looks angry. "Baby, you need a better plan than that. You have to be able to defend yourself," he scolds.

I start to cry harder – deep, pathetic sobs that make my shoulders shake. Nate puts his arms around me, drawing me into a reassuring embrace. "I'm sorry," I manage to say, not certain why I'm apologizing.

"Shhh... don't apologize," Nate says softly. "I'm not angry with you. It just scared me to see you so unprotected here." He kisses me gently before adding, "I want to be sure that you're safe, even when I'm not here, okay? I'm going to teach you how to shoot."

At the shooting range, Nate holds out a gun and I accept it gingerly. "This is a .38 Special," he tells me, standing behind me as I aim my gun at the target board. "It is pretty accurate, and it doesn't have much of a kick-back."

"So, what you're saying is, even a girl can handle it," I say.

"Exactly," he teases, shooting me a wink.

I shoot several rounds under Nate's coaching, startled by the kick each time I fire the gun. I miss the target more times than I hit it. Nate shakes his head and makes a clucking sound with his tongue as he evaluates my target sheet, pointing out the lack of holes. "We'll pick you up some pepper spray instead," he says.

"Will that be before or after you pick me up a new bedroom door?" I quip.

CHAPTER THIRTY-FOUR

NATE CALLS ME AT WORK the next morning. "Meet me for lunch?" he asks.

I groan. "Oh, Nate, I can't. I have so much work to do. I think I'm just going to work through lunch today."

"I'll make it worth your while." His voice is soft, seductive. I picture his devilish, dimpled grin from the other end of the line.

"Okay, you've twisted my arm," I say, giving in.

Terry enters my office to drop off some research files for *Aidleman, Inc.*, the new client I blindly pitched to Lance. I wave her over to my desk. "Okay Nate, I've got to go, but I'll meet you at noon. Usual spot?"

Shaking my head, but smiling happily to myself, I hang up the phone. I know I'll have to work extra hard to concentrate on the new files until I get to see him again.

I am buried in my research when Lance walks into my office and takes his usual seat across from me. We discuss the new client for a few minutes and I feel a twinge of guilt when Lance congratulates me on my *find*.

"Since you'll be heading up the research, I'd like you to present the information to the rest of the execs – bring everyone else up to speed," he tells me.

I nod. This type of thing should make me nervous, but it doesn't. Speaking to a group of people doesn't bother me. In fact, I feel a sense of empowerment at my ability to command the attention of everyone in the room, especially when presenting something I'm passionate about. It's the one-on-one interactions that I'm not any good at.

"Oh, I almost forgot," Lance tells me. "I brought the proofs for the new billboards with me."

I sigh heavily, noticing the manila envelope in his hand for the first time. He opens it up and takes out several sheets of photo paper – each containing multiple pictures of me. Setting the photos on my desk, Lance leans in closer to view them with me. The faint smell of cigarettes hits me and I am instantly dizzy. *Remain calm.* I grip the edge of my desk, trying to steady myself.

"What's wrong?" Lance asks. Clearly, I do not have a poker face.

"Oh, nothing, I… umm... just didn't know that you smoked," I say lamely.

"I don't," he says, looking genuinely confused.

Am I losing it? Did I imagine it? I grapple with my emotions as my thoughts bounce around my head like the steel balls in a pinball machine. Finally, Lance interrupts my thoughts. "Oh, I was just outside talking to

Levi from Payroll while he was on his smoke break," he explains, lifting the collar of his shirt to smell it. "Are you saying I stink, Emma?" he teases.

I offer a tight smile. "No, you're fine. It just, uh, surprised me." I do my best to remain composed. "I'll forgive your stinky-ness this one time," I add, trying to recover. Lance chuckles before returning his attention to the photographs.

We mull over the proofs and each select our top three. I thought I'd be embarrassed about studying photos of myself alongside my boss, but I'm secretly relieved at how they turned out. The photographer did a fabulous job and somehow managed to make me look reasonably photogenic. Scooping up the proofs, Lance thanks me once again for agreeing to do the photo shoot (as if I had much of a choice) before he leaves my office.

I dart into the ladies' room before going out for lunch. I've just entered the stall when I hear two women come into the facility. I recognize one of the voices as Diana Segard, an administrator with a cubicle down the hall from my office. I don't recognize the voice of the other woman.

"Can you believe Lance is going to put her on his billboards now?" Diana scoffs. "The man could have anyone he wants. I'm not quite sure why he wastes his time on her. I mean, she's pretty and all, but she seems so frigid."

Suddenly I find myself straining to hear. *Are they talking about me?* "I know," I hear the other woman chime in. "Rachel in Accounting calls her 'the Ice Queen,' but it's so obvious what's going on. She might as well formally announce at the next staff meeting that she's sleeping her way to the top."

More shocked than hurt by this display of catty office gossip, my first impulse is to hide in the stall until they leave, but my irritation gets the better of me. I exhale slowly, channeling a dignified demeanor, and walk out of the stall.

Diana and the woman I don't recognize are standing at the sinks. I gain instant satisfaction from their shocked expressions. I square my shoulders and approach them, squeezing between them to use the middle sink. *I'll show them Ice Queen.*

After drawing out the process of washing my hands, pretending to be oblivious to the uncomfortable silence in the room, I turn to face them. They are both too stunned to move. "The executives as a whole made the decision to put me on the billboards, not Lance," I say firmly. "And I got where I am today because I worked hard for it. If you two put in a little more effort back at your desks, instead of spending time in here gossiping about how you think everyone else is moving upwards, it might do your careers some good." The words discharge from my lips like poisonous darts and I let them land where they may.

Diana's face turns crimson and the other woman's jaw drops open. Satisfied, I walk away, head held high. I may have just sunk to their level, but I still feel pretty good about it. Screw the high road.

At lunch, I relay to Nate every detail of my encounter in the ladies' room. We are squeezed together in a cozy booth in the back corner of the restaurant and he is tracing my knee with his index finger. "Emma, they're just jealous," he says. "I wouldn't let it bother you. I'd say you handled yourself rather well."

"They're calling me the *Ice Queen*!" I exclaim, as if that is somehow worse than suggesting I am sleeping with my boss.

Nate lets out a playful snort. "Well, I think I can tell them first hand that just isn't true." He moves in closer to me, his lips locking with mine. His hand moves further up my leg, making my pulse quicken.

"Behave yourself," I demand, not really wanting him to stop.

Nate's hand glides even further up my thigh, the tips of his fingers grazing my lace panties. "Nate," I say more firmly, "this kind of affection is not exactly permitted here." My eyes dart around the restaurant to see if anyone is watching.

"Well, I've never been much of a rule follower. I like to test the boundaries of what's forbidden. You should try it," he teases.

I am about to remind him that tasting the forbidden fruit didn't work out so hot for Eve, but I am distracted by him nibbling on my ear.

It takes all my self-control to go back to work. I want nothing more than to head back to Nate's house and let him finish what he started. It's actually Nate that convinces me to go back to the office, promising that we'll pick up where we left off when we both get off work. Begrudgingly, I drive back to my office after agreeing to meet him at his house around five.

Lance calls a two o'clock meeting for all senior executives. I suspect that he will be announcing his plans to attend the annual consulting conference in New York. Lance chooses just one senior executive to attend with him each year. It is a coveted opportunity, so all the executives have been buzzing with anticipation for the past week.

I know the chances of Lance picking me are slim, given that I have been a senior executive for the least amount of time; not to mention, as co-owner, Eldon Banks has input on who goes on the trip and I'm fairly certain he doesn't admire me as much as Lance does. Despite the low probability, I can't help but be hopeful.

I check the clock on the computer and stand to leave my office. As an afterthought, I grab my leather notepad, embossed with my initials. It was a welcoming gift from the other execs – posh, flashy – and so not me. But the gesture was sweet, and I don't want to appear unappreciative.

The first order of business at the meeting is to play an ice breaker game. Everyone hates this type of activity, but no one has the heart to tell Lance. He is convinced it promotes team building, so we all humor him. Today's ice breaker is a game where a beach ball is tossed around the conference room and the person holding the ball has to say something positive about someone else in the room before tossing the ball to that person. I like *most* of the other senior executives, so I shouldn't have a problem coming up with a compliment, but I feel like I am still finding my place amongst them and I dread what they may say about me.

To begin the game, Lance tosses the ball to Bart Parsons, one of the oldest execs. He frowns and looks around the room. I get the impression he's not the type to freely hand out compliments. "I enjoy how Kathy is able to keep everyone in the loop on important events," he says. With that, Bart tosses the ball to Kathy Smith. I stare at Bart's expression for a hint that he's being sarcastic. Everyone knows Kathy has a big mouth and an ear for gossip. If the expression wasn't so old, I'd swear the term *chatty Kathy* was inspired by her.

My attention is now on Kathy, who seems pleased with the compliment. Perhaps she regards her gossiping as a talent. I silently pray that she won't choose me but search my brain for the appropriate compliment to dish out if she does. I can feel myself start to perspire at the thought. Kathy doesn't choose me though. She enthusiastically compliments Nick, a handsome exec in his mid-thirties, and the game continues.

During the few minutes allotted for the ice breaker, my name is not mentioned, nor is the ball tossed in my direction. I should be relieved, but instead find myself likening the situation to being picked last in gym class. *Throw me the ball. Pick me. Pick me.* Realizing how silly I am being, I push my adolescent memories aside and force myself to focus on the rest of the meeting.

"And now, for the moment we've all been waiting for," Lance draws out his announcement, "I would like to announce my decision to invite… (he pauses and glances around the room) …Emma to join me in New York."

The announcement startles me, catching me flat-footed, and I can feel an uncomfortable heat creep up my neck and across my cheeks. "Wow, thank you Lance." I try to remain professional, but I imagine that I must both look and sound like a giddy school girl.

Everyone claps courteously, but I sense some agitation from a few of the older execs. I glance over at Eldon, who casts a small nod in my direction, but his steely expression doesn't change. I smile politely at everyone. Lance goes on to explain his decision, talking about the advantages of new talent and the positive impact I've made to the company's bottom line.

Uncomfortable with his praise, I tune him out and concentrate on looking both humble and gracious. When the meeting is adjourned, several of the executives congratulate me as we head out of the conference room. For the most part, their well wishes would appear genuine.

I follow Lance to his office to convey my appreciation. "Thank you for choosing me," I begin.

Lance holds up his hand to stop me. "No need to thank me. No one deserves this more than you. I want you to know that." Unable to help myself, I thank Lance once again before heading back to my office. I feel even more obligated to do a good job for the company, so I bury myself in my work until it's time to go home.

CHAPTER THIRTY-FIVE

I RUSH TO NATE'S HOUSE from work. I can't wait to tell him about my upcoming trip to New York. Traffic seems unusually slow and I find myself yelling at no one in particular. "Come on people, drive like you have somewhere to be."

Nate is already preparing dinner when I arrive at his house. He has given me a key, so I let myself in. I have barely removed my jacket before Nate pulls me close to him and kisses me.

"I missed you like crazy today," he murmurs seductively in my ear.

"Not as much as I missed you," I say, my body temperature rising. "So, what's for dinner? It smells delicious."

"I am making us chicken tortellini," he announces proudly.

"What's the occasion?" I ask, searching my brain for some forgotten holiday or anniversary.

"You," he says, shooting me a sexy wink.

Nate leads me back into the kitchen. I notice he is wearing a kitchen towel tucked into his pants like an apron and I don't know if he's ever looked sexier. One dark tendril of hair is tickling his forehead and he brushes it back with his arm.

"Dang, you're beautiful," I blurt out.

Nate smiles and winks at me again.

I try to help prepare the salad, but he refuses my assistance. "Oh, no you don't," he says. "You just relax. I got this."

I can't help but gawk as Nate finishes preparing the dinner. He smiles when he tastes the sauce, then tosses the salad a final time. He sets the table and lights a candle. Finally, he pulls out my chair, offering me a seat at the table. I give him a quick kiss on the cheek.

"What's that for?" he asks.

"For being you," I tell him, taking my seat.

Once he's plated the food and has taken his seat, I bring up my upcoming trip. I am chattering about it excitedly for several minutes before I realize that Nate has grown quiet.

"And it will be just the two of you there?" he finally asks.

Uh oh. I am exasperated when I realize where the conversation is going. For being the most gorgeous person on the planet, Nate sure gets jealous a great deal. I want to explain the importance of the trip to him, but I don't want to ruin our evening together, or his beautiful dinner.

"I don't have to go," I say, trying to sound cheerful. "I was just flattered that he picked me. I was thinking of turning him down though. I don't want to fall behind on my studies." I glance across the table at Nate to see if he's buying my act.

"Is that what you want?" he asks. I can see his mood darken before my eyes.

"Yes, of course," I say. I wonder if I am convincing, or if the disappointment in my voice gives me away.

Nate just offers a nod and I change the subject. In a few short minutes we are back to laughing and joking around. All the while, in the back of my mind, I am mourning my trip. It meant so much to me to go, but Nate means more. *Pick your battles*, I tell myself.

At bedtime I find it hard to sleep. I think Nate is aware that something is bothering me, but he doesn't say anything. We shut off the lights and I put a pillow over my head to block out my thoughts. The silence in the room is stifling, but I finally manage to fall asleep.

My eyes flutter open and I find myself in a park, sitting under a large oak tree. Nate is beside me, stroking my hair. "I hate it when everything is not okay between us," he says.

"Me too," I admit. "Sometimes it's just hard for me to explain myself to you."

"Try," Nate prompts. He laces his fingers in mine and my resistance melts at the warmth of his touch.

I am braver. Nate is calmer.

"It's just that this conference is a unique opportunity for me. And being chosen is a big deal. If I don't go now, I may never be chosen again," I explain.

"Why didn't you just say so?"

"Well, if you saw the look on your face…"

"That obvious, huh? I'm sorry, Emma, I just don't care for this Lance character very much."

I roll my eyes and assure him once again that Lance is just a friend.

"I just want you to be careful," he says.

When I wake up, Nate is awake beside me and stroking my hair, just like in our shared dream. He smiles down at me.

"Okay," he replies.

"Okay, what?"

"Okay, if this business trip means that much to you, I won't stand in your way."

Sitting up in bed, I kiss him happily. "Thank you for understanding."

"Emma, I want you to be able to tell me anything," he says.

"I did."

"No, not in a dream," he says. "Here. Now." He pulls my hand to his chest and dips his head to kiss my fingertips. I feel electricity jolt through my body. "I'm not always going to agree with you," he continues, "but you have to promise that you'll always be honest with me. I don't want you to miss out on the things that are important to you, and I don't want there to be any regrets between us."

"I promise," I tell him. "No regrets." And I mean it with every fiber of my being.

CHAPTER THIRTY-SIX

AFTER KISSING NATE GOOD-BYE at the airport, I join Lance at the ticketing kiosk. I wave my cellphone in front of the barcode scanner and my boarding pass appears on the screen. I hit the print button, then glance down at my ticket. "First class?" I ask aloud, surprised.

"Hmm… our travel agent must have made a mistake," Lance says, winking in my direction.

"I see what's going on here," I accuse, playfully. "You can't handle flying coach, and you didn't want to be alone."

"Guilty," he says.

We check our bags, wade through the nightmarish maze of the security line, then head for our gate to await the boarding call. We sit near the service counter and watch an elderly couple in matching polyester blue pantsuits walk hand in hand toward the female agent perched behind the counter. The agent forces a smile and I hear the old man softly ask what the price of two first-class upgrades would be. Clearly disappointed with the answer he's given, he turns away from the counter.

Without a word, Lance stands to his feet and walks over to the counter. Towering above the elderly couple, he exchanges a few words with them before leaning in close to speak with the agent. The agent's forced smile morphs into a genuine grin as I watch Lance go to work on her. He smiles and points in my direction, then continues to talk to her. I can tell he is putting on the charm, buttering her up. Before long the woman hands Lance two rectangular sheets of paper and does the same for the elderly couple.

"What was that all about?" I ask when Lance once again takes a seat beside me.

"I hope you weren't too attached to our first-class seats," he tells me.

"You gave that couple our seats?" I am shocked. "Lance, that is so sweet."

He shrugs, looking somewhat embarrassed at the compliment. "Well, they were so fragile, and the old man was hoping to get a first-class seat to make his wife more comfortable. This is their first plane ride in years and they're going to visit their new great granddaughter."

The agent announces that it's time for first-class members to board. I look over at Lance and pretend to pout. He chuckles to himself and hands me a newspaper to read while we wait. When it's finally our turn to board, I look to the far back of the plane in search of row twenty-three where my newly assigned seat is located. It's a far cry from row two with the wide leather seats.

"Up there in first class that old couple is having *your* drink," I whisper wickedly to Lance as he squeezes into the seat beside me.

He smiles and shakes his head. "At least it's a nonstop flight."

Before takeoff, a stewardess with brown, curly hair and a painted-on smile commences with the safety procedures. An unwieldy curl from her over-processed perm keeps creeping towards her mouth as she speaks, and I find myself concentrating more on that than what she is saying. When the plane finally lifts off the ground, I look around at the worried expressions on the faces of some of the passengers. I am always amazed at how many people are terrified of flying. I just find it boring, so I've come armed with a book and headphones.

It's still early, and I know I should rest, but I'm afraid I'll have another nightmare and don't wish to have a plane full of witnesses when I snap out of it. Lance keeps the flight interesting, though. I learn that he loves to people watch and is quick to point out anyone worth watching. First, there is the guy with the chronic itch. Lance pokes me in the ribs each time the man goes on a scratching frenzy. Lance chuckles softly at the way the nearby passengers try to inch away from the man and his incessant scratching. It's no use though; they are prisoners in their tiny assigned seats.

The next person of interest is the little girl sitting in front of us that I would guess is no more than three. She reminds me of my niece, Libby. She talks endlessly to the poor man beside her, who is doing his best to look like he's sleeping. The mother tries to quiet the young girl, but it's of no use. I spend much of the flight enjoying the girl's strange tales.

CHAPTER THIRTY-SEVEN

NEW YORK IS AS BUSTLING AND STIMULATING as I could have ever imagined – an electric jigsaw puzzle of lights and yellow taxis. "You're not going to call it a day once we check in, are you?" Lance asks once we've hailed a taxi and are headed towards the hotel.

"What did you have in mind?" I ask.

"I thought we could take the rest of evening to explore New York," he says smoothly.

While I know Nate would be less than thrilled about the idea of me traipsing around New York with Lance as my tour guide, I am so excited that I push away my guilty thoughts. "Sounds perfect," I say.

After checking into the hotel and tipping the bellhop to take our luggage up to our rooms, Lance hails another taxi cab. "You're not the least bit curious to find out what our rooms look like first?" I ask.

"I come here every year, remember?"

"Oh, right. I forgot. Well, I guess I'll have to trust you that our rooms are satisfactory," I say in my best snobby voice, but judging from the posh lobby, I have no doubt that they will be.

For our first stop, Lance and I visit the Museum of Modern Art before it closes for the evening. I try to hush Lance as he sarcastically compares a piece of art to something he recalls painting in the second grade. Overhearing him, a member of the staff walks over to patiently educate him on the evolution of modern art and the importance of keeping an open mind.

"I can't take you anywhere," I laugh as we make our quick exit from the museum. Lance is laughing too, but he looks a little sheepish.

It's a long elevator ride to the top observation deck of the Empire State Building, our next must-see location. Lance looks nervous and I wonder if he's afraid of heights, but he doesn't admit it. I take several photos with my phone and peer in wonder through the tower viewer while he clings desperately to the deck rails. We wrap up our tour by visiting Rockefeller Center, where I am rendered speechless by the beautiful gardens. As I stare in envy at the couples holding hands and strolling through the center, I wish for the thousandth time that Nate was with me, but I am still having an amazing time.

I welcome the cab ride back to the hotel. My feet are aching, and I am exhausted, the jet lag taking its toll. "I can't wait to get back to my room and get into a nice, hot shower," I mutter aloud.

"Is that an invitation?" Lance pipes up.

I slug him in the arm. "Will there be a session on sexual harassment at this seminar?" I ask, batting my eyes innocently.

"Well, I hope so for your sake. After all, it is *highly* inappropriate to invite your boss to your room for a shower when you're on a business trip together," he quips.

I shake my head at him and he smiles back at me. Pulling up to the hotel, the valet helps me out of the cab. Lance drops a tip in the valet's open palm and the two of us make our way into the lobby. It's a flurry of activity as a host of staff rush about putting up banners and setting up booths in preparation for the conference. Lance and I pass by a few of the booths before pausing outside of the hotel restaurant.

"Do you want to grab a quick bite to eat?" he asks.

My stomach growls in response. "I'd love to, but I'm afraid I may fall asleep at the table," I tell him. "I'm just going to order room service." I excuse myself and head for the elevator.

When I reach the top floor, I make my way down the hallway, following the numbered signs until I reach my room. I fiddle with the key card, excited to see what waits for me on the other side of the door. When I step into my room, I am not disappointed. It is exquisite! I rush to the balcony to see what the lights of New York City look like from the top floor of a luxury hotel. The views are amazing, but my time on the balcony is short-lived, interrupted by the incessant ringing of the telephone from my room. I rush inside to answer the phone by the nightstand table.

"Hello?"

"Hello, ma'am, it's the front desk. I just want to be sure everything in your room is to your satisfaction."

"Yes, thank you," I say. Hanging up the phone, I wonder to myself how the front desk was aware I had checked in at that very moment. Do they have cameras in the elevator? Do they get a notification whenever my key card is used? However they do it, it's a bit unsettling.

After fishing my cell from my purse, I throw myself onto the plush king-sized bed. I call Nate and chat about my evening touring New York. He is doing his best to sound excited for me, but I can tell he's still apprehensive about me going on the business trip alone with Lance. "How is your room?" he asks.

"Empty without you," I tell him, stressing the word *empty*. After saying our goodbyes, I drift off to sleep, exhausted from my day.

Lance and I browse the conference agenda over an early breakfast. The first scheduled session is at eight o'clock. My enthusiasm waivers when I realize it is a motivational speaker, but I keep the thought to myself.

I lose Lance somewhere after the second session. The conference is enormous, with multiple sessions offered during the same timeslot. I seize the opportunity to network on my own – and to sneak in a call or two to Nate during the breaks. At lunchtime, I wander to the banquet hall by myself, hoping to catch Lance and spare myself the agony of dining alone. My eyes dart around the dining area until I finally spot him at a table-for-four in the far back of the room. I also spot that he is not alone. He is accompanied by a slender, blonde woman. She throws back her head and laughs at something Lance says. She then touches his arm flirtatiously and leans toward him from across the table.

I smile and shake my head, ever amazed at how easily Lance can attract attention from the fairer sex. I am about to find another place to sit when Lance looks up and motions me over. I hesitate at first, not wanting to be a third wheel, but decide to join them.

"Emma, this is Jillian. Jillian, this is Emma," Lance says. He stands and pulls back a chair for me.

I extend my hand to shake Jillian's. "Are you sure I am not intruding?" I politely ask.

"Of course not," he says.

I see a flash of annoyance on the woman's face, but she quickly masks it with a tight smile. "Please, join us," she chimes in.

After lunch Jillian tags along with Lance to the next session, so I choose a different one and politely avoid the two of them for the remainder of the day. When the final session ends, I head to my room early, skipping the scheduled seafood dinner. I call Nate. He's much more chipper than the previous evening. I prop the phone on my shoulder and let him talk about work while I massage my temples. When I notice the long pause, I speak up.

"You still there?" I ask.

"Yes, are you?" Nate teases.

"Sorry. I don't know if it's the time zone change, or the fallout from sitting in these sessions all day, but I'm tired."

"Okay, okay, I'll let you go to bed," Nate says laughing.

"I do miss you," I say.

"Miss you too. Now get some sleep."

I fall asleep the moment my head hits the pillow.

The faceless man once again haunts my dreams. Like so many dreams before, I am being chased through the woods. I feel the man's hot breath on my neck – smell the stench of cigarettes. The burning in my lungs is almost unbearable. I stumble and fall to the ground, the undergrowth cutting into my hands.

When I wake up, I am chilled to the bone and it takes me a few moments to remember where I am. My lungs feel like they're on fire. My imagination is working overtime and I smell the faint odor of cigarettes lingering in the air. Although my hands appear unscathed, they sting from the dream. I hug my pillow, wishing that Nate was here to protect me; to hold me.

CHAPTER THIRTY-EIGHT

FOR THE SECOND MORNING IN A ROW, Lance and I meet for breakfast in the lobby. He senses that I am upset the moment we're seated.

"What's wrong?" he asks, looking alarmed.

"Oh, it's nothing," I lie.

"Emma, don't take this the wrong way, but you look awful," he says. "Tell me what's going on."

After some coaxing, I confide in Lance that I have been having nightmares since my attack. He listens intently, his face set in a grim line. I remain vague about my dreams. Lance is a friend, but I don't feel comfortable telling him about Madame Destiny's theory and the degree to which I've entertained its merit.

Lance reaches across the table and grabs my hand. "Emma, I am going to say something, and I really hope you know that it's because I have your best interest at heart."

"Okay," I say, not sure what to expect.

"Do you ever wonder if your detective friend is the one who attacked you?" he asks, nervously smoothing his hair with his free hand.

"Nate?" I exclaim, appalled at the implication.

"Hear me out," Lance says. "You were dating this guy, right?"

"Yeah," I reply.

"Okay, and not long after you broke up, you were attacked, correct?" I nod in agreement.

"Well," Lance says, "then miraculously your ex-boyfriend takes over your case and is suddenly back in your life?" His accusations hit me hard and my anger sparks. I jerk my hand away and stand to leave.

"That is enough!" I tell him firmly. "Nate is the best thing that has ever happened to me. How dare you suggest such a thing!" With that, I turn on my heel and stalk back to my room with Lance staring after me.

I attend the morning session without Lance. When I spot him several rows in front of me, I pretend not to notice him. At lunchtime, Lance catches me in the buffet line and tries to make peace, but I am not ready to call a truce just yet.

"Lance, now is not the time." He stalks away to eat lunch by himself.

Back in my hotel room, I play back Lance's accusations in my head. He has some valid points. I know Nate was angry when we broke up. Perhaps he tried something drastic to get me back?

Tears stream down my face as I think back on my dreams. Both my masked assailant and Nate are able to invade my dreams. Hadn't Madame Destiny said that the darkening of dreams was rare? What are the chances that two different people would have the power to do such a thing?

Curling up in a ball, I reflect on my nightmares, then my beautiful dreams with Nate. When I am with him, I rarely dream about the man in the ski mask. When I do encounter a nightmare, it's often after Nate and I have had some sort of a disagreement. Could the intruder and Nate really be one and the same? Their build is similar. What if Nate used the cologne and cigarettes as a ruse to keep me from suspecting him? Perhaps that's why he volunteered to take over my case. Feeling sick at the possibility, I run to the bathroom to throw up. I return to bed, miserable and confused. Out the window of my hotel room I watch the sun dip low in unison with my sinking spirits. I don't call Nate. I just pull the covers over my head and cry.

The next morning, I check my cellphone. I see several missed calls and texts from Nate. I feel guilty, but I can't bring myself to call him back. I attend the final portion of the conference and then head for the airport with Lance. We drive in silence.

"I am sorry, Emma," Lance finally says. "I was way out of line. The detective seems like a nice guy."

I know Lance knows Nate's name and I wonder why he refuses to use it. "It's fine," I say, cutting him off. "Let's just drop it."

Lance nods, looking away. I soften my voice. "Really, it's fine. I know you meant well. Thank you again for inviting me on this trip. I hope that I didn't spoil it for you."

Lance brightens a little. "Of course not. I had a great time, Emma." I know he is just being nice and is probably regretting his decision to bring me along, but I pretend to believe him.

The flight home is brutal. The plane is sweltering, and I'm convinced we're destined for the seventh circle of hell rather than home. I still haven't talked to Nate and am worried how I will explain why I didn't return his calls. I have an extra glass of wine to calm my nerves. The liquid courage goes down smooth.

Nate is waiting for me when I land in Seattle. One look at him and I know Lance's accusations are ridiculous. I feel terrible for even considering them. I run to Nate, bounding into his arms.

I can tell Nate is baffled. "I was worried about you," he says. "Didn't you get any of my calls and texts?"

I don't want to lie, but I also don't want to hurt him by telling him I had entertained the idea that he could be my attacker. "Well, the conference kept us pretty busy," I say lamely.

It is obvious Nate is a little put out by my response, but I kiss him softly on the mouth. "I really missed you," I tell him. "Next time I go on a trip, I'm going to insist on taking you along."

This seems to appease Nate and he smiles. Lance wanders over to us. "Thanks for bringing my girl back safely," Nate says. His voice sounds casual, but his arm tightens possessively around my waist.

"Emma is an incredible woman. She's a real asset to *my* company." I can't help but notice how Lance exaggerates the word *my*. I am exasperated at this pissing contest taking place as if I am not standing here.

"I'll see you tomorrow, Lance," I interject, trying to break the tension. Lance nods his head and walks away.

"You can loosen your grip on my waist now," I say to Nate. I want to be mad at him, but I still feel too guilty for having paid any heed to

Lance's accusations. I know Nate would be hurt and furious if he ever found out.

The silence between us on the car ride home is deafening. The road seems to stretch on forever. Nate tries to ask about my trip, but I add little to the conversation. My guilt settles over me like a wet blanket.

Back at Nate's place, I am edgy when we get ready for bed. I know now that Nate is not the attacker, but the guilt I feel for having even considered it is consuming me. I want to tell him the truth, but I know it will crush him. Fearing that I will reveal too much if coaxed, I do my best to keep any conversation to a minimum as I shut out the light and climb into bed.

As if sensing my apprehension, Nate does not try to be amorous with me. This only makes me feel worse. Although he gives me a tender kiss goodnight and drapes an arm around my waist, I can tell he's angry and hurt in reaction to my outward coolness towards him. After spending several days apart, I imagine this is not at all how he pictured our reunion would be. *Oh, Nate, everything will be better tomorrow,* I cry out in my head, praying that Nate can somehow hear me as I drift off to sleep.

I am sitting on a park bench, overlooking the waterfront. Nate is beside me, his hand resting casually in mine. "Baby, I want you to know that you can tell me anything," he tells me.

Contemplating what to say, I sigh deeply. "I'm afraid to." My throat tightens, and I steal a glance at Nate.

"Afraid?" he asks. His eyes darken, but his voice softens. "Why, Emma? You know I would never do anything to hurt you."

Guilt engulfs me. I do know that. Now. Or at least I should. "It's not that, Nate," I say. Tears spring to my eyes. "I'm afraid if I tell you, it'll be me that's hurting you."

"Your silence is hurting me. Do you have any idea what it's doing to my imagination? Emma, please just tell me. Did something happen with Lance on your trip?"

"Yes, but…"

Nate exhales deeply. "Okay, let's talk about it." His words come out slowly. He drops my hand and turns to look at me. "Did he kiss you?" I can tell he is trying his best to remain calm as he searches my face and waits for an answer.

"No, no, it's nothing like that." Nate looks temporarily relieved, but his relief fades once I reluctantly tell him what Lance had accused and I had so foolishly considered.

As expected, Nate is angry. "You actually believed that?" he says in disgust, springing to his feet.

"Only in that moment. I was so stupid. Nate, please forgive me," I beg. I start to cry as he stomps away.

I wake up in tears and Nate is out of bed, glaring down at me. I scramble out of bed, grabbing for his hand. He pulls away from me and my heart catches in my throat.

"It's not fair that you can invade my dreams like that," I try to reason with him. "I never would have told you that in person. I don't think that now."

"The fact that you believed it at all is enough," Nate says coolly. "Emma, I would never hurt you. Not ever. It makes me sick that you could think that of me, even for a minute."

A wave of nausea sweeps over me and I wonder if I've lost Nate for good this time. Terrified at the thought, I swallow all my pride and launch into an apology. "I had a few moments of confusion and stupidity, Nate. I am so sorry. There is no excuse. Please Nate, please don't leave me." I am sobbing. I know I look like a pathetic mess, but I don't care. I know I will be wrecked if he walks out.

"Dammit Emma, I'm not going anywhere," he says. "For someone that always looks for the best in everyone, you sure have a way of believing the worst about me."

I can tell Nate is furious, but he steps towards me. He places his left hand on my waist and lifts my chin with his right. My heart is racing as I try to anticipate his next move. His thumb brushes my cheek and I stare intently into his solemn, green eyes.

"Nate, if it seems that way it is only because I feel like you are too good for me. I keep waiting for this thing with us to end."

"This *thing*?" he interrupts. "Emma, you really need to get it through that pretty head of yours that this is not just a *thing*. I am not going anywhere."

It's obvious that Nate is still angry, but I kiss him bravely. I am afraid that he will turn away from me, but instead he kisses me back. "I promise that I am not usually this unsure of myself," I say, stepping back. "I am usually more of a take-charge kind of girl." I laugh nervously, trying to lighten the mood.

Nate manages a laugh. He cradles my face in his hands, wiping away my tears with his thumbs as he studies my face. "I know. I love you, even if you are sort of crazy." I feel myself blush as he leans in to kiss me again. The man has the patience of a saint.

"I guess this experience gives a whole new meaning to the phrase, *don't go to bed angry,*" I mutter. Nate laughs again. This time it's a deep, throaty laugh, and I know all is forgiven. I bury my head in his chest and silently vow to never doubt him or hurt him again.

CHAPTER THIRTY-NINE

HE SITS QUIETLY IN HIS VEHICLE, sketching her face as he waits for her to come home. He doesn't need to see her in person to capture her likeness in his drawing. Her face is etched in his memory – it invades his every thought and haunts him while he sleeps. He wakes each morning with her taste on his lips and her scent lingering in the air.

While he waits, he is patient at first; but after several hours he grows agitated. He's consumed several sodas and needs to urinate. It is rude of her to keep him waiting, he thinks to himself. "A woman who is a tease makes me angry," he mutters aloud to no one. "The way she tosses around her hair and laughs with those pouty lips – she knows exactly what she's doing."

He thinks to himself that he'll soon have to teach her a lesson. It's then that he realizes she must be at that cop's house again. He wants to vomit at the thought of another man touching the woman that should rightfully be his. He slams his fist into the steering wheel, then races away, screeching his tires and cursing aloud to himself.

CHAPTER FORTY

I AM NERVOUS ABOUT GOING into work. Lance is my friend and I don't want things to be awkward between us. I delay my arrival by swinging by my house to check on it and to grab fresh clothes. Pulling up to my driveway, I sigh deeply when I notice my overgrown lawn and realize that I will either need to find the time to mow it or pay the neighbor kid once again.

On the drive to work, I rehearse aloud what I plan to say to Lance. I am so deeply involved in a conversation with myself that I almost fail to notice the large billboard to my right. But I do notice it. It's impossible to miss the bright, boldly displayed advertisement for Danner and Banks Consulting, and the woman staring down traffic in a neatly tailored skirt suit – *me!* I have no choice but to pull over to take a closer look, a combination of morbid curiosity and, surprisingly, pride. I admit to myself that the billboards look great as I climb back into my car and head the rest of the way to work. I pass another one before I reach my destination.

When I arrive at my office, Lance is already waiting for me outside the door. I open the door and motion him in. When he closes it behind us, it puts me on edge.

"Are we cool?" he asks after a brief pause. His gray eyes are intense.

"Yes, we're fine. I'm sorry, Lance. I overreacted. I know you were just trying to help."

"No, I overstepped. You're just a really good friend, and I don't want to see you get hurt." Lance, usually so sure of himself, looks like a lost little boy.

"I am still really glad I was given the opportunity to go to New York," I tell him, smiling up at him.

"And I am still glad that I chose you to go with me, Emma."

"Did you see the billboards?" I ask, switching topics.

"They look fantastic," he says. The tension between us is lifted.

"They really do," I admit aloud. "The photographer did a nice job."

"The photographer… yeah, that's what made them great," Lance mutters, his voice dripping with sarcasm. I can't help but laugh, remembering how put out Lance was when the photographer asked him to leave the room.

"Okay, fine, *I* made them look great," I say. My conceited statement provokes a laugh from Lance and I know we're back to the way things were.

I leave work an hour early. I have a date with Nate and I want everything to be perfect. Although I know he has forgiven me for New York, I still feel terrible and am determined to make it up to him.

When I pull up to my house, I notice my freshly cut lawn and realize Nate must have done it. I wonder when he had the time. I can't fathom it being possible for the man to be any more perfect as I unlock my front door and head into the bathroom to grab a quick shower and prepare for my date.

I am shaving my legs when I hear my cellphone ringing. At first, I am inclined to ignore it, but I wonder if it's Nate and don't want to miss a call from him. I rush out of the shower and grab my cell from the night stand. "Hello?" I answer, out of breath.

"Hi sweetie, it's Grandma." I smile at the sound of my grandmother's voice. She's not the typical picture of a woman with grandchildren in their twenties. My grandma looks very youthful. She loves to go out dancing and is known to still sing karaoke on occasion.

"What's up, Grandma?" I ask, sitting down on the bed with my towel draped around me and my wet hair soaking the bed sheets.

We chat about the voice lessons my grandma has been giving at the community center. She asks if I've been seeing anyone and I tell her that Nate and I are back together. I smile when my grandmother gives a low whistle and tells me what a *hunk* she thinks Nate is.

After promising that Nate and I will both be attending the family reunion, I say goodbye to her and make a mad dash back into the bathroom to finish getting ready for my date.

When Nate saunters into my bedroom, I am putting the finishing touches on my makeup. I turn and stare at him, contemplating the way he makes me feel. On the one hand, he makes me feel invincible, like I can do anything. He both encourages and challenges me. On the other hand, sometimes he makes me feel small – not from anything he says or does, but simply because of who he is. His presence fills the room, takes up every bit of space, and sometimes I wonder where I fit, or if I fit at all.

Nate casually grabs my hand, interlacing his fingers with mine. Suddenly we are the same again. I am part of him, and he is a part of me. I look up at him and grin. "Ready to go?" he asks.

He surprises me with reservations to *Lunar*, a ritzy restaurant in Seattle that's nearly impossible to get into. "How did you manage this?" I ask, obviously impressed, as Nate helps me out of the car and tosses his keys to the valet.

"I just told them that I had a famous girlfriend."

Nate is grinning, and at first, I am confused; but then I realize what he's referring to. "So, you saw the billboards."

"I did." He is clearly amused.

"Well, what did you think?" I am bustling with anticipation.

"I think you looked all-business, yet sexy."

"Really?"

"You're probably going to cause some traffic jams," he says. His tone is serious, but his eyes dance with humor.

"So, are you going to tell me how you really managed to secure a reservation at this place?"

"I know people," he says casually, shrugging his shoulders, but he still doesn't reveal how he managed such a feat. I guess some things will just have to remain a mystery.

The hostess seats us at one of the linen-covered tables along the window. The waterfront views outside are incredible, but pale in comparison to the view across the table from me – Nate, dressed in black slacks and a button-up dress shirt. Although he's wearing a tie, it's loose and the top button of his shirt is undone. I stare at his neck, resisting the urge to lean across the table and plant a kiss on the exposed skin just above his collar.

"You look beautiful tonight," Nate tells me, echoing my own sentiment. I am wearing the flirty cream dress that I wore when I first saw him at the police station, shortly before we got back together. Only this time I've traded in the strappy sandals for dangerously high heels, but somehow Nate manages to remain taller than me.

Nate orders us a bottle of wine and politely declines the waiter's help, offering to pour it himself. With delicate finesse, he fills our glasses, perhaps a little too generously.

"Are you trying to get me drunk, Nathan Mitchell?" I playfully accuse. He smiles in response. His expression is that of an angel and a devil all rolled into one.

I must admit that I do get a little tipsy at dinner. I feel giddy as Nate helps me inside my house and I'm uncertain if it's him or the wine that's gone to my head. I tell him that he's beautiful and he kisses me softly on the cheek. In the bedroom he patiently removes my cream dress and helps me out of my shoes, planting another tender kiss on my shoulder and sending tingles down my spine and into my toes.

As Nate helps me into bed, I am flirting shamelessly. Although I am being far from a lady, he remains a complete gentleman. I love this man and all his confounding chivalry.

Nate slips into bed beside me, caressing my back and tenderly moving my hair aside to place a soft kiss between my shoulder blades. I want to turn to look at him, but my eyelids feel too heavy. When I drift off to dream, I think how I can't imagine life without him. I dream of us and am happier than any one person deserves to be.

CHAPTER FORTY-ONE

I HANG UP THE PHONE, excited. My younger sister, Nikki, is coming to visit from Nevada and bringing Libby, my adorable four-year old niece. It's been over a year since I've seen them, and I miss them both like crazy. Bubbling just beneath the surface of my excitement, I feel a little apprehensive. It's unusual for my sister to make such a last-minute trip and I sense that something may be wrong. When I last saw Nikki, it was me making a last-minute trip to Nevada.

୨୧୨୧

Nikki's boyfriend, Libby's father, had picked up and left town unexpectedly. I had always suspected he was a loser, but Nikki had adored him and was crushed when he left. She begged me on the phone to come see her. "I need your help," she pleaded, and like I had done countless times when we were kids, I swooped in to rescue her.

When I arrived in Nevada, Nikki's emotions and finances were both in shambles. She free-lanced as a fashion designer and, although I had to applaud her for doing what she loved, the pay was not always steady. I helped Nikki get out of a lease for a house that was too grand for her meager income and got her into a smaller house that she could afford on her own, complete with a modest yard for Libby to play in and a cozy den for Nikki to work on her sketches.

Luckily Libby was too young to fully realize what was happening, and other than asking a few times where her dad was, she remained a happy and vibrant toddler. Nikki, on the other hand, cried night after night and I wound up staying with her for nearly two weeks before I felt comfortable flying back to Washington. She went through a real rough patch, but Nikki is strong, and she eventually bounced back.

꧁꧁꧁

As I prepare the guestroom and give the bathrooms a quick scrub, I wonder to myself what sort of trouble Nikki might be in this time. Not wanting to spoil the excitement of her upcoming visit, I shrug the thought away and focus my energies on putting fresh sheets on the guestroom bed.

Nate offers to drive me to the airport to pick them up. I am hesitant because I haven't yet told Nikki that Nate and I are dating again, but it's sweet of him to offer, so I accept.

I chat animatedly on the way to the airport and Nate smiles and laughs as I relay forgotten stories from my youth and the predicaments Nikki and I used to get ourselves into. Despite my excitement, I am a bit nervous about Nate meeting her. She's always been the more outgoing one in our family – "the pretty one," as I remember one of my aunts saying when we were little.

Nikki's eyes are blue like mine, but not as pale. Her hair is blonde in contrast to my dark mane. I feel the familiar jealousy rising within as I remember all the attention Nikki used to get when we were growing up. As if sensing my apprehension, Nate reaches over and squeezes my hand. He lifts my hand to his mouth and playfully grazes my fingertips with his teeth.

My pulse quickens, and desire builds within. I wriggle my hand from Nate's grasp and place it on his inner thigh, running my hand slowly up his leg and grazing the zipper of his jeans. I can hear Nate's breathing getting heavier and a smile tugs at the corner of his mouth. "Don't make me pull this car over," he threatens playfully, and I cast an innocent look in his direction, as if I have no earthly idea what he is talking about.

After arriving at the airport and finding the correct gate, I spot Nikki at the baggage claim. Her hair is pulled into a loose pony tail, adding to her already youthful appearance. Nikki rushes over to hug me, and my jealousy disappears.

Nikki glances at Nate and prolongs our hug. "He is gorgeous," she whispers in my ear, and I suddenly realize she has never even seen a picture of him. I smile and wink at Nate.

My niece, Libby, is pulling on Nikki's pant leg and clutching a teddy bear. I can't believe how much she has grown. Libby's hair is blonde like my sister's, but short and curly. She looks like a little cherub.

I crouch down so that I am eye level with my niece. "Do you remember me?" I ask. Libby nods, but I'm not sure that she does recognize me. I wrap her in a tight squeeze anyway, and she returns my hug.

Nate offers to take the bags, always the gentleman. It's hard not to notice how Nikki is fawning over him. I expect to feel annoyed, but instead I find her behavior amusing. Nate switches one of the bags, freeing up his right arm so he can slip it around my waist. I lean in a little closer, putting Nikki's brazen flirting to a screeching halt.

"Who wants to go out for ice cream?" Nate asks as we pull away from the airport.

"Yay," Libby says excitedly from the back seat, and we chuckle at her childish enthusiasm, knowing we all feel equally enthused.

Nate drives us to a small, family-owned ice cream parlor in Seattle. "How did you ever find this place?" I ask as we walk through the revolving double doors. "It's adorable." I feel as if I've been transported back to the 1950s.

"I used to come here as a kid," Nate tells us. The image of him as a young kid with a mop of black hair and ice cream all over his adorable face pops into my head and it makes me smile.

Although it's a small shop, there are a surprising amount of ice cream flavors. After we each order our flavor of choice, the four of us squeeze into a corner booth. I scoot in extra close to Nate, eyeing his waffle cone of peppermint mocha ice cream and wondering if he'll agree to a trade. "Don't even think about it," he teases, but he still offers me a bite.

With a mouthful of ice cream Nikki asks, "So, what made you two get back together again?"

"Well, you get straight to the point, don't you?" I retort, but I'm not sure what to tell her.

"I couldn't stay away," Nate says, coming to the rescue. He puts an arm around my shoulders and plants a quick kiss on my cheek.

We commence with small talk, but the question of why Nikki is in town still burns in the back of my mind. I know that I shouldn't ask in front of Libby, but I can no longer stand the suspense of wondering what kind of trouble Nikki might be in. "So, what brings you to Washington?" I finally blurt out.

"Well, now who's getting straight to the point?" Nikki says, but she sounds light-hearted.

"Well, spit it out," I prod, trying to sound more relaxed.

"Prepare yourself, but I was offered a job," she says proudly.

"That's amazing," I tell her. "What's the job?"

"It's only temporary," Nikki says. "There's an up-and-coming fashion company in Seattle that is temporarily hiring designers to help launch their new line. But," Nikki explains, "if I do good work, and the launch goes well, there may be more work for me in the future."

"So, how long does this job last?" I ask, relieved that Nikki is not in any trouble, but also wondering how long I will be obligated to play host to my sister. I love her, but we haven't been known to get along after too much time together.

"Oh, I'll only be in town for a week," Nikki says. "Most of my sketches I can send in from home, but the investors want to meet me in person and observe how I work under pressure." Nikki is beaming with excitement.

I am about to express how happy I am for her when Libby interrupts. "Did you guys live back in the gray days?" she asks, licking her ice cream and looking lost in thought.

"The gray days?" Nikki repeats. I'm also confused.

Nate chuckles. "The black and white photos," he says, pointing at the row of pictures hanging above our booth – memoirs of the ice cream shop's early days.

We do our best to stifle our laughter, not wanting to hurt Libby's feeling. "Libby," Nikki explains patiently. "The world didn't used to be gray. It's just that the cameras people used back then to take pictures didn't record things in color."

"Oh," Libby says, mesmerized by this fact as she continues to lick her ice cream and study the photos.

Nikki kisses the top of Libby's head and for just a moment I feel the familiar twinge of jealousy. But this time my jealousy isn't about any attention Nikki is getting. I wonder if Nate will want to have children someday. We've never discussed it.

"You've been quiet," Nate tells me later when we're alone and snuggled comfortably on the couch. Nikki is in the guest room, tucking Libby in for the night.

"Oh, I was just thinking…" I trail off.

"You're wondering if you and I will ever have kids," Nate says. It's not a question.

"Geez detective, don't I get any private thoughts?" I murmur, a little embarrassed.

"I think having kids with you would be amazing," Nate tells me. He cups my chin in his hand and I smile up at him. "But let's not get ahead of ourselves," he teases, planting a kiss just above my jawline. "I'm not ready to share you just yet."

When Nate shakes me awake from yet another nightmare, I can't help but find the humor in our routine. "Just think," I tell him, "with how often you wake up to my screaming and have to coax me back to sleep, you already have this parenting stuff down."

"You see why I don't want to share you yet?" He laughs as he rubs the sleep from his lovely green eyes. "I already have my hands full with you."

I am about to tell Nate about my dream when I'm interrupted by a knock on the bedroom door. "Is everything okay?" I hear Nikki call from the hallway.

"Everything's fine. You can come in," Nate calls out.

I glance over at Nate and shoot him a dirty look before tossing the blanket over his bare torso. "You're very naughty," I whisper.

Nikki slowly opens the bedroom door and pokes her head in before entering the rest of the way. "I'm sorry for... whatever I'm interrupting," she says. I can feel myself shrink a little. "I just heard screaming and got a little worried."

"I was having a nightmare," I explain, somewhat mortified.

"Does this happen often?" she asks. She is looking at Nate instead of me.

"Since the attack," Nate explains, his hands balling into fists. He tugs playfully on my hair. By now Nikki is staring at me, her face drawn into a look of pity. I hate pity.

"It's not a big deal," I tell them both, doing a poor job of masking my irritation. "Lots of people have bad dreams. Now if everyone will stop treating me like a freak, I'd like to go back to bed now."

CHAPTER FORTY-TWO

IF NIKKI HAD GIVEN ME MORE NOTICE, I could have taken time off work to spend the week with her and Libby. Instead, Summer graciously offers to entertain them during the day while I am at the office. Her work schedule allows more flexibility than mine. I worry at first that Summer and Nikki will not get along, both so accustomed to being the center of attention, but I am relieved, and frankly a little shocked, when they hit it off.

I do manage to slip away early from work most days, which allows me more time to spend with my sister and niece. In the evenings we go to the park or do some shopping. Nate buys Libby a little fishing pole and we all go fishing off the docks. I love to watch Nate with Libby. When he helps Libby reel in her first fish, her squeal of delight, mixed with fear, has us all in stitches. Nate is so patient with her and I know he'll make a wonderful father someday. Not to mention that dressed in jeans, a faded t-shirt, and a ball cap, with his dark hair peeking out the sides of his hat, he's exceptionally sexy.

My mom drives over frequently from Seattle to have dinner with us or to join us on our shopping trips. It's nice to have my family together, but it also makes me remember my dad and the huge hole left in our family when he died. Nikki was too young to remember much about him, but I can tell us all being together makes my mom think of him as well. A brief glimpse of poignant reminiscence fills her eyes and I sense the deep pain behind her pretty smile.

On Thursday I announce that I am going to bed early, exhausted from four days of staying up late to visit with my family. Nate offers to stay behind and tidy up the kitchen. "I'll meet you in a few," he tells me. "Sweet dreams." He winks, and I smile at the private joke between us. Awake or asleep, I'm certain I'll see him soon.

When I do drift off to sleep, the landscape of my dream has changed. I'm alone on a park bench, but the scenery is desert-like and everything around me is dry. The sun is sweltering, almost suffocating. Nate approaches me, a small bouquet of flowers in his hands. "For me?" I ask.

He hands them to me, looking nervous. He takes a seat next to me on the park bench. "We need to talk," he says, clearing his throat.

"Okay," I say, still unconcerned. I sniff the flowers, already wilting in the hot sun. They have a strange odor.

"I know I said I was ready for all of this, but after this week, with your family and everything, I just wonder if things are moving too fast."

I turn to face him. His words infuriate me. He promised he wouldn't change his mind about us. "So, what are you saying?" I ask slowly. Only I

212

think I already know what he's saying, I just don't want to accept it. My throat tightens, and my ears start to burn.

"I'm saying we just need some time apart," he says. He doesn't even look at me. He stares off into the distance as if he's searching for a more interesting view.

I want to scream at him. I want to pound his chest and tell him that he lied to me. I know I probably deserve this for what I've put him through, but still, I don't know how much more of this I can handle.

"How much time?" I finally ask.

"I don't know… a few days… maybe a few weeks." Nate's voice trails off. He offers me no more than a sideways glance.

"If that's what you need," I tell him flatly. The flowers fall to the dry earth. I trample them beneath my feet as I run away.

When I wake up, my pillow is damp from my tears. Nate is still sleeping, so I crawl out of bed and look down at him. He looks peaceful and I resist the urge to hit him with a pillow. After a lengthy, hot shower, I dress slowly. When I'm finished, I open the bathroom door, hoping to find Nate still asleep. I'm not yet ready to face him.

When I reenter the bedroom, Nate is sitting up in bed. I shrug to myself. I suppose this time is as good as any to talk things out. He looks up at me and smiles. I just gaze back at him, trying to keep my face void of any emotion.

"What did you dream about last night?" I ask. Despite my best efforts, I can hear the bitterness in my tone echoing back in my ears.

"I honestly don't remember," Nate says. "I don't think I did dream."

I stare at him – outraged at his blatant lie. Does he really want to drag this out? "I'm going to work," I say flatly.

Nate stares after me, scratching his head as if he's confused. I never realized what a great actor he was. It makes me question everything.

Work is painful. The workday drags on endlessly. I am determined not to let my personal life interfere with my career, but I find it hard to concentrate. Or be productive. Or not break anything. To my credit, I don't cry.

I leave work at exactly four o'clock. Staying late will only delay the inevitable. Besides, I have my sister and niece to think about. I drive the long way home and take the opportunity to test the sound capacity of my speakers. I will probably sustain permanent hearing damage, but the pulse of the music is soothing. It helps drive away the emptiness that I am all too familiar with – the emptiness that, until last night, I had dared to believe I would never again have to endure.

When I arrive home from work, I find Nate in the kitchen helping Nikki prepare dinner. Summer is here too. In the far corner of the kitchen, Libby sits cross-legged on the floor, talking intently to the tiny toys lined up in front of her. Her pretty, blonde curls bounce as she shakes her finger at one of the toys, scolding it for talking out of turn. I had hoped Nate and I could have a rational discussion about what happened last night, but I know it will have to wait. Maybe it's for the best. I'm in no hurry to end things with Nate. But if he wants out, I'm not going to force him to stay, no matter how much I want him to.

Seeing me enter the kitchen, Nate walks over and kisses me on the cheek. I smile faintly, wondering if it's just a habit for him. "What's wrong, Emma?" he asks.

He appears wide-eyed and innocent, and my body burns with rage. As if he doesn't know. "We can talk about it later," I tell him. I keep my tone even, hoping the others in the room don't notice the resentment I feel.

"So, what's for dinner?" I say more cheerfully, looking around the room and avoiding Nate's gaze.

"We're trying a new recipe," Summer speaks up. I've never known her to cook, so I hope either Nate or Nikki have had more of a hand in dinner than she has.

"Sounds good," I manage.

Dinner is good; at least the food is. From what I can tell, everyone seems to be enjoying the conversation – everyone but me, that is. I barely utter three words. I smile and nod, not wanting to spoil anyone else's evening, but inside I'm dying.

After dinner, I offer to play with Libby and I do my best to avoid the questioning looks from Nate. Looking a little lost, he busies himself by helping Nikki and Summer with the dishes. I can hear the three of them laughing and joking around from the kitchen and I quietly seethe from the living room couch while I help Libby comb out her doll's hair.

When it's time to turn in, I find myself wondering if Nate will make an excuse to go back to his house. I'm stunned when he takes me by the hand and leads me down the hallway towards my bedroom – the bedroom we may be about to share for the final time.

After he closes the door to my room, he turns to face me. "Emma, are you going to tell me what's wrong?" He seems so patient, his question so honest. It confuses me. It infuriates me.

"You know exactly what is wrong," I tell him. "Are you hoping that I'll just forget what you told me last night?" My hands are shaking, and I take a seat on the bed.

"What are you talking about?"

"Last night, when you told me you were having second thoughts and that we might need to take a break." The words spew out of my mouth like hot lava from an erupting volcano, but I don't cry. Maybe I'm all cried out.

Nate just stares at me. "So, what, you have nothing to say about it?" I spit out.

"Emma, I never said those things."

"Yes, you did," I argue. "Don't act like I'm crazy." A tear escapes and runs down my cheek. I didn't realize that I had any tears left.

"I don't think you're crazy," Nate says, "but I'm telling you, I never said that. When do you think you heard me say that?"

"In our dream," I tell him. "I guess your subconscious is willing to reveal more than you are." Nate has the indecency to grin and I want to slap him. How can he find anything funny at a time like this?

"Emma, I didn't dream about you last night," he tells me. "To be honest, I had a very strange dream that I quit being a detective to become a chef. I probably ate too late or something."

"What?" I ask, bewildered and embarrassed. Nate takes my hands in his, sitting down next to me on the bed.

"Did you ever think for a moment that your dream was just that – a dream? Nothing more." He speaks softly. He's not angry, which amazes

216

me given how I've behaved. I feel so relieved and foolish at the same time. If patience is a virtue, Nate may very well be the most virtuous man I've ever met.

"I'm so sorry," I tell him. "I really thought that… It was just so real." I press my fingers to my temples, trying to process my disbelief and relief all at once. I wonder how many times Nate is going to put up with my distrust and insecurities before he tires of it.

Nate puts an arm around me and pulls me closer to him. "It's okay, although you did have me going there for a while wondering what I did. I mean, if you think about it, if I was already thinking of leaving, would I really have suffered through cooking in a kitchen full of women?"

I laugh and wipe the tears from my cheeks with the back of my hand. "I guess not," I mumble.

"So, just to get this straight, you dreamt all of this last night and then spent all day stewing on it?"

I nod. "I had a rotten day today," I admit.

"I can imagine. I suppose when I acted all chipper this morning you wanted to punch me in the face." This really gets me laughing. He knows me so well.

"Ice cream?" Nate suggests, as if it's the only acceptable solution to diffusing our situation. He pulls me to my feet and slips his arms around my waist, cupping my buttocks in his hands. *Hmm… virtuous? Maybe not.*

I turn and kiss him squarely on the mouth. "Ice cream," I confirm. He takes my hand in his and we head to the kitchen for a late-night snack.

CHAPTER FORTY-THREE

PROVING MIRACLES STILL HAPPEN, my sister and I manage to go the entire week without a single fight, something that would have been impossible for us when we were kids. We hug goodbye at the airport and I promise Nikki that I will visit her soon. Nate crouches down next to Libby to ruffle her hair and give her a kiss on the cheek. He produces a stuffed puppy from behind his back and presents it to her. Libby jumps up and down excitedly, her blonde curls bouncing as she clutches it tightly. I can see her little heart melt. She's not the only one. My heart puddles like a Popsicle in the blistering summer sun.

Nikki kisses Nate on the cheek, thanking him profusely for the thoughtful gift. Nate smiles and shoves his hands in his pockets, a little embarrassed by the fuss. I can tell that both Nikki and Libby are taken with Nate, and it makes me happy. We exchange a few more pleasantries before Nate and I both lean down and give Libby one last squeeze.

"I'm being squished like a bug," she says, trying to wriggle free. "I feel like a fly being squashed between two fly swatters."

We laugh at the exaggerated description of her predicament and I realize how much Libby reminds me of Summer. I seem to be surrounded by a bunch of drama queens.

Nate and I drive back to his house. We've spent the last week at mine and I can tell he's anxious to be back in his own bed. We order Chinese food, both too exhausted to cook.

When the food arrives, Nate answers the door and gives the delivery man a generous tip. He brings the food into the kitchen, where we dish up our plates and head into the dining room. Nate has slipped off his shirt, shoes, and socks and is moving about in jeans and bare feet, something I find extremely sexy. I light a couple of candles to set the mood and I take a seat across from him.

I don't realize how famished I am until I take the first bite of food. I gulp down the rest, barely coming up for air. Nate is also inhaling his food. I catch his gaze and smile up at him with a mouthful of Chow Mein.

"Let's go to bed early," Nate says, winking at me from across the dinner table.

"Oh Nate, sometimes you are not very romantic," I tease.

"I'll show you romantic," Nate says, scooting his chair back from the table. He playfully strums an air guitar as he sings a couple lines from a sappy love song. I am laughing riotously at his performance.

"Hey, I'm trying to be romantic here," he says, pretending to be hurt. "What's so funny?"

"I finally found something the great Nathan Mitchell isn't good at," I laugh. "Singing!"

"What?" Nate feigns shock. He tosses his imaginary guitar and rises from the table, chasing me into the bedroom.

Scampering towards the bed, I trip over my own feet and topple onto the floor below the footboard. We are both laughing hysterically.

"You still interested in making love to the world's biggest klutz?" I ask.

"Only if you're willing to be with someone that can't carry a tune in a bucket," Nate says.

"Absolutely."

CHAPTER FORTY-FOUR

I TRY TO CONCENTRATE ON MY STUDIES but am distracted by the rain tapping on my window. I nearly come out of my skin when I hear the wind scoot a chair across the front porch. Annoyed with my jumpiness, I dial Summer's number.

"Want to go shopping?" I ask the second she answers the phone.

"Who are you and what have you done with my friend Emma?" she teases.

"Nice," I say. "I am just tired of being home and want to do something."

"What's Nate doing today?" she asks.

"Why does he have to be doing something? Maybe I'd just rather spend the day with you," I say defensively.

Summer is quiet, and I know she's not buying it. "Okay, fine. Nate is working with the Seattle Police Department on a case and I'm all alone." I am pouting, but I don't care.

Summer laughs. "You two crack me up. Someday I hope I can find someone that consumes me the way you two are so clearly consumed by each other."

I pause, trying to decide if Summer is being serious or if she's teasing. I've never known Summer to want a serious relationship with anyone, but her voice sounds sincere. "Meet you at the mall in an hour?" I suggest, not sure what else to say.

"Sounds great," Summer agrees.

"So, you were joking about wanting to be in a serious relationship, right?" I ask Summer as we stroll through the department store.

"And why shouldn't I be in a serious relationship?" she asks, flipping through a rack of clothes without really looking at them. The crossness in her voice takes me by surprise.

"Oh, don't get me wrong, I think it would be great," I tell her. "I've just never known you to want to get serious about anyone."

Summer is unusually quiet, so I hold her gaze, trying to gauge her expression. "Summer, are you already seeing someone that you are getting serious about?"

Her face turns scarlet and I am shocked. "You are? Oh my word. I can't believe this! Who is he?"

She is suddenly giddy. "His name is Michael and he's an investment banker. He's super sweet, and so gorgeous."

I smile as I listen to Summer describe Michael in great detail. Some of the specifics I can do without. Sometimes she has no filter. Nate would die if I revealed some of the things about him that Summer is so eager to share about Michael.

"I am so happy for you," I tell her. "Geez, I feel like a jerk that I haven't even met him."

"Well, you've been a little preoccupied lately," she says teasingly.

"Have your parents met him?"

"Don't be ridiculous. They'd freak and think I was knocked up or something." I chuckle, realizing that Summer has probably never been remotely serious enough about a guy to bring him home to meet her parents. "Hey, I have an idea," Summer says. "How about if you and Nate meet up with Michael and me for dinner tonight? It can be a double date."

"That's not a bad idea. You're sure Michael won't mind?"

"Oh, in his line of work he's used to meeting new people, so he won't mind at all. Plus, I want to get your opinion of him. I can't get too serious with someone without first making sure my best friend likes him."

I smile but start to feel a little guilty. I never asked Summer for her opinion of Nate. I wonder what she would have said if I had asked her point blank. Although I value Summer's opinion and would be devastated if she told me she didn't like Nate, I also know that nothing, even my best friend's disapproval, could keep me away from him.

Back at home, I call Nate to see what time he'll be back from Seattle. He assures me that he'll be home in time for dinner. I broach the idea of dinner with Summer and Michael. I can tell that Nate was hoping for a quiet evening alone with me, but he graciously agrees to go. I smile to myself, grateful that Nate is content with making me happy.

The four of us meet for dinner at a little sushi restaurant downtown. Summer wasn't exaggerating. With his blonde hair and generous dimples, Michael is gorgeous. I can't help but notice what a handsome couple they

223

make as they walk into the restaurant holding hands. When they take a seat across from Nate and me, I squeeze closer to Nate, suddenly conscious of how plain I must look in comparison to everyone else at the table. Nate is studying the menu when he leans over to whisper in my ear.

"I'm having a hard time finding anything on this menu as appetizing as you." His lips brush against my ear, sending a tingling sensation down my spine.

This makes me smile and I reward him with a quick peck on the cheek. "So, tell me about yourself, Michael," I say, turning my attention away from Nate.

Michael talks briefly about his job as an investment banker, but then steers the conversation to stories from his childhood. Like Summer, he doesn't seem to be defined by his career. His tales about growing up in a household with six older sisters have the rest of us in stitches. Summer is beaming, and I know she is relieved that we are all getting along.

"It was nice to meet you, Michael," I tell him when the evening is over.

Michael hugs me, then shakes Nate's hand. "It was nice to meet both of you. Hopefully we can do this again soon."

Summer gives me a hug. She looks like she's about to hug Nate but settles for shaking his hand instead. Summer has always acted a little awkward around Nate. I suspect it's because he's the only man who seems immune to her charms and the poor girl isn't sure how to handle it. As Summer and Michael walk towards their car, Summer looks back at me and I give her a quick thumbs-up. She is all smiles at my acceptance of her new boyfriend.

As Nate and I get ready for bed, I replay the night's events in my head. I thought dinner went exceptionally well, but I also know that Summer still isn't convinced that Nate likes her, a notion that has stayed with her since she and I first met Nate. Smiling to myself, I think back on that day.

৯৯৯৯

Summer and I were running late to a concert and I was driving too fast. I panicked when I saw the flashing lights behind me and quickly pulled over.

"Leave this to me," Summer had said, fully expecting to flirt her way out of trouble. But neither of us were prepared for the police officer that showed up at my driver's side window.

"You ladies must have somewhere you really need to be," the officer I would later get to know as Nate had said. I had to bite my lip to prevent my jaw from dropping. Leaning into my window was an intimidating but gorgeous cop with dark hair and smoldering green eyes. A familiar wave of insecurity swept over me, and I was lost for words.

"You see officer," Summer cooed, "I haven't been feeling very well, and Emma here was just trying to get me home…"

"License and registration," Nate demanded, cutting Summer off. I could tell she was furious at his dismissal.

I tried a different approach. "To be honest, officer," I told him, "we were running late for a concert and I guess I took a chance we wouldn't get pulled over." My eyes darted to his, then I quickly looked down at my steering wheel while handing him my license and fumbling around in my center console for my insurance card.

I thought I saw the slightest hint of a smile on Nate's face when he took the documents I handed him and headed back to his squad car.

"Humph, he's a stick in the mud," Summer grumbled. I knew her pride had been wounded, so I said nothing.

Nate returned a few moments later and handed me back my things. He then tore a ticket out of his notepad, folded it in half and handed it to me. "Slow down next time, okay?" I nodded, and he walked away.

My heart was still pounding, and I couldn't be sure if it was because I'd just received my first ticket, or if it was due to the affect Nate had on me – perhaps a little of both.

It wasn't until after the concert that I opened up the ticket slip to see what going fifteen miles per hour over the speed limit had cost me. My mouth fell open when I read the ticket. It was blank, except for Nate's full name and his personal cellphone number.

It took all my courage to call the number Nate left me. I tried to sound convicted when I told him that I was shocked by his blatant misuse of police resources. Nate had chuckled and asked me out on a date anyway. We hit it off immediately.

ౖ౿ౖ౿ౖ౿

"You have to flirt a little with Summer," I yell at Nate from the bathroom, my mouth full of toothpaste.

"What?" Nate asks, poking his head in.

I quickly wipe off my mouth with the hand towel. I still don't want Nate to see what a mess I make brushing my teeth. "You have to flirt more with Summer," I repeat.

"That's what I thought you said," Nate replies, smiling. "Why?"

226

"Summer is used to guys fawning over her. When you don't at least flirt a little with her, it makes her think you don't like her," I explain.

"That may be the silliest thing I've ever heard," Nate says good-naturedly.

"Well, that's Summer," I say, laughing and nodding my head in agreement. I return my toothpaste and toothbrush to the drawer and turn to face him.

Nate is quiet for a moment. "That won't bother you?" he asks more seriously.

"Well, I'm not telling you to start undressing her with your eyes in front of me or anything," I clarify. "Besides, she's my best friend. A little harmless flirting is fine by me."

"Well, if I must," Nate teases, feigning exhaustion as if I've asked a great task of him.

I laugh. "But, just so we're clear," I add, "if you flirt with anyone else, I may smother you in your sleep." I shoot him a wink and slip past him through the bathroom door and into the bedroom.

Nate grabs the hand towel and playfully slaps me on the rear with it. "You got it," he says.

CHAPTER FORTY-FIVE

AFTER YET ANOTHER LONG DAY at the office, I drive directly to Nate's house – a routine that has become second nature to me. I let myself in, mildly irritated that I have once again beat him home. I head to the bedroom but kick off my shoes before I reach the doorway. I discard my clothing in the hamper and pull on the silk PJs Nate bought for me to keep at his house. "You see, they're both cute *and* comfortable," he had tried to explain. I found it adorable Nate worried he'd hurt my feelings if he admitted his dislike for my threadbare sweatpants.

I go to the refrigerator to see if there is anything I can whip up for dinner. After staring at its contents for a full minute, I close the fridge door and opt for ordering a pizza instead. Since Nate isn't around to object, and I'm feeling a little displeased about it, I order the pan crust – although I'm fully aware the hand-tossed crust is his favorite.

When Nate finally does arrive home from work, he is filthy, and I'm shocked by his ratty attire. His hair is matted to his forehead and there is a streak of dirt running across his jawline. When he approaches me, I find myself taking a step backwards.

"Nate, I don't want to hurt your feelings, but you stink!"

He smiles, and I am horrified. "Nate, your teeth look almost brown!" I am reeling at his change of appearance. Normally he's so clean and well put together.

"Sorry, I should have warned you. I've gone undercover as a homeless person for that carjacking case," he explains as he rubs some sort of gummy substance off his teeth with the sleeve of his tattered jacket.

I want to tell him that he shouldn't put his filthy jacket anywhere near his beautiful mouth, but I resist the urge. "Undercover? I didn't know Edmonds had the resources for that type of thing."

"We usually don't, but since I'm teaming up with the Seattle Police Department, we're able to combine our resources."

Underneath all the grime, Nate beams, and I can tell he is proud of the work he's been doing with Seattle. "Is it dangerous?" I ask, not really wanting to know the answer.

"Nah," Nate tries to assure me, but I notice the tiny twitch his jaw makes.

"You suck at lying," I tell him.

Nate leans in to kiss me and I push him back. "Sweetie, I love you, but you've got to shower," I tell him, giving him a playful shove towards the bathroom.

"Don't I get to eat first?" he complains, eyeing the leftover pizza on the island in the kitchen. I feel a twinge of guilt for ordering the pan crust.

"And risk coming down with some sort of disease because you're so filthy? I don't think so."

"Care to join me in the shower?" he asks.

"I'll give you a five-minute head start to get yourself cleaned up," I tell him. My annoyance from earlier vanishes, replaced by deep, scorching desire.

CHAPTER FORTY-SIX

"YOU WILL SOON BE MINE," I hear a man whisper, and my eyes shoot open. The man in the ski mask is leaned over the bed. I pull the covers to my chin and inch closer to Nate, only he's no longer lying next to me. Realizing that I must be dreaming, I squeeze my eyes shut in hopes the man will disappear.

"Go away!" I scream.

I can hear the man's wicked laughter. "I will stay as long as I choose," he says. "And I will do to you whatever I choose."

Pulse racing, I crawl further under the covers and plead with my mind to wake me from this terrible nightmare. I can feel the man clawing at the sheets as I remain huddled in a ball beneath them. The bed shakes violently as the man jerks at the covers, unleashing profanities and demanding that I come out to face him.

"Emma, baby, it's me," Nate says, shaking me awake.

231

"What happened?" I ask. Nate is stark naked and dripping wet.

"I was in the shower and I heard you screaming in your sleep. You must have had another nightmare." I want to deny it, but I can't. I feel the tears seep down my face.

"We had a break in a case, so I was getting ready to head into the office, but I can stay with you if you need me to," he says. I want to beg him to stay, but I know if he's even mentioning it, that it must be important for him to go in.

"I will be fine," I tell him, wiping my eyes. He shoots me a look. "I promise," I say more convincingly. "I'm going to head into work soon too."

Finally convinced that I won't fall apart without him, Nate leaves to work and I decide to go for a run. It's not like me to exercise without Summer forcing the issue, but work has been stressful, and with the fitful night I had, I am hopeful that the morning air will clear my head.

After tugging on my sneakers, I zip up my rain jacket and head outside. It is starting to drizzle, but the light wind feels good against my cheeks. I can feel my damp hair curling around my forehead as I head towards the waterfront.

The fresh air feels fabulous and I think to myself that exercise really might be a good thing to get into. I take several cleansing breaths and settle into a steady pace that passes for more of a jog than a run. Not having any music to listen to, I concentrate on the rhythmic sound my shoes make when they hit the pavement. Each street light I pass feels like a small victory.

After a few minutes, I think I hear someone running behind me. I strain my ears to listen, convinced that I hear a second set of footsteps. I am correct. The footsteps are distinct, and they are gaining ground. My blood runs cold and I feel like I'm back in one of my nightmares. My pace quickens, and I dart down a more populated road. The footsteps get closer and I am now at a full sprint. I curse myself for deciding to go running and I can't help but wonder if, in this case, exercise really will be deadly.

Attempting a quick glance over my shoulder, I lose my footing and fall hard on the pavement. "Are you okay, ma'am?" A teenage boy in running shorts crouches down beside me, his face filled with concern.

"Yeah," I say, rattled. "I'm not used to running I guess."

"Well, sorry if I scared you," the kid says. "I was trying to find the right moment to pass you."

"I guess I am a little slow," I admit, dusting the gravel and dirt from my knees, but not bothering to try and stand.

"Nah. Your pace is fine. I'm just practicing for a track meet so I'm trying to improve my time."

The kid helps me to my feet before he continues on his way. I turn and walk back towards Nate's house. My days of running alone are over – at least for now. My heartbeat finally returns to normal once I am safely behind locked doors, but I am now convinced more than ever that exercise is not for me.

CHAPTER FORTY-SEVEN

WHEN NATE CALLS ME AT WORK, I can hear the excitement in his voice. "I think we may have him, Emma," I hear him say.

"The man who broke into my house?" I can scarcely believe it. Could all my nightmares soon be over?

"Yes." Nate is talking fast. He sounds out of breath. "There's been a rash of break-ins around town over the last month, and the burglar finally slipped up. We have him here in holding."

"And you really think it's the same guy?" I ask, my voice filled with hope.

"We're not sure, but there's a very good chance. I'd like you to come down to the station and participate in a lineup."

My excitement dulls. "Nate, the man wore a ski mask. I didn't see him. Not to mention that he must have been wearing contact lenses."

"I know, Emma, but you heard him speak. I just want to see if you recognize his voice." I shudder at the thought of hearing the intruder's voice again. "Emma, I'm going to pick you up and I'll be right there with you the whole time," Nate assures me, sensing my hesitation.

I pace nervously in front of the vending machines in the police station lobby. "We're ready for her," I overhear a woman tell Nate, and I recognize her as Elena Mendoza, the city prosecutor.

Nate takes me by the elbow and leads me into a cramped, poorly lit room. I know he's trying to squelch all appearances of a personal relationship between us, not wanting to jeopardize the lineup. I enter the room, purposely keeping my back to the large window.

"Emma, it's time," Nate whispers in my ear. I realize I have been closing my eyes. I take a deep, cleansing breath, then turn to face the glass window.

"They can't see you," Elena assures me.

I've seen enough cop movies to know how this works, but I never dreamed that I would experience it firsthand. There are six men standing on the other side of the glass, each dressed similarly in jeans, a dark shirt, and sneakers. I look at each of their faces, trying to envision them as my assailant. A man's voice over the intercom instructs the first man to step forward and read a line from the piece of paper he is holding.

"Tears won't help you," the man reads.

Although the voice isn't familiar, the words are. I start to tremble, and I feel the floor sway beneath me. Nate grabs my arm to steady me and I resist the urge to bury my head in his chest.

"I'm okay," I reassure him. I can see the doubt cloud Nate's face and I can tell he's ready to put an end to the lineup. I square my shoulders. "I can do this," I say more firmly.

I hear the same phrase five more times as each man steps forward. Although my throat constricts, and I shudder each time, I can't be sure any of the voices match the man who attacked me.

All eyes are on me when I shake my head *no*. "I'm sorry," I say. "I just can't be sure."

"Don't apologize," Nate says. "It was a long shot."

An idea hits me. "Did you say you caught the guy in the act of burglarizing someone's house?" I ask.

"That's right," Nate says.

"Was he wearing a ski mask?"

Both Nate and the prosecutor nod and excitement bubbles in my belly.

"I'd like to smell it," I tell them.

I can see their stunned expressions, and I realize they must be thinking I've finally gone off the deep-end, but I keep my voice firm. "More than his voice, I would recognize his smell," I explain. "I want to smell the mask he was wearing."

Nate leaves the room and returns momentarily with a plastic evidence bag containing a black ski mask. I can feel my heartbeat quicken in anticipation. Nate puts on plastic gloves and retrieves the mask from the bag. He hands me a pair of gloves, and I yank them on before reaching for the mask.

I will my hands to stop shaking as I bring the mask towards my nose. I smell a slight scent of sweat and the faint odor of hair gel, but nothing more. "It's not him," I say, handing the ski mask back to Nate. I am having trouble processing what I feel. Is it relief? Disappointment?

"Are you sure?" Nate asks. It's easy for me to interpret what he's feeling. The disappointment in his voice is unmistakable.

"I'm positive. The man who attacked me was a smoker. He also wore very strong cologne. I'm telling you, it's not him."

Nate returns the ski mask to the evidence bag and hands it to a clerk standing just inside the room.

"Thank you for your time," Elena tells me, extending her hand to shake mine. "I'm sorry for having dragged you down here for nothing. We do have enough to book the perp on at least one burglary and I think he'll be ready to cop to a few others as well. I only wish I could tell you that we found your intruder."

I am touched by her kindness. "It was really no trouble," I say. "I'm glad it will bring a few families some relief that you caught this guy." I put on a brave face, but a heavy weight is settling deep in my gut. My nightmares are not over.

"I'll drive you home," Nate says. I do my best not to display my amusement at his professional tone as he once again takes me by the elbow and leads me to entrance of the police station.

Nate looks lost in thought during the drive home. "Emma, I'm sorry that I got your hopes up," he apologizes. "I really thought we had our guy."

"Oh, Nate, don't apologize," I beg him. "I know how much we both wanted this to be the guy."

He reaches over and holds my hand, lacing his fingers through mine. "Wouldn't you rather hold my elbow?" I ask, smirking when he glances over at me.

"When we get home, I'm going to kiss that smart mouth of yours," Nate warns. I giggle, licking my lips in anticipation. The weight is temporarily lifted.

CHAPTER FORTY-EIGHT

I KISS NATE GOODBYE before he heads off to work. "Are you sure you have to work on a Saturday?" I ask, still holding out hope that he'll change his mind.

He smiles, moving closer to tousle my hair and place a kiss on my forehead. I playfully pinch his rear. "Hurry back to me," I command. "Don't forget we have that *exciting* family reunion in a few hours."

"Looking forward to it," Nate says, and I can't quite tell if he's being sarcastic.

I watch Nate from the doorway as he makes it to the car in just a few, long strides. Even after spending so much time together, he still makes me quiver and I wouldn't have it any other way. I close the door and reflect on our morning together. Despite his easygoing demeanor, I can tell Nate is growing weary with his caseload.

It is easy for me to compartmentalize my career from my home life. When I am at work, I pour all of myself into the job and have been successful in doing so. But when I'm home, I don't take my work with me. Like a switch, I turn it off. Nate also has a proclivity for working hard, but his approach is different from mine. He lives and breathes the job. Like everything else in his life, he approaches his work with deep, emotional intensity – something that I find both sexy and frustrating. His tougher cases weigh on him and spill into his private life. I do my best to be understanding, but sometimes I can feel his workload taking a toll on my own life.

The phone call I receive just hours later rocks me to my very core. "Emma, it's Tony." It takes me a moment to recognize the voice as Tony Garza, the police officer from Seattle that Nate has been working with.

"Tony, what's wrong?" My chest tightens. *Please, please let Nate be okay.*

My heart sinks when Tony tells me that Nate has been shot. He's not sure how bad, but Nate's undergoing emergency surgery at Harborview Medical in Seattle. I am biting down on my shirtsleeve to keep the sobs from escaping my lips. *Hold it together.*

I am not sure if I even thank Tony for the call before I slam down the phone and rush out of the house to drive to the hospital. I wasn't aware that my car could go as fast as it does. When I reach the hospital, I am still sporting my pajamas and my hair is in disarray. I charge through the emergency room door and spot Tony and several other police officers standing by the soda machine. Tony sees me and rushes over. "How is he?" I am pleading for good news.

"The doctors are still working on him. We haven't heard yet."

"I need him to be okay, Tony. He has to be okay." I know I am falling apart, but I can't bring myself to pull it together. Tony pulls me into his arms and pats my back like one would a small child. Under ordinary circumstances I would feel silly, but instead I feel comforted.

"So, what happened?" I finally ask, hoping that I don't sound like I am placing blame.

Tony begins to fill me in on the details leading up to the shooting. Halfway through the story, I realize that I shouldn't have asked. I know now that I will only worry more about Nate.

From what I can gather, Tony and Nate were staking out one of the main suspects in the carjackings. The suspect made Nate and Tony, who ended up chasing him through the streets on foot. When Nate cornered the man, and tried to arrest him, the man pulled a gun and shot Nate several times in the chest. Nate was wearing a bulletproof vest, but the handgun was of such high caliber, one bullet partially penetrated his vest.

Just when I think I can't stand the wait any longer, a doctor in full scrubs, including something resembling a shower cap on his head, enters the waiting room from the surgery ward. He eyes the group of police officers and makes his way over to us. As if on cue, Nate's parents come bursting into the emergency room with Brandon close behind them. Despite the chaos, Nancy is still perfectly put together.

We huddle together closely, anxious to hear the doctor's prognosis. He tells us that Nate pulled through surgery well and is going to be okay. "The blunted bullet broke two of his ribs and bruised his right lung, causing excess fluid to accumulate," the doctor explains. "We were able to drain the excess fluid and we've introduced antibiotics to prevent pneumonia. The healing process should be fairly short."

Without thinking, I hug the doctor and plant a kiss on his cheek. He looks a little stunned, but he smiles and pats my head. "I'm sorry, you must get that a lot," I say, laughing despite my awkwardness and the medical crisis at-hand.

"Not as often as I'd like," he says good-naturedly before walking away.

We are forced to wait another hour before we're allowed to see Nate. Brandon sits by himself in the corner of the waiting room while his father, Martin, nearly wears a hole in the floor pacing back and forth in front of the reception area. Nancy sits quietly, displaying a poised demeanor with her hands clasped firmly in her lap. Most of the officers stay at a respectful distance, but Tony sits beside me, patting my shoulder and making casual conversation. I am now uncomfortably aware that I'm still wearing my pajamas, but everyone is polite enough not to mention it.

After some time passes, I glance at my cellphone and notice several missed calls and texts from my family members. I realize that in the chaos, I forgot to let my family know that Nate and I would not be attending the family reunion as planned. I step into the hallway to make a phone call to my mother.

Trying to keep from melting down emotionally, I give her a quick summary of events. After reassuring her that everything is fine and telling her for the hundredth time that there is no need for her to come to the hospital, I request that she relay the information to the rest of the family, as well as to Summer. "I will call you later with an update once I've had a chance to see Nate," I promise her before I end the call.

When I step back into the main waiting area, I notice that another man has joined our growing party. It takes me a few moments to recognize him as Frank Jefferson, Nate's friend that I didn't care much for after being introduced to him at Nate's birthday party. I have no rational explanation for my negative reaction to this man. I don't recall meeting him before the party, and he behaved well-enough, but something about him puts me on guard. I'd hate to use the term *woman's intuition*, but it's the best explanation I have. I offer a tight smile of appreciation for his concern, then look away to avoid his gaze, taking a sudden interest in the dated wallpaper pattern pasted over the waiting room walls.

"How is he?" I hear Frank ask.

I don't have the energy or the patience to deal with this man. Thankfully, Tony fills him in on the details and I am spared further dealings with Frank.

CHAPTER FORTY-NINE

IT'S ALL I CAN DO NOT TO SCOLD NATE when I first enter his hospital room. He promised me he'd be safe. Hooked up to an IV drip, and adorned only in a hospital gown, Nate looks fragile for the first time, and my heart aches to be near him.

Entering the room behind me, Nancy scoots past me and rushes to Nate's side. Her strong resolve disappears, and she begins to weep inconsolably. I'm shocked to witness that her cool disposition is nothing more than a façade, and I wonder how much of that trait Nate inherited.

Nate tiredly motions me over with a small wave of his hand. I walk to his bedside and lean in to kiss his forehead. "That's all you have for me, eh?" he asks. "I'd hoped since you were already in your PJs..." His voice is hoarse, but I'm happy to see that he hasn't lost his sense of humor.

"Nate, be a gentleman," Nancy interrupts, somehow managing to compose herself again. Martin and Brandon are waiting quietly in the doorway, along with Tony and several other officers. I do not see Frank amongst the individuals huddled in the doorway and I am thankful. *Why does he bother me so much?*

"You can come in, but only for a few minutes," I hear the nurse tell them.

The room is a sea of blue as the uniformed officers fill the cramped space. There is a brief exchange as Nate's friends wish him a speedy recovery, but they disperse before the nurse can kick them out.

"Tony, hold up a bit," Nate calls out. Tony pauses by the door and turns to look at Nate. "What happened to the guy who shot me?"

"We caught the sonofa…um, the guy," Tony says, correcting his language after glancing sheepishly at Nate's mother, and then at me. "I heard word from the precinct that he's singing like a bird and rolled over on his partners. The judge served up warrants and we should have them all in custody by the end of the night."

Nate smiles, but I can tell he's disappointed. "I wish I could have brought some of them in personally," he voices his regret.

"Hey, it was your hard work that helped crack this case. Now you sit back and rest," Tony demands before politely excusing himself from the room. Nate's family also steps out, and I am finally left alone with him.

I want to tell him how scared I was and demand that he never put me through this again, but I know it would be selfish, so I refrain. "I love you so much," I tell him, lost for anything else appropriate to say.

Nate gives me a tired smile and squeezes my hand. "This is a terrible way to get out of going to the family reunion with me," I banter.

"Well, I ran out of ideas," Nate quips in response to my lame joke.

"The doctor says you should make a speedy recovery. You may even get to go home tomorrow. It's a good thing too because…" I trail off, realizing that Nate is looking at me strangely.

"You are handling this rather well," he compliments, searching my face for evidence that I might fall apart.

I take a long, deliberate breath, choosing my words carefully before I respond. "Hopefully this isn't something that I'll have to get used to," I finally say. I hear my voice crack and immediately stop talking.

"It's okay to cry, Emma, you don't have to be brave on my account," Nate says. I want to do more than cry. I want to scream at Nate that his close call was almost more than I could bear, but I remain stone-faced. It's selfish to think about how I'm feeling at a time like this. I want to be strong for Nate.

"I am not going to cry," I reassure him. "But," I continue, "if you make me go through this again, I may just shoot you myself."

CHAPTER FIFTY

HE WATCHES FROM THE PRIVACY of his vehicle as the woman helps her lover out of the car. The couple embraces outside the house, and he thinks to himself that he will need to make her pay for flaunting her lover in front of him so carelessly. When the moment comes, he'll take his time with her. Perhaps she'll see reason.

When he first received the news that her lover had been shot, he wanted to give a medal to the person responsible. Now, after learning the shot would not prove fatal, he no longer feels as generous.

He fights the urge to watch longer, knowing he needs to be careful not to get caught. Quietly he starts up his vehicle, passing the woman's house just as she shuts her door. He knows the woman believes she is safe in her house with her cop lover. But soon she will find out that is far from the truth.

CHAPTER FIFTY-ONE

I BRING MY LAPTOP TO BED, hoping to catch up on the overwhelming amount of unread email cluttering up my in-box. I'm breaking my strict personal rule to not bring my work home with me, but my workload has grown so much, it's been a struggle not to fall behind. My eyelids grow heavy, but I push myself to keep on working.

Just a few more emails, I tell myself as I fight to stay awake. I hear a sound from the hallway and conclude that Nate must have let himself in. When my bedroom door opens, I look up to greet Nate with a smile.

The smile freezes on my face when I see who is standing in my bedroom doorway. It isn't Nate at all. It's the man that I've grown to hate even more than I fear. "Well, hello Emma," the man in the ski mask says wickedly.

I snap my laptop shut and stare at him, trying to keep my wits about me. When he approaches, I notice that his form is hazy – out of focus. *You're dreaming*, I tell myself. I must have fallen asleep. The observation should comfort me, but since I have no way to know how much this man can hurt me in our shared dreams, my feelings of dread increase with every step he takes towards me.

"Why don't you just tell me what you want?" I scream at him.

"Oh, I think you know what I want." His tone is cruel, pure evil.

Leaping out of bed, I fumble for the pepper spray that I now keep in the top drawer of the nightstand. The drawer is empty. I'm agitated that my subconscious didn't bother to place such an important object in my dream world.

"Looking for something?" the man asks. I can tell he's toying with me. His movements are slow, meticulous.

With cat-like speed, I try to dart around him, but he stiff-arms me and I drop to the floor, staggered. Before I can stop him, the man is on top of me, pinning me beneath him. I claw and bite.

"You won't win," I tell him determinably. The man erupts into wicked laughter. The room begins to spin, and I close my eyes, willing myself to snap out of my terrible dream.

CHAPTER FIFTY-TWO

FOR THE FOURTH NIGHT IN A ROW, I find Nate gently shaking me awake from another nightmare. I feel terrible, knowing that I should be taking care of him after his recent surgery rather than the other way around. "I'm sorry that I keep waking you up, Nate," I tell him as I sit up in bed. "You should be getting your rest."

"There's no place I'd rather be than here with you." He plants a kiss on my cheek and nuzzles my neck.

A dull ache shoots up my neck and spreads across my skull. I gingerly touch the back of my head. I can feel a small lump forming and it frightens me. Lately my nightmares have escalated. Not only does the masked intruder invade my dreams with more frequency, but he appears to be on a mission. In some of my dreams I see him rifling through my personal files and searching the rest of my house. He seems to be looking for something, and he grows increasingly agitated at his lack of success.

I try to downplay my terror as I recount my most recent dream for Nate. "I'd hate to say it," Nate tells me, "but I think you should go visit Madame Destiny again."

I glance at him to see if he is joking, but his expression is sober. "Really?" I ask.

"Yes, really."

When Nate and I arrive at Madame Destiny's doorstep, she invites us in, only this time she greets me with a warm hug. "Thank you for agreeing to see us so late, Madame…"

She cuts me off. "Please, just call me Katie." I smile at her. She looks like a Katie.

I introduce Nate to Katie before we all take our seats in the living room. Katie offers us some tea, but Nate and I both decline. "So, what did you need to see me about?" she asks.

I fill her in on the nightmares, but also find myself talking about the dreams Nate and I share. I leave out the intimate details but provide enough information to let her know that we can both communicate in my dreams and hint that our encounters are far from nightmarish in nature.

"Oh, so you're a sensitive," Katie replies, smiling to herself and sounding very matter of fact.

"I'm sorry, a what?" I ask.

"A sensitive. Someone who is very receptive to certain things. In your case, this sensitivity kicks in while you dream. Oftentimes, this is triggered by a traumatic event. In your situation, Emma, this was probably sparked by the harrowing experience of your break-in."

251

Or break-up, I think to myself. I glance over at Nate to see if he's smirking, but his face remains expressionless. "What surprises me," Katie continues, "is that this never happened to you when you were younger."

"What do you mean?" I ask.

"I more often see dream sensitivities in children. Children are more innocent and the realm between reality and their imagination can be blurred. When they grow up, children often lose their gift."

I know I must appear unconvinced, but Katie continues. "The human brain is an amazing and complex organ, and its potential is vastly unknown. It is very common for children to have imaginary friends, vivid dreams, and even frequent occurrences of déjà vu. These events are often dismissed by adults as an overactive imagination. After a while, children become convinced that the adults are correct and they simply 'outgrow' the phenomenon."

I am quiet for a moment as I reflect on my own childhood. "I had one experience when I was seven," I finally admit, my voice barely above a whisper.

Nate looks surprised. "On the night my dad died," I explain. "I was sleeping, and he came to me in a dream. He told me that things were about to change and that I would need to be strong for my mom and little sister. My mom woke me up that same evening to let me know about the car accident."

I dab at my tears as the reality of that night hits me. "I just thought I'd had a foretelling dream," I continue. "Now...now I'm not so sure." Nate places his hand over mine and I stare into his eyes, wondering what unknown issue remains between us that gives him the power to invade my dreams. *Does he too have something important to tell me?*

I realize that I need to know the answer, no matter how painful. I turn my focus to Katie. "What you said before, about unresolved conflict…" I start.

"You're wondering if there is something unresolved between you two," Katie answers for me, glancing back and forth from Nate to me.

I nod, surprised at where this conversation is heading. When I arrived, I thought we were only going to discuss my nightmares. "We spoke before about your dreams being darkened," she continues. "What we didn't touch on, because I didn't think it applied at the time, was the awakening of dreams."

I feel a skeptic look cross my face, but I recover quickly and hope Madame Destiny, rather Katie, didn't notice. "This is even more rare," she continues. "Not only does at least one party have to possess the power of dream sensitivity – but both individuals must have a keen sensitivity to one another. I guess some might classify the pair as the purest of soulmates. Because many people never meet their true soulmate in the romantic sense, these cases are most often recorded with identical twins or where there's a strong bond between a mother and her child."

Nate nods and casually pats my hand as I squirm uncomfortably in my seat. "So, just because we're still able to share our dreams doesn't mean there's any unresolved…" I trail off, unsure of my own emotions.

"With the awakening of dreams, it's not so much about dreaming about one another, but about waking up – waking up and realizing what you both want and having the strength and courage to embrace it. What you two have is very unusual, but a very beautiful thing. Cherish it," Katie says.

I breathe a sigh of relief. "And these nightmares I keep having? I really feel like I've moved on, but this man keeps invading… or rather, *darkening* my dreams as you put it."

"You've moved on, but he hasn't. You see, you've already opened this doorway to him. You still need to find out what he wants. It's the only way to stop this from happening." I try to hide my disappointment. I had hoped that Madame Destiny would have all the answers.

"There's got to be something she can do," Nate interrupts, sounding as desperate as I feel.

Katie looks pensive. "There is one thing she can try," she offers.

"I'll try anything," I speak up, somewhat miffed that they are talking about me as if I'm not in the room.

Katie pauses. "You can practice controlling your dreams. As much power as your attacker has over you, you have the ultimate control."

"It doesn't feel that way," I mumble.

Katie patiently continues. "Emma, when you have a nightmare, I want you to focus on remaining calm. Count backwards from ten, and then project all of your energy towards keeping this dark stranger at bay. If you keep calm and concentrate, you may be able to form a protective shield with your mind."

"I'm not sure if I *can* keep calm," I admit.

"You're stronger than you give yourself credit for. You've already managed to push this man out of your dreams before he can do any real harm. Learning to further control the situation will just take some practice." I shudder. To practice, I'll have to endure more nightmares. I dread the practice.

"But remember," Katie continues, "the best thing you can do is figure out who this guy is and what he wants. You are lucky to have a detective here to help you with that." She casts a wink in Nate's direction.

"How did you know...?" I begin, but then stop myself. Of all the outlandish things we've discussed over the past two visits, her declaring Nate as a detective without me mentioning it is probably the least bizarre.

Nate and I both thank Katie for her time and head back to the car. Nate opens the passenger door for me, then climbs behind the wheel. Taking my hand, he turns it over and plants a soft kiss on my wrist. "See, you're pretty much stuck with me," he quips. "It's fate." I can't be sure, but I think I sense some relief on his part.

"If I were you, I'd run away now while you have the chance," I tease back, although there's a ring of truth to my suggestion.

As we pull out of the drive, I try to process my feelings. I am doubtful that I will be able to control my dreams the way Katie suggested, but I'm still satisfied with the outcome of our visit. I didn't realize before this evening just how much I was worried the dreams between Nate and I were somehow unhealthy. I realize that I have been waiting for some unresolved conflict to rear its ugly head and break us apart.

I also think back on our conversation about my childhood and know that I will treasure the last memory of my father more than ever. What I once believed was a dream was really my father's final visit to say goodbye. I sigh happily and lay my head on Nate's shoulder. He kisses the top of my head and we drive the rest of the way to my house without speaking. Content with the comfortable silence that settles between us, neither of us feel the need to fill it with idle conversation.

CHAPTER FIFTY-THREE

WHILE ON OUR MUCH OVERDUE LUNCH DATE, I steal another glance at Summer and try to read her mood. She has been perplexingly quiet during the entire meal. I also notice that she's not as put together as usual. Her purple blouse is wrinkled, and her hair is pulled back in a loose, lopsided braid. I continue to study her as I reach across the table for one of her untouched fries.

"Michael doesn't want to get married," Summer finally blurts out. I am momentarily speechless.

"Summer," I finally say, "you've only been dating just a short time…"

"I don't want to get engaged right now," Summer interrupts, looking abashed and horrified. "All I'm saying is that Michael told me that he *never* wants to get married. To anyone. The man doesn't believe in the institution of marriage. How can I carry on a relationship with him when I know it's not going to go any further?"

I quietly ponder what Summer said. I realize that she really must be falling for Michael if she's worried about whether or not he'll commit. With any other man Summer has dated, hearing that the guy was not interested in anything long-term would have been music to her ears. "When did he tell you all of this?" I ask.

"Last night," Summer admits. "We were hanging out at his place and I spotted a wedding invitation on his fridge. When I asked if he was going, Michael made some offhand comment about not wanting to witness the biggest mistake of two people's lives. I thought he was joking, but when I pressed him on the matter, he said that he didn't believe in marriage."

"Oh," I say. "So, how did you respond?"

"I broke up with him."

"You what?"

"I know, I know, it may have been a rash decision, but my life has been a series of temporary relationships and I was hoping he'd be the one to change all of that." Summer buries her head in her arms. I scoot my chair next to hers and put an arm over her shoulders in an awkward attempt to comfort her. Typically, it's Summer comforting me through my latest drama.

While reaching into my purse to find some tissue for Summer, I freeze when I see Frank Jefferson walk through the door of the restaurant. I crouch lower in my chair, hoping he won't see me.

"What's wrong?" Summer asks, dabbing at her eyes with the edge of her napkin.

"Don't look over, but there's a guy that just walked in and I don't want him to see me. He is a friend of Nate's, but something about him just creeps me out."

Summer does her best to turn and look at the guy without being too obvious, a challenge I am quite certain she fails at. "Oh my God!" Summer exclaims.

"What?" I ask, instantly on edge.

"I went on a date with that jerk," she reveals.

"Really?"

"Yeah, don't you remember, Emma? He and I stopped by your house before going out so that I could borrow a necklace, and I introduced you." I scan my memories, trying to recall. "You're right, Emma, he is a creep," she says.

"Why, what did he do?"

As usual, Summer has me sucked in.

She shudders. "Let's just say the man doesn't know how to back off when a girl is not interested. We went to a club together and I had to have the bouncer throw him out. I ended up taking a cab home by myself."

I feel awful for Summer's experience but am a little relieved that my judge of character wasn't too far off base. I am also thankful that Frank's entrance seems to be the distraction Summer needs. Temporarily forgetting her drama with Michael, she begins to launch into stories of past dating disasters, more humorous in nature, and before long the two of us are swapping stories and laughs.

CHAPTER FIFTY-FOUR

I AM COOKING DINNER WITH NATE when my phone rings unexpectedly. "Hello?" I answer, not recognizing the number.

"Um, hello. Emma? Can we talk?" It takes me a few seconds to recognize the voice.

"Michael?" I ask.

"Err...yes. Is this a bad time?"

"No," I say, casting a look of confusion in Nate's direction. "What's going on, Michael?" I repeat his name for Nate's benefit.

"Summer broke up with me," he says, sounding miserable.

"I know, she told me."

"She told you? What did she say? What did I do?" Michael is firing off questions more rapidly than I can respond, and I smile to myself at how desperately sweet he sounds.

"What did she tell you?" I prompt, wondering how Summer was able to end a relationship without cluing the guy in as to why she was doing so.

Then I think about how I ended things with Nate before, and suddenly realize I have no room to judge.

"She didn't really tell me anything. I thought everything was going fine, then she started acting kind of weird and quiet. All of a sudden, she told me that things weren't working out – and she left. She won't even return my calls!"

"Michael, I really don't want to get involved."

"Please," he interrupts. "I really care about her. I just want a chance to fix whatever I did."

"Okay," I say hesitantly. "Come over and we'll talk." I hang up the phone after giving him my address, hoping that I made the right decision by agreeing to speak with him.

"What was all that about?" Nate asks.

"Drama, drama, drama," I tell him, filling him in on the events at hand.

When Michael takes a seat in my kitchen, Nate hands him a beer, then leaves us alone to talk. Feeling both awkward and sympathetic, I explain Summer's reasons for breaking things off with Michael – hoping that I'm not betraying Summer's confidence by doing so.

"She wants to get married?" Michael looks confused, but to his credit, not repulsed.

"No, no. It's not that she wants to get married now or anything. In fact, if you asked her, she'd probably run screaming for the hills. She just doesn't want to pursue a relationship with you if there's no chance for marriage in the future."

Michael looks baffled. "I'm going to be frank," I continue. "Summer has never wanted a serious relationship. With anyone. The fact that she even cares whether or not there would be one with you speaks volumes. But Summer is also a smart girl. She's not going to get too attached to someone she can't, um, *keep*, for lack of a better word."

"I'm an idiot," Michael says, taking a long swig of his beer. "I didn't think Summer even cared about that sort of thing. Otherwise, I wouldn't have brought up my feelings on marriage so casually."

"Why don't you believe in marriage?" I ask, unable to harness my own curiosity.

Michael sighs and takes another drink of his beer. "My parents. I saw what it did to them." He goes on to relay a gut-wrenching story about two people that loved one another so deeply but were all wrong for each other. "Something that started out as a young couple madly in love turned into misery and ended in a bitter divorce. I watched two strong people pick at each other until there was nothing left but an angry woman and an empty shell of a man. I don't want that for me, and I certainly don't want that for Summer."

I pat Michael on the arm, thinking how close I had been to ruining my own chances of happiness by breaking things off with Nate. "Michael, not every marriage is like your parents'. My parents had a beautiful marriage until my dad passed away. Nate's parents still do; and Summer's. Sometimes by running away from something, you're actually causing yourself more pain. Trust me on that."

The doorbell rings, interrupting our conversation. I hear Nate answer my front door and invite someone in. I am perplexed when I hear Summer's voice as she heads toward the kitchen. She enters the room with

Nate close behind her. "I called her," Nate explains in response to the look of confusion that must be plastered all over my face.

I glance over at Summer to see if she's angry about my interference, but she is only looking at Michael, who jumps up, pushes aside his half-empty beer, and crosses the room towards her. He hugs her fiercely and Nate and I slip away to the living room to allow them their privacy.

"Do you think they'll work it out?" I whisper to Nate, taking a seat next to him on the couch.

He shrugs his shoulders, feigning lack of interest. "Oh, don't try to pretend like you don't care. You're the one that called Summer."

Nate smiles at me. "I just thought you'd want me to call her."

"Does this look like the face of someone that's convinced? Admit it. You're just as much of a hopeless romantic as I am," I accuse.

"I could sympathize with the guy, that's all," Nate says, and the familiar guilt washes over me. Nate reads my face and plants a quick kiss on the tip of my nose. "It's okay," he reassures me. "It all worked out for us. No permanent damage done."

I smile and scoot in closer to him, painfully aware that I don't deserve him, and grateful that he's too love-struck to realize it.

CHAPTER FIFTY-FIVE

I WANT NOTHING MORE than to lie naked in bed with Nate for the rest of the evening, but I made plans and am not one to bail when I give my word. I sit up in bed and search the floor for my clothes.

"Where are you going?" Nate asks, trying to coax me back into bed.

"I'm going out for drinks with some ladies from work, remember?"

"Nope, must have slipped my mind," Nate says. I give him a pointed look, knowing he's lying. He runs his finger seductively over my bare shoulder.

"Are you sure you don't want to come back to bed? I'll bet we can have way more fun here than you'll have with your friends." Nate's smile is alluring, and very tempting.

I reach deep within to find my resolve. "Keep it in your pants, sailor," I tease, offering Nate a quick kiss. "You're going to make me late."

Nate puts up his hands in a position of surrender, giving in. "Will you be here when I get back?" I ask, sounding hopeful, but not wanting to be selfish.

"If you promise to make it worth my while when you get home."

I am in such great spirits that not even the unwelcome arrival of Diana Segard manages to sour my mood. I watch her closely as she saunters over to our table, stuffed in her skinny jeans and wearing a top that ceased to be appropriate after junior high. Perhaps my assessment of her attire is harsh, and *mildly* exaggerated – but I'm still smarting from our encounter in the ladies' room at work. At the start of the evening, we sit on opposite ends of the table and do our best to avoid each other. But after Diana gets three or four drinks in her, she starts talking to me like we're the best of friends and I do my best not to smirk at the red lipstick smeared across her teeth. Her dangling earrings bobble back and forth as she prattles on. I humor her with friendly conversation, but also know to watch my back.

My original plan was to stick to water, but I don't want to suffer any probing questions from Diana or anyone else at the table. From what I've observed of Diana, she'd be the first to report back to the other gossipers at work how I didn't have any alcohol and am most likely pregnant. Instead, I spend the evening nursing a beer.

I still get asked several questions about Nate, but it doesn't bother me. The more drinks the other ladies consume, the more personal the questions become. *Is he good in bed? Do you just want to jump his bones all the time? How hot is his scar from the bullet wound?* I smile and laugh at the incessant questions, but don't give anything away.

I'm deflecting the latest inquiry about Nate when I catch a piece of the conversation at the other end of the table. "I mean, the man creeps me out," I hear Tamara in Accounts Receivable admit.

"Who creeps you out?" I interrupt.

"Well, I'm not sure it's okay to say in front of one of the executives," she says, flustered.

"Your secret is safe with me," I tell her, raising my beer in salute.

"Eldon Banks," she offers. "Something about that man scares me."

The ladies at the table nod in unison.

"You want to know a secret?" I say. All eyes are on me. "He scares me too," I say good-naturedly. They have a point. The man is one of the most intimidating people I've ever met.

Nate is fast asleep when I get home. I try to slip quietly into bed as not to wake him, but he stirs and pulls me closer to him. I realize he's been sleeping naked and I feel my pulse quicken.

"How's my party girl?" Nate teases, nibbling on my earlobe. Sleepiness slurs his speech.

I turn to face Nate and smile. "I had one beer," I say in mock defensiveness.

"Wow, you are a wild one, aren't you?"

"You're about to find out."

CHAPTER FIFTY-SIX

WHEN I FALL ASLEEP, I get the opportunity to practice controlling my nightmares. The scene is familiar. I am being chased through a dense forest. As I pick up speed, Katie's advice comes back to me. It's as if I can hear her whispering to me from somewhere above the trees. *Concentrate. Control the situation.* I slow my pace and start to count backwards from ten. Nine...*I am in control.*..seven...*I am brave.*..four...*I am stronger than I think.*..and then at one, I step through the heavy cloak of fear, and turn around to face my attacker. He sneers at me – at least that's what I imagine beneath his dark mask.

I stare at him, imagining that I am creating a force field with my mind. He steps closer to me, snickering. I close my eyes and concentrate harder. I silently will the man to back away, but instead I hear another footstep come toward me. I clear my throat and do my best to sound in control. "When I open my eyes, you will be gone," I tell him fiercely. And then I feel his gloved hands around my neck and I am gasping for air.

Nate shakes me awake. I start to sob and bury my head in his bare chest. He wraps his arms around me, not saying a word. "I tried," I croak. "I'm not brave. I'm not strong. I'm helpless." Nate still doesn't speak; he just strokes my hair and lets me cry. Safe in his arms, I drift back to sleep.

CHAPTER FIFTY-SEVEN

AT WORK ON MONDAY, Diana Segard stops by my office to request a brief meeting. I do my best to keep my face void of emotion as I invite her to take a seat across from me.

"Would you like coffee or anything?" I ask, making an effort to be polite when what I really want to do is kick her out of my office.

"No. Actually, I came to apologize," Diana tells me. I am caught off-guard.

"For what?" I ask, although I know she is referring to her previous gossip session about me in the restroom.

"You're being kind. Listen, I know I can't expect us to be friends, or even expect you to trust me, but I have felt terrible about that day in the ladies' room ever since. I am really not typically like that. I guess I just got caught up in the action."

"It's fine," I try to reassure her, wanting the awkwardness to be over.

"No, it's really not. Please, just know that I truly am sorry." I find myself starting to feel sorry for her. I also sense that her apology is genuine, so I accept and assure her there are no hard feelings between us.

Lance interrupts us with a knock on the door, putting an end to our session. "What was *that* all about?" he asks as Diana slinks past him and out of my office.

"Oh, nothing. Trust me, you don't even want to know. It's a girl-thing," I tell him, smiling up at him from my chair.

"Oh, come on, tell me," Lance prods. I don't budge but do let him know that his need to hear gossip far outweighs that of any of the girls I've met around the office. Lance doesn't even try to defend my remarks. Instead he chuckles and throws his arms up before making his exit.

Finally, alone with my thoughts, I dive into my work. A phone call startles me and I pick it up on the first ring, not bothering to wait for Terry to field the call.

"Emma Taylor speaking."

"Hi, Emma. It's Mr. James… err… Tyrell, from *Angry Gamer*."

I get a sinking feeling that there may still be a problem. "What can I do for you, Tyrell?" I ask, still not comfortable with addressing my client so informally.

"I wanted to thank you again for helping us launch our last game. You really stepped in at the end there and got us out of a bind, and I never really thanked you."

Relief washes over me, and I find myself smiling. "You are most welcome. Thank you, sir."

Mr. James continues. "We never did find out how our competitor got some of our information. Unfortunately, that will have to remain a mystery, but our new product is doing well, and I already have my development team working on the sequel."

I thank him for the update before politely ending our exchange. My curiosity is peaked and more than ever I am convinced that the leak might be within my own consulting firm. Not wanting to arouse suspicion from any of the employees, I head to the records department to do some research. The desk clerk, a young redhead no more than twenty, smiles politely at me when I approach her. She guiltily puts down her science-fiction book.

"What can I do for you?" she asks. I get the sense she doesn't get many visitors.

I request to see all client files for both *Angry Gamer* and *Moxley's*, the two clients that raised concerns of a possible breach of information. I expand my request to include a handful of additional clients where Danner and Banks Consulting had to offer a partial refund due to customer dissatisfaction with the outcome of our company's recommendations.

Although I did not work with most of the clients in question, each incident had been brought up in a meeting at one point or another. As isolated incidents, none seemed significant, but when putting them all together...

The desk clerk types feverishly on her keyboard before responding to my request. "I'm sorry ma'am, all of those files have been checked out."

"Excuse me? All of them?" I am exasperated. "By whom?"

"Mr. Banks called down here personally a few weeks back. He asked me to bring him the files right away. You can imagine my shock when Mr. Banks himself..."

"Thank you," I say, cutting her off and heading back to my office. It's getting late, so I make a mental note to investigate further in the morning. Now more than ever I find Eldon Banks' actions peculiar – and suspicious.

CHAPTER FIFTY-EIGHT

HE GRABS HIS SKI MASK from the hall closet, stuffing it into the pocket of his jacket. He is practically bursting with excitement as he prepares for the night ahead. Meticulously, he packs a bag of overnight clothes, a sturdy rope, and a gun. As an afterthought, he tosses in an extra blanket and some lubricant.

He drives to the gas station to fill up his vehicle. No one will recognize him in this car. He bought it at auction six months ago, licensed it under a shell corporation he was sure couldn't be traced back to him, and has had it garaged ever since. He purchases the gas with a prepaid card and heads into town.

His erection swells as he prepares himself for the night ahead. Tonight is the night he will finally be with Emma, and no one will be around to stop him.

CHAPTER FIFTY-NINE

LEANING IN CLOSER TO THE BATHROOM MIRROR, I examine my face for any remaining traces of makeup. I sigh loudly, disheartened that I will once again be going to bed alone. I miss Nate and am disappointed that he will be working late.

I thought that wrapping up the carjacking case would lighten Nate's hectic work schedule. Instead, he was promoted to lead detective and has been supporting the Seattle Police Department more frequently. There has even been talk of him making a permanent transfer to Seattle.

Absentmindedly, I run my fingers over the new silk negligée draped over the bathroom towel rack. I had planned to wear it as a surprise for Nate. I consider trading it out for my old nightshirt, but slip into it instead, hoping it'll make me feel like Nate is here with me. As the fabric skims my torso, my stomach growls, and I realize I forgot to eat dinner. I had been waiting, holding out hope Nate would get off earlier than planned, and somehow amid all my moping, eating slipped my mind. Now the thought of dinner is at the forefront of my brain, but I'm also too lazy to wander to the kitchen to find something to eat. I shrug and reach for my toothbrush and toothpaste instead.

After brushing my teeth and tidying up the bathroom, I walk into the bedroom. It is here that my whole world stops.

"Hello, Emma," a man says menacingly from behind his dark ski mask.

Please be a dream, please be a dream.

To my horror, the man is perfectly in focus and I know it's not a dream. At first, I wonder how the man got into my house, but then realize that I failed to set the alarm. I glance over at the nightstand drawer, wondering if I can make it to the pepper spray before the man has time to catch me. My instincts tell me to run, but my feet feel glued to the floor.

As the man edges closer, I find myself paralyzed with fear. *Move. Move.* I finally turn to run, but I am too late. He grabs me and puts a foul-smelling cloth over my mouth and nose.

"You're mine now," he says. It's the last thing I hear before losing consciousness.

CHAPTER SIXTY

I TAKE A DEEP BREATH, willing myself not to panic. *Think. Think.* I try to assess the situation rationally. I am blindfolded, and my wrists are tied behind my back; my feet, bound at the ankles. The room smells musty, a combination of wood smoke and moss. My head is pounding. I wonder why I am so cold, but then remember that I am only wearing a silk nighty.

Suddenly the room gets brighter. My blindfold still prevents me from seeing, but I think someone must have turned on a light. Unfamiliar footfalls approach. Not sure what to expect, I try to shrink into the wall as if it will guard me from whatever is about to come.

My blindfold is lifted, and I blink rapidly, my eyes rebelling against the sudden brightness. A man is inches from my face. I smell the stench of cigarettes. *Don't vomit. Don't vomit.* My vision comes into focus and it's all I can do not to scream. *Lance? It's Lance!*

"Oh, my beautiful Emma. You look surprised," Lance says. I've never heard him sound so condescending.

"Where am I?" I ask, my eyes darting around the room as I try to recognize my surroundings.

"Oh, just an old family cabin. You're the first girl I've taken here," he sneers cruelly.

I am confused. "Lance," I question softly, "what is going on?" I try to keep my voice steady but know that I am failing.

"Oh, Emma, like you don't know. After all, I've been buying your silence for the past several months. At least, that's what the police will think if they investigate."

"What do you mean?" I squeak.

"Well, Emma," Lance starts, his eyes boring wickedly into mine, "there's the small matter of your quick rise to the top. Honestly, will anyone believe you did that solely on your own merit?"

I feel like I've just been slapped in the face. *I believed it.*

"But you were still so persistent, so I started paying for you to go back to school." My heart is sinking. I've been such a fool. I feel tears welling up in my eyes. "Finally," he says, "you were such a glory hound I was forced to make *you* the face of *my* company. Your pretty face must be on at least ten billboards between Edmonds and Seattle."

I am so angry I can no longer hold back my emotions. My once bright future at his company – my future in general – now looks so bleak. Bitter tears stream down my face, but my bound wrists prevent me from wiping them away. Lance smiles menacingly and begins to pace the floor. "Please, Lance. I don't understand." I am terrified, but I also want an explanation.

When he begins to talk, I am overwhelmed with growing disbelief. Lance has been stealing information from our clients. Our clients trusted us. They provided us unlimited range to their financials and trade secrets. Lance has been betraying that trust, selling proprietary information to the highest bidding competitor.

"But it couldn't have been you that attacked me in my house," I say, trying to reason with the insanity of the situation. "The man that attacked me…"

"Talked like this," Lance interrupts. I shudder. His voice has changed, and memories of that night come flooding back. The voice is a perfect match. And then I remember the impressions. Lance had always been a big hit in the office with his voice impressions. When we were on his yacht, he charmed the pants off our clients with his talents. I am baffled.

"But why did you attack me in my house? What did I ever do to you?" I ask.

"Terry thought you were beginning to suspect," Lance replies. "I wanted to scare you into silence. I also needed to be sure you weren't bringing evidence home to compile a case against me."

"Terry?" I am shocked. *My assistant is involved?*

"Yes. You were starting to dig into old files and having the administrators do extra research, looking for irregularities."

"Lance," I interrupt. "I was doing my job. Some of our biggest clients were questioning why our recommendations didn't pan out. On paper it all worked…" I trail off as the magnitude of the situation hits me. Lance has been double-crossing our clients. He has been ripping the rug out from underneath them by stealing information and giving higher paying companies a leg up.

I remain silent, slowly processing all the information. "You know, instead of looking at me like I'm some sort of a monster, you should actually thank me," Lance interrupts my thoughts.

"*Thank* you?"

"Terry thought we should have gotten rid of you from the start. I talked her out of it." He crosses his arms smugly across his chest.

The thought of my assistant plotting my demise not only makes me shudder, it makes me question whether I have any aptitude for judging someone's character. I sit for several moments in stunned silence. "But, you don't smoke," I finally say, trying to make sense of it all, and still unwilling to accept the truth as it's being presented to me.

Lance laughs, but his face is unsmiling. "Usually don't anymore. Quit those things years ago. But occasionally I allow myself one when I am under extreme stress. I think breaking and entering or kidnapping qualifies."

Rendered speechless, I gaze silently up at Lance. He stares down at me, his gray eyes boring into mine. Although the red contacts are gone, I now recognize the familiar shape of his eyes. I shiver violently, my thin nighty offering little protection from the cold. Lance grabs a throw blanket from the couch in the next room and tosses it over me. I can feel him staring at me as I do my best to huddle underneath it.

Lance's gaze softens, and I get the sense that there is more that he wants to say. His expression is one of torment, as if a private battle wars in his mind. I can no longer take the silence and give into the need to ask more questions.

I speak slowly, doing my best not to agitate Lance further. "When you attacked me, were you thinking of…" I trail off, not sure that I want to know the answer to my question.

"I will admit it took a lot of self-control not to take you that day," Lance says. His words are almost soft, and I tremble with revulsion. "But that would have opened up a bigger investigation," Lance says, "which was too risky."

"I've wanted you for a long time, Emma," he confesses. "I guess I've still been holding out hope that you wanted me too. I thought someday that you would… umm… join me." He crouches down beside me, tenderly brushing the hair out of my eyes and wiping my tear-stained cheeks. The small blanket doesn't cover my legs, and Lance strokes my exposed thigh.

I try my best not to show how repulsed I am by him. "I have dreamt of you often over the past several months," Lance admits. "The dreams were so real, so vivid. You were such a fighter." Lance looks lost in thought and I know he must be reflecting on our shared dreams with fondness. I consider the irony, knowing that I have only regarded them with terror.

I shudder, recognizing if Lance had known how real the dreams were, there was no telling how far he would have gone. Realizing that his attraction to me gives me a hand to play, I channel all the flirtatious ploys I have seen Summer use on men throughout the years. I gaze at Lance through slightly lowered eyelids. My mouth is pulled into a seductive pout.

"Lance, we can work this out," I say, keeping my voice firm and husky like I've heard Summer do so many times. I stare directly into his eyes, holding his gaze.

For a moment, it seems to work and Lance leans in closer. He repositions the blanket so that it covers more of me. "Do these hurt?" he asks, softly running his fingers over the ropes binding my ankles.

"A little," I say. He looks conflicted, as if he wants to loosen them but knows that he shouldn't.

"You know, as much as I want you to join me, I know that it can't happen. I see the way you look at that detective. You've never looked at me that way. I've just been kidding myself into thinking that could ever change." As Lance speaks, I'm not sure if it's me he's trying to convince, or himself.

"It doesn't have to be this way," I tell him. My voice is a whisper and Lance is so close to me that my lips graze against his cheek as I speak. Inside, my stomach is churning violently, but I manage to keep my voice steady.

Lance pulls back to study my face. I can see that he is fighting with his own emotions. Finally, he speaks. "Emma, I'm sorry, but it does." He kisses me on the forehead, and then stands to walk away. I lower my head in defeat.

CHAPTER SIXTY-ONE

LANCE PACES BACK AND FORTH in the cramped bedroom of the cabin. He knows that he should get rid of Emma – she will never agree to go along with his plan. More importantly, she will never agree to be with him. Their trip to New York made that abundantly clear.

The problem is that he wants her. He wants her bad. He thinks back on all the nights he dreamed of her. In every dream he was closer to taking what he wanted, but she was strong, and she always fought him off. His dreams were so realistic, always leaving him wanting more.

Struggling with his emotions, Lance touches his fingers to his lips, remembering the one time that Emma had allowed him to kiss her – and she had kissed him back. She had tasted like vanilla and smelled like cinnamon. That intimate exchange had kept him going over the past several months. It gave him hope that Emma did care for him, as more than a friend.

But Nate had come back into the picture, dismantling everything that Lance had worked so hard to build. Lance punches the wall in anger, scraping his knuckles on the rough surface of the cabin wall. He knew what he had to do. Emma would die tonight – but not before he took what he'd been longing for, what he felt should rightfully be his.

CHAPTER SIXTY-TWO

LANCE IS GONE, and by my estimations I have been alone for about an hour. He didn't replace the blindfold and I'm at least grateful for that. I am cold and the sinking feeling in my stomach is being overpowered by growing hunger pains. *Why did I skip dinner?*

I just want Nate. I know he was working late. *Will he be home yet?* I wonder what time it is. I'm not sure how long I have been Lance's prisoner, but the lack of light coming through the cabin windows suggests it's still the middle of the night. *What will Nate do if he calls me and I don't answer? Will he come for me?*

I try hard to formulate a plan, but I feel both physically and mentally exhausted. Inwardly I scream at myself. *Stay awake. Think. Think.* Ignoring my silent pleas, my eyelids start to feel heavy. As my exhaustion takes over, I drift into unconsciousness.

My eyes open and I am in Nate's bedroom. My surroundings are slightly fuzzy, a detail I've learned to use to help me distinguish my dreams from reality. For a moment I have a fleeting hope. If Nate joins my dream, I can tell him where I am at and he can come rescue me. I look around, but the room is empty; the bed still made. I realize Nate must not be asleep yet, and my heart sinks to my toes.

I am about to abandon all hope when an idea pops into my head. I look around the room for a pen and piece of paper. After finding what I need in the drawer of the nightstand, I scrawl a quick note. *Help. Lance. Family cabin. I love you.* I place the note on Nate's bed, and then lie down on his bed and wait. I wait for the rescue that I know will probably never come.

I wake up to Lance standing over me with a plate of food, and I am so hungry that I am grateful to see him. The offering of food provides me with a glimmer of hope that he might be planning to let me go. "Thank you," I tell him. Lance doesn't say anything in return. He just stands over me with a blank expression.

I polish off my food, all the time wondering how long I was asleep and praying that Nate found my note. I gather I must not have been out for long. The windows are still dark. "So, what are you going to do with me now?" I ask. I speak calmly, but I can feel my pounding heart threatening to escape from my chest.

"Well, as far as I know, no one else suspects what I have been up to. With you out of the picture, things can go back to normal." Lance's voice is like steel. Any tenderness from before has faded.

The faint hope I felt just moments before disappears and I start to shake, my dinner threatening to resurface. "Lance, please. *I* didn't even know."

"You eventually would have put it together, Emma. You're a smart girl. It was just a matter of time. I couldn't take the risk."

I am still shocked. Lance and I have spent so much time together, and I never suspected he was capable of violence. It makes me sick to think about our trip to New York and how Lance tried to make me believe that Nate was the one who attacked me. He seemed so genuinely concerned, he had nearly convinced me. "I trusted you," I say, stupefied. "I thought you were my friend." I sound like a naïve child.

Lance leans down and cocks his head to one side. "Aww... are you saying we can't be friends anymore?" he says callously, stroking my cheek with the back of his hand.

"You won't get away with this," I seethe.

"Watch me," Lance says. While watching him walk away, I have a sinking suspicion that he might be right.

When Lance leaves the room, I know I need to work fast. I've given up hope that he will let me go, and my time is running out. To my horror, I am also beginning to realize that the only reason Lance would have for keeping me alive until now is to carry out what he wanted to do so badly in my bedroom all those months ago. The thought both repulses and terrifies me, fueling my urgency to escape. I struggle with my bindings, but they are tight. I wonder if Lance was a boy scout as a kid. *Stupid knots.*

After kicking off the blanket, I lie flat on the ground and manage to maneuver my feet through my arms so that my hands are now tied in the front of me rather than behind my back. From this position, I can more easily untie my feet. I quickly loosen the ropes around my ankles – and then I run.

When I bolt out the front door of the cabin, the chilly night air shocks my system. I suck in my breath and make my way to the woods, hoping the trees and the darkness will provide the cover I need to escape. The cold ground stings my bare feet and the smell of moss and rot fills my nostrils, but I continue to run, fueled by the sound of Lance's enraged screams behind me. It is almost like my dream. I am running through the dense foliage, my assailant close behind. Only this time he's not wearing a ski mask, and Nate isn't here to save me.

The thin, silk negligée provides little warmth against the crisp night air. I plunge onward in the darkness, the fading glow of the cabin porch light offering modest illumination. I should be grateful for the cover of night, but I'm also terrified of being alone in it and of what may or may not be waiting for me in the woods. The tree branches whip at my body and face while the ground cover tears at my bare feet. My legs feel like rubber and my lungs scream in protest, but I press on, driven by sheer terror. I wonder how long I'll be able to keep up this pace when suddenly a shot rings out. For a split second, I think someone has come to rescue me. Then I feel a blinding pain in my back and I black out.

CHAPTER SIXTY-THREE

I FEEL COLD AND I KNOW THAT I HAVE LOST a great deal of blood. I think I hear Nate's voice, but I can't open my eyes. I struggle to regain consciousness, but something keeps pulling me below the surface.

"Stay with me, baby," I hear Nate say.

I sink further below the surface of consciousness and am back at Olympic Beach. Nate and I are lying on a blanket on the sand. He holds me close and I cuddle up next to him. I feel so tired.

"Don't leave me," Nate pleads, pushing the hair out of my eyes.

I am confused. I'm not leaving him. I'm lying next to him. All at once the waves are upon us. I am sucked under. It's dark and the water is cold as ice. I am gasping, and I feel the air being squeezed from my lungs.

A strange beeping sound keeps playing in my ear. *Wake up. Wake up.* The rhythmic beeping becomes a long, flat tone. I hear more voices. They are becoming frantic. "Clear!" I hear someone yell. Pain jolts through my body. *Stop. Stop.* The pain is fierce, but I find myself unable to scream.

Blackness surrounds me, and all goes silent. The pain subsides, and I hear a familiar voice in the darkness. "Emma, wake up." The man speaks softly, but urgently. His voice is known to me, but I know it's impossible.

I slowly open my eyes. "Dad?"

"Yeah, sweetie it's me." He is just as I remember him: strong, caring – larger than life.

"Is it time for me to go with you?" I ask. Shockingly, I am not afraid, but I know that I'll miss Nate. I'll miss my mom and Nikki and Summer...

"No, no it's not time yet."

"But I'm so tired," I tell him. My words are slurred.

"I know pumpkin. But you have people here that still need you. You have to be strong Emma. You have to wake up."

"Wake up!" another voice screams from somewhere in the darkness.

My eyes flutter open and it takes me a moment to realize where I am. The room smells heavily of rubbing alcohol and latex. There is a pain in my right hand. I look down and notice I am hooked to an IV. I struggle to sit up, but a coursing pain shoots through my body. I wince in response and opt to remain flat on my back.

"No, babe, don't move." It's Nate. I am so relieved to see him. He rushes over to me. I look up at him and am alarmed at his appearance. His expression looks pained – his green eyes are red and puffy.

"Nate, have you been crying?" I ask, surprised. I have never seen him cry.

I expect Nate to look embarrassed, but he doesn't. "Emma, you were shot. I thought we were going to lose you. Luckily the bullet missed any major organs, but you'd lost so much blood by the time I found you. That was the worst experience of my life." His voice trails off.

Nate's hands are shaking. I want so much to hold him – to comfort him with my body the way he's done for me so many times. But I'm in no condition. "Nate, you saved me. I'm fine." He looks unconvinced. "How did you find me?" I ask, trying to distract him.

"I went home from work last night dog tired. I should have gone to bed right away, but I needed to unwind, so I stayed up to watch a stupid TV show. When I finally went to bed, I, uh, I found your note." His eyes stare directly into mine, as if he's trying to determine if I understand the meaning behind his words – or perhaps wanting reassurance that it was more than a dream.

"So, it worked!" I say in disbelief. "I have to admit, I was a little skeptical."

"Oh, Emma, that was so smart. Not many people would have kept their wits about them enough to think of an idea like that."

I swell at Nate's praise. "I was so scared," I confess. "But part of me knew you would come for me." The last portion is a polite exaggeration, but I feel it's warranted given the circumstances.

"Of course, I wasn't the only one who found you," Nate says, playfully raising one eyebrow. "Half of the police squad saw you in that cute little nighty."

"I told you my sweatpants and t-shirts are much more practical," I say weakly.

"I'm beginning to agree." Nate smiles at me, but his forehead remains creased as if he's frowning. I can tell he's worried about me. I imagine I gave him quite a scare. I remember how helpless and frightened I felt when I got the call that Nate had been shot. The memory still makes me shudder.

Before I can dwell on the matter further, my mom and Summer come rushing into the room with Michael trailing behind them. They each give me a hug, making me wince each time, but I try not to show my pain. I am so glad to see them.

I can tell that my mother and Summer have both been crying. "Geez," I say, "who turned on the waterworks in here?"

"It was pretty touch and go there for a while," my mom says, her voice barely a whisper. Her eyes well up with tears again and she squeezes my hand.

"Nate kicked the crap out of that jerk," Summer cuts in. Her lip is trembling and Michael hooks a protective arm around her waist. I glance over at Nate.

"You got him?" I ask.

"We got him sweetie," Nate says. He speaks so softly, and his expression is pained. I want to hold him or have him hold me. I fight once more to sit up, but the pain knocks me flat on my back.

Nate is by my side again, protectively inserting himself between my mother and me. "Baby, please. Stay lying down."

Resting my head on the pillow, I close my eyes. I have a nagging feeling that I am forgetting something important but am unable to determine what that *something* is. Suddenly, my eyes snap open when I remember my conversation with Lance. "Wait," I say, "Terry Peters, my assistant. Lance said that Terry was involved."

Nate quickly dials a number on his cell before stepping out of the room. I can hear him in the hallway, barking out orders as he paces in front of the doorway.

The precinct calls an hour later. Terry was apprehended at the bank, attempting to withdraw all the funds from a bank account she and Lance shared. In her car, the police found several bags of clothes, more cash, and a fake I.D. – evidence that she planned to run.

I find it nearly impossible to imagine my assistant as a criminal, and more to the point, someone that wanted me dead. I shiver at the thought and Nate calls the nurse to request another blanket for me, misreading my tremor as a sign that I am cold.

CHAPTER SIXTY-FOUR

FOR THE DURATION OF MY HOSPITAL STAY, Nate barely leaves my side except to grab us food or check in at work. He even insists that the nurses bring him a cot to stay the nights with me. I am going stir crazy staying in bed, but I do love having Nate all to myself every evening. That is, until the hospital staff interrupts us to draw blood or check my vitals.

During the day, my room is bustling with visitors. Nate's parents and brother visit, as well as my mother and Summer. My sister threatens to fly up, but I convince her to stay home. In addition to family and close friends, several of my coworkers also pay me a visit. Of biggest surprise to me is the visit by Eldon Banks. He enters my room with Robert, the company janitor, close by his side. I think of them as an odd pair, but then remember Lance mentioning that Robert was a family friend of Eldon's.

Eldon and Robert take a seat in the hard, outdated chairs at the foot of my hospital bed. Sensing the overcrowding in the room, Nate politely excuses himself under the guise of tracking down a soda. An awkward silence unfolds before Eldon clears his throat and begins to speak.

Although he will not go into detail about the damage control being done back at the office, he assures me that my job is waiting for me when I am able to return. I am touched by the gesture, but uncertain at this point if that is even an option I wish to pursue.

"There is one thing you should know before you go back to work," Robert speaks up. "You won't be seeing me around when you return."

Confused why Robert feels the need to tell me about his upcoming plans, I try to respond politely. "Oh, have you found another job?"

"No, ma'am. You see, Eldon didn't hire me on as a janitor. He hired me as a private investigator."

My mouth quite literally drops open and my eyes dart back and forth between the two men. "What?" is all I manage to say.

"Let me explain," Eldon says. "It had come to my attention that someone may be leaking confidential information within our company. I had Robert investigate and narrow in on a few key suspects." He pauses.

"Me? *I* was a suspect?" I say, not bothering to mask my anger and hurt.

"Well, at first, yes," Robert says, "but we cleared you. You have to admit, Lance did a pretty good job of making it look like you could be involved. But once I bugged your office..." Robert trails off as if suddenly realizing he said too much.

"And why the hell wasn't I notified about any of this?" Nate says angrily from the doorway, and I wonder at what point he re-entered the room.

"You were too close to the case," Eldon tells him bluntly.

293

"So, what? You've been spying on me? Did you know it was Lance?" I am spitting out accusations, unable to remain calm.

"He was on our list," Eldon explains, "but we just couldn't be certain. I am so sorry, Emma. We didn't think that you were in any immediate danger."

"Well, Mr. Banks, clearly you guys were wrong," I say, waving my hand around the room as if anyone needs reminded that we are in a hospital.

"And I deeply regret that, Emma," he says. "And please, call me Eldon." It's the first time he's requested me to do so, and my anger subsides a little because I know the significance of the request. It means he *does* respect me and value me as an employee.

After more apologies and assurances from Eldon that he would like me to return to work once I am able, he and Robert (assuming that is even his real name) leave my hospital room. When I'm finally alone with Nate, and trying hard to absorb everything I've just learned, I take the opportunity to break down and have a good cry.

The doctor comes in later to give me an update on my progress and inform me that I will need to stay for another couple of days. While I am anxious to get back home to my own house, I enjoy my nights in the hospital. Nate and I share many vivid dreams. I no longer think of him as someone who darkens my dreams. Instead, I invite him into my dream harbor – a safe place of refuge we both share. Here we can hold each other tightly, to make love without limitations. I am not in any pain.

I half expect to see my dad again, but I don't. I suppose I will never know if the encounter with him was real, or just a dream, but I'm quite certain it saved my life. Seeing him gave me the strength to fight to live. It makes me miss him though, even more than usual. I don't share the dream with Nate. It's personal – just between my dad and me.

When I am finally released from the hospital, Nate insists on pushing me in a wheelchair to his car. I try to refuse him. "Hospital policy," he mocks, trying to make his voice sound nasally. I'm not sure what nurse he is trying to imitate, but it makes me laugh.

"Your place or mine?" he asks, helping me into the car. After a brief exchange, we settle on mine. During the drive home, the anticipation of finally sleeping in my own bed, and getting to sleep there with Nate, begins to build.

Back at my place, Nate turns down the bed and helps me undress. After arranging the pillows, he strips off his clothes and helps me into bed. He slips under the sheets, spooning my body with his as he drapes a long, muscular leg over mine.

"You know, if you moved in with me, we wouldn't have to keep deciding whose house to stay at." Nate's lips are inches from my ear and my body tingles at his suggestion.

"And just what is wrong with you moving in with me?" I tease, craning my neck to look at him while trying to contain my excitement.

"My place is bigger," Nate says matter of fact.

"You sir, are a snob," I try to sound defensive, but I can't hide the happiness in my voice. I squirm out of Nate's grasp and turn to face him.

"Well, what do you say?" Nate asks, looking a little nervous while he waits for my answer.

I chew on my bottom lip as if I'm contemplating, but I've already made my decision. When you come face-to-face with your own mortality, it changes you, puts things into perspective. I realize now that a house can no longer be my only refuge or safe harbor – it's those I love and those who love me. I've learned that it's okay to venture out and put my faith in others.

"Well," I finally say, "I'll have to sell this house. Then there's the matter of me needing a little more closet space…" Nate knows I am teasing and he cuts me off by pulling me closer and kissing me.

"Say yes," he whispers in my ear.

"Yes!" I cry out. Nate kisses me again, careful to bypass my still tender wound as he strokes my back. I know things between us won't always be perfect. The waters will get rough. But I don't mind the waves. Like stones tumbled in the sands of the sea, our conflicts help smooth us out, keep us polished.

"Does anyone deserve to be this happy?" I ask.

"We do," Nate says, and I don't feel any need to disagree with him.

Acknowledgements

Thank you to my family and close friends for putting up with me over the past *several* years while I obsessed over writing my first novel. Your encouragement kept me going and offered me the strength (and courage) to put this novel out into the world. A special thanks to my husband, parents, sister, and two of my wonderful sisters-in-law for reading early versions of this novel and providing me with feedback. Finally, thank you to my two brothers for helping with cover design. I love you all and am so grateful for your support.

About the Author

Blake Channels was born in Tri-Cities, Washington where she resides today with her husband and two children. She graduated from Washington State University and is a wife, mother, and office professional by day and a writer in her heart and soul – and whenever her busy schedule allows. In addition to writing romance novels, Blake enjoys spending time with family and friends, camping, and curling up with a good book.